Brave Heart

Brave Heart

by

Susan E. Westoby

Pharaoh Press
Roby Liverpool L36 4HF.

Dedication

To GRAHAM

A Brave Heart for putting up with me.

ISBN 0 9525543 0 5

Cover design by G.S.Design Partnership. Rainhill.

Published by
Pharaoh Press. Roby. Liverpool L36 4HF

Printed and bound in Great Britain
by
Stephenson Print. Prescot.
Merseyside.
L34 5SD

Elenor cowered, terrified, beneath her scant bedcovers as the roaring drunken sounds of the revelry in the hall below increased in intensity.

She had escaped from the table after snatching only a few mouthfuls of food, thankful that Gerard, her husband, had been too deeply involved in an argument with one of his knights to do more than grunt as she excused herself. Fervently now she prayed that she would stay forgotten up here in the cold and dismal room which served more often as her prison and torture chamber than as a haven for rest and sleep.

A crash as a chair overturned made her jump then she whimpered softly as a howl of laughter sounded close, approaching up the stairway.

"Please! Please sweet Jesus make them go past. Have mercy dear Mother of God, I shall die of fear. Make them go past!"

For one brief hopeful moment she thought her plea may be answered as the stumbling steps seemed to go on past her door, then she shrieked in despair as the broken old lock shattered once more beneath a kicked assault and her husband leaned there in the doorway.

There was silence for a few seconds and Elenor's mind fought to prepare itself for whatever horror was to come.

Gerard sniffed and wiped his sleeve across his nose, grinning at the pathetic picture of his young wife, white - faced and shaking, scarcely able to control her own bodily functions and striving for breath as she stared at him.

His companions fought to see over his shoulder as he belched then pushed his obscene bulk forward into the room. They crowded after him, whooping and laughing anticipating the sport they knew their lord delighted in.

"No!" She knew he loved it when she screamed, when she ran from him. Knew he loved to watch her vain attempts to escape, yet she could not help herself and with that despairing cry of denial she flung herself from the bed clad only in her shift, and across the room, away from him. Inexorably he advanced on her and her eyes darted desperately from face to face as his men and their trollops closed in around her. No mercy. No pity. Only hard, greedy lustful eyes and slack, anticipating mouths.

Joan! The woman who was, in theory, her maid hung to one side, her expression like stone, her lips in a tight thin line as she watched her mistress press back against the wall as though willing the stones to open and swallow her up. No help there. Should she have expected it? Gerard had more use from Joan than his wife did, Elenor knew that.

The group grew still as she backed herself into a corner

"Well now my dear wife.? What sort of welcome is this for a loving husband?"

Roars of laughter greeted Gerard's remark and he glanced around with drunken enjoyment.

"Come now my sweeting, don't be afraid - you know you love this as much as I do."

With a speed of movement remarkable in a man of his bulk he had grasped the neck of her shift and ripped it down and away from her pale slim body.

She screamed again, knowing it was music to his ears, yet still unable to stop it, and the crowd cheered, encouraging him as he fastened his fingers in her long silky hair and dragged her, fighting desperately, trying to throw herself on the floor, clutching at the furniture, towards the bed.

"Keep still, you bitch..." she almost struggled free and he raised his fist and smashed it once, twice, three times into her face.

The blinding flash of pain was abominable, and she felt the sticky flow of blood start warm down her nose and in her mouth, her senses whirling as he threw her on her stomach onto the bed.

Elenor would have welcomed unconsciousness but it was cruelly denied her and she heard the crowd urging Gerard on as he fumbled with his clothes, unlacing himself to take her from behind. He preferred to mount her like an animal knowing he could inflict more pain on her that way and insanity fluttered on the edges of her mind like some great blind moth, jumbling her brain and making her giggle crazily.

Surprise made Gerard pause a second, then he grabbed hold of her soft hips and plunged himself into her with a shout, a shout echoed by the sodden crowd around him, a shout blotting out his wife's screams as he rode her viciously and hard, slapping at her as he would a horse to urge it on.

He grunted like a rutting pig, the paunch of his belly flopping obscenely onto her bottom. On and on, it seemed to last forever, perhaps because he was so drunk and Elenor stared blindly into nothing as the pain seemed to tear her apart. Other hands than his invaded her soft body, fumbling, pinching, even biting her and her sweat and tears mingled with her blood to stain the cover of her bed.

Finally, mercifully, he jerked to his climax and collapsed on top of her, almost suffocating her, crushing her with his weight and she lay like one dead praying that this would be the end of her ordeal. It seemed she was to be lucky this night for when he regained his breath he pushed himself away from her, smacking his hand onto the back of her head and sending jolting pain through her nose which she knew must surely be broken.

"Clean yourself up you slut! You're beginning to bore me and I must think of some way to be rid of you... when it suits me!"

Everyone laughed again at that and as they trooped from her room there were sly slaps and kicks, especially from the women, which Elenor suffered without a sound or a movement. Only Joan, the maid, did not abuse her, and that could have been because Gerard slung his arm about her neck and dragged her with him pressing slobbering kisses to her ear and neck in a revolting parody of affection.

Elenor lay still long after they had gone and all was quiet, then she uncurled herself from that protective foetal position which her body had taken up in an almost reflex spasm, and eased herself slowly and painfully to the edge of her bed. There was cold water in the pitcher on the table and she dipped her fingers gratefully into its depths, gently washing away the blood, the sweat, the semen and even the gobs of spittle which sullied her body. Finally she dried herself on the bedcovers and slid carefully into bed, rolling onto her side and staring blankly into space.

The stubs of candles guttered and went out, leaving the room dark and cold and desolate, a haunting reflection of her mind and spirit.

The pain of her face and the burning ache in her stomach and between her thighs made sleep an impossibility.

Arguments with her God spun round and round in her head voicing bewilderment at what she had done to deserve such a life as this; hated, abused and tortured for no reason.

She knew Gerard had married her for the rich dowry she had brought with her as the only daughter of a doting father and she was intelligent enough to suspect that after the death of her parents it would have been tempting for her overlord to sell her to the highest bidder. Gerard had made no secret of the fact that it was merely her lands and fat coffers which had attracted him to her. Powerless, with no friends nor family to safeguard her interests, she had protested to Lord de Vere, her protector in law, of her aversion to the marriage. He had pretended sympathy but the lure of Gerard's bribe had been too great.

"It is the way of things with all women my dear. Love often comes much later after a marriage. Believe me all will be well, for Lord Gerard is a fine, upstanding and proven warrior who is well able to look after his wife."

So she had been spirited away from her home in Normandy to cross that grey and wrathful strip of water that was the Channel and she had been brought here to Fernrean, incarcerated in the castle which Gerard had built and furnished with money he had milked from her lands in Normandy.

A shout and the slamming of a door close by made her flinch and stifle a moan, holding her breath as the seconds went by until the lack of any further sound allowed her to relax again. Elenor's room was separated from that of her husband by a small antechamber. There were three further such apartments built around the circular keep. Gerard had designed his stronghold after castles he had seen in Sicily and the stone had been plundered from ancient ruins in the forest around the village.

Many had crossed themselves and muttered of bad luck at that but Gerard had sneered and boasted that he made his own luck and that his stronghold at Fernrean would be the finest in William's new kingdom of England.

Elenor shivered, then forcing her aching limbs to move, she slid out of bed and in the dim gloom she cuddled her arms about herself and went to search through the chest at the side of her bed for a fresh shift. There was very little left of the things she had brought with her from Normandy. Gerard had helped himself to anything he wanted for presents for his women - especially Joan. Climbing gingerly back into her bed Elenor puzzled over the relationship between her husband and her maid. Although what he showed the woman could scarcely be termed 'affection' , he was certainly never brutal and cruel with her as he was with his wife.

Joan had been installed as Gerard's woman well before Elenor's arrival and although Elenor hated and loathed her husband, she had found the situation highly embarrassing when Joan had become her maid.

Joan, however, had gone about her tasks with an expressionless calm which had disconcerted Elenor at first but to which she had soon become accustomed.

Warmth slowly began to creep over her as she huddled beneath the bedcovers and the shock of her husband's assault began to recede.

Nothing he did to her now could ever be as bad as the nightmare which had been her wedding night.

At seventeen years of age, Elenor had known very little of the sexual side of the relationship between a man and a woman and she could not control a shudder of loathing for the inhuman beast who was her husband. He had taken her, brutally and repeatedly, on the banqueting table in full view of all his followers and the servants. Screaming, bleeding and naked, she had pleaded for mercy, for help and then, finally for death, but this had only seemed to inflame his lust all the more and she had soon learned to take all he gave as silently as was humanly possible.

She suddenly remembered his words as he had finished with her earlier,..." You're beginning to bore me and I must think of some way to be rid of you!" In Gerard's terms that must mean he intended to kill her! But surely he would never be able to get away with that - to murder his wife!

Then she shrugged, talking aloud to herself

"Well nobody stops him doing exactly as he pleases now - surely murder would be nothing at all to him - or to the spawn of Satan who follow him!"

Her own voice frightened her and she clenched her fists and beat them helplessly on the bed.

"Do something! I must be able to do something! I will not be abused and murdered without fighting - I -will - not!" The courage and spirit of her Viking forbears which had made it possible for her thus far to survive her life with the maniac who was Lord Gerard de Beauvrais now came once more to her aid and fortified her - gave her the strength to face whatever lay ahead with cunning and determination.

"For let us face the fact that Gerard is not overbright. Surely anyone with normal intelligence could defeat him- not by force of arms perhaps but I am most capable of outwitting him. If I can conquer my fear and think - just think!" God! She would go crazy - crazy with fear and desperation!

She sighed and snuggled down into the bed allowing her fatigue to overcome her and sleep to enfold her in its welcoming arms. She would think about it all on the morrow, for now her beaten body needed rest.

The hand which awoke Elenor the next morning was not gentle, neither was it brutal. It was obvious that Joan had served her master late into the night for she was heavy - eyed and dishevelled. She said nothing, merely setting down a fresh pitcher of water on the table next to the bed and cutting two large hunks of bread from a loaf for Elenor's breakfast.

Elenor was used to this silent service and made no attempt to get out of bed, nor to eat or drink anything.

The dull pain in her face and jaw did not really encourage the desire to chew anything, especially the hard bread which formed her usual breakfast.

She watched Joan slyly from the corner of her eye. Finishing her tasks quickly Joan seemed nervous and wiped her hands down her skirts looking over at Elenor as if she wanted to say something but could not decide whether to or not.

In the end she left, quickly and without a backward glance.

Stiffly Elenor rose from her bed and washed herself as thoroughly as she could with the small amount of water she was allowed. Gerard did not believe in bathing - it weakened the system he said. He simply covered any body odours with a heavy musky perfume which turned Elenor's stomach. Shivering, she dried herself and dressed then attempted to eat something. Dismally she considered how thin she had become since arriving at Fernrean and although she had no mirror she knew she must present a pitiful sight; beaten, bruised, half- starved and poorly dressed.

Suddenly Gerard was there in her room. She had not heard him enter through the connecting doors but she forced herself not to react with her usual fear and loathing.

He was suffering badly from the night's excesses, which helped her, for he was unsteady on his feet and his vision was blurred. He clutched at the bed hangings.

"Stir yourself, bitch. We are to have visitors. The King..." he belched and closed his eyes briefly "The King is coming here to Fernrean - honouring us with his presence." He sneered his contempt for William."These uprisings - these rebellions have him running round like a scalded cat." He paused consideringly."I say one thing in his favour - he's a bastard when he's roused!" He laughed at his own joke then groaned.

"You!" He fixed her with his unsteady gaze,"You're sick. Too sick to come out of your chamber. I shall play the devoted, worried husband. No-one to disturb you.

Rest is essential - ha ha!" He was pleased with what he saw as his own cleverness, then he frowned as he realised he did not seem to be having his usual terrifying effect on her.   He leaned close. His breath stank and with an enormous effort of will she did not flinch away. Disconcerted he raised his fist, but lowered it again slowly as she showed no sign of having noticed the gesture."Do you know..."   He paused."Your face looks like a boiled turd!" He laughed hysterically, then turned to leave, forgetting her strange behaviour as he concentrated on the impending visit of King William.

As the door slammed behind him, Elenor felt the hate and fear rise up once more and threaten to choke her. She loathed his huge sneering face and lank, greasy hair, worn longer than most other Norman lords, an affectation which surprised her considering his lack of personal hygiene. Suddenly she realised what he had been saying - The King was coming to Fernrean!

Her breath caught in her chest as she swung around, her fists clenched to her mouth in excitement and hope.

If the King was in Fernrean Gerard would find it impossible to continue his systematic abuse - and if she could not find a way to turn this to her advantage, then she was a fool - and deserved everything her husband might mete out to her.

A commotion in the courtyard below caught her attention and she leaned out of the window embrasure to see what was happening.

Gerard was down there arguing fiercely with a strange knight mounted on a grey warhorse.

The knight bent low towards the dishevelled Gerard and spoke urgently, punctuating his words with a clenched fist. Gerard was shaking his head, spreading out his hands and shrugging. In the next moment the knight grabbed the front of his hauberk and dragged him close, spitting out some sort of threat then throwing Gerard backwards and whirling his destrier round, shouted to his followers. They left the upper bailey in a thunder of hooves with the lord of Fernrean lying in the dirt behind them.

The first glimmer of amusement in more than two years lightened the fine - boned features of his lady. Elenor put her hand to her mouth to stifle a laugh at the sight of the fat beast who was her husband, struggling like a cockroach on its back, roaring to his men to help him up. She dodged quickly back into her room in case he should happen to glance up and see her, then allowed her laughter to bubble forth.

Things were changing for her, she knew it! Perhaps the Holy Virgin had heard her prayers and was giving her some sort of chance of life, some opportunity to escape the present hell of her existence!

Cautiously moving back to the window she watched as Gerard was helped to his feet and his henchmen made ludicrous attempts to brush him down. Angrily he pushed them away then swung around gesturing to them to follow him into the keep.

Elenor cast her eyes about for some occupation should he decide to come into her room, sliding quickly in behind her embroidery frame as she heard his angry shouting on the stairwell."I'll have de Touron's guts if he treats me like that again... in fact I'll have his guts anyway..."

I wonder who he will find to do that for him- thought Elenor nastily."

I like it not my lord - They want us to get too deeply involved - the risks are too great. I say tell them to go to hell!"

"Hell is where we'll go if William discovers us..."

"Quiet you fool!   This is no place to discuss such matters."

Her head was bent over her needlework and she was humming a little tune as her door opened suddenly.   She looked up and his piggy brown eyes glared at her suspiciously.

"Hah! About time you did something useful you bitch..."

"Yes my lord." She answered him pleasantly and he was taken aback.

"My lord..."   His man spoke from behind.

"Yes, yes. You! Stay securely in here or I'll have your hide."

"Yes my lord."

He stared, then sneered and went out and she heard the key turn in the half-broken lock.

Her legs lost their strength and she leaned on her embroidery frame for support for a moment before stiffening her resolve and forcing herself to move as silently as possible over to the door which opened onto the separating antechamber between her room and Gerard's.

She could hear the muffled jumble of voices from the room beyond and she knew she simply had to know what they were saying. For some reason she knew it was vitally important to her.

Gently, oh ever so gently, she turned the handle of the door.

It opened without a sound and she paused, her heart hammering like a drum. The voices were much louder, clearer, more frightening in what they were saying.

'Tis too soon, and I like it not so close to Fernrean. If aught should go wrong - the finger would point straight at us. You should not get involved my lord."

Elenor blinked. Something dark and dangerous was afoot and she found herself desperate to know more. She eased herself into the room and in a few steps she was close enough to hear them clearly.

"... too dangerous my lord. Thus far we have done our work in secret, no names, no faces to our scheming. I think that the reason they wish to involve us more is that if aught goes amiss we share the responsibility and the punishment."

"We need to use men not known for their allegiance to us. Some brigand or Saxon rebel who would do the thing and not ask why or wherefore."

"And where do we find such men? Could we trust them? I think not. This is less and less to my liking."

"But think lord. If we were to succeed.

To kill the Bastard!

There would be no reward too great, nothing we could not ask for!"

"You are right in that!" Gerard's voice held excitement."Instead of this paltry barony - this poverty - stricken, unproductive plot. Instead of that puke of a wife-an heiress! Rich lands! Aye! I could well do with some of that! But we must be certain. We must be sure of success Nothing must go wrong, nothing must lead them back to us should we fail."

Elenor could not believe what she was hearing. This plot to kill the King! Sweet Jesus if they found her here she was dead - and she knew that that death would not be quick and merciful!

Trembling, she eased her way back towards her own room, terrified that a sound - a whisper of sound - her breathing - even the thunderously loud beat of her heart would alert them. Suddenly her chamber seemed the safest most desired haven in the world and when she finally reached its drab interior and the door closed behind her with a click which she felt in her cringing flesh, she was gasping for breath.

Gerard must be mad! His excesses had sent him over the brink into lunacy where he thought he could do as he wished and get away with it. To kill William!

Elenor knew enough to realise that Gerard must have allied himself with enemies, probably highly placed enemies, of William.

Some of his barons opposed him even now, wanting more than he had given them and stirring up remnants of Saxon rebellion. She knew enough of William's methods of restoring order to his realm - something at which he was highly experienced - to know that to betray him was to die!

Sitting carefully on the edge of her bed she took deep breaths to calm herself, realising what a gift this could be to her plans. If only she could reach William and warn him - betray Gerard!

To do so would be some fine revenge!

She groaned. May as well try to reach the moon.

Their voices were suddenly loud again in the passageway outside her door and Elenor leaped to the protective barrier of her embroidery frame. They went on past her room, however and she relaxed as the argument, which was still fiercely in progress, faded into the distance.

Elenor collected together the coloured silks for her embroidery and sat down to thread her needles and settle to the work on the frame. It helped to calm her nerves and order her thoughts as her fingers deftly pushed the sharp steel through the heavy cloth. Her eyelids were badly swollen with bruising and after a while the close work became difficult but her mind was busily active, ferreting through every possibility of escaping and reaching William the King.

The light had started to fade before she finally stretched and pressed a fist to her brow to still the feverish aching which her desperate scheming and subsequent discarding of various plans had caused.

It was no use. She could see no way out of Fernrean - no way of reaching William - no escape from the beast to whom she was married. It was surely time for the evening meal yet Joan had not come to summon her to the hall. She would be glad to stay in her room and avoid the harsh glare of the torches on her ruined face and the laughter and raucous jibes made at her expense. Yet she was suddenly hungry, and her stomach rumbled to agree with the thought.

She had eaten nothing since she had broken her fast with the two slices of bread Joan had brought. Small wonder she was so thin!

As though summoned   by her mistress's thoughts, the door opened suddenly to admit the Saxon maid.   Obviously greatly agitated yet making an effort to control herself, Joan stared almost wildly at Elenor.

"What is it Joan? What do you want?" She was surprised at the aggression in her own voice, yet her maid seemed not to notice, moving away from the door towards her mistress, her finger on her lips to warn her to be quiet.

"My lady, we all do as we must to survive. I no more than you, you understand that. Yet this..." She turned away just watching Elenor from the corner of her eye ,"This business with the King."

There was a silence in which the tension and suspicion could almost be tasted.

"I don't know what you mean. You refer, I suppose, to King William's visit here." God! She must be so careful. There was no possibility of her trusting Joan. Not Joan who seemed so openly contemptuous of her. And yet - if Elenor could use her to further her own plans...

"Aye lady, to the King's visit here - and more." Joan's fingers were tightly clenched together. "It could be the death of us all. The King is well known for his lack of mercy to any who oppose him or may betray him, and if this madness continues we will all die. Even you lady."

Elenor's heart was racing. "You must be clearer Joan. I am not so stupid yet what you are saying means nothing to me."

The maid's face was pale and her eyes held fear and desperation.   "They..."she   swallowed convulsively. "They mean to kill the King."

She moved suddenly closer to Elenor, her face less than an inch from that of her mistress, and hissed a threat. "And I said none of this if you value the miserable life you have."

Elenor matched her venom. "I care not for the threats of a serving woman. You are in more danger than I, for you may betray your lord or your King, while I have said nothing - done nothing."

They glared at each other, two women in terror with no-one to trust, no-one to care for them, nor defend them from the loathsome creature who held their lives in his hands.

Elenor grasped the maid suddenly by the shoulders, surprising them both with her strength.

"Now listen. You may have been favoured by him where he hates me - God only knows why - but this will be the death of us all if we do not do something. We have no-one to trust but each other. Now tell me what you know."

After a brief moment of indecision, Joan nodded fractionally and Elenor let her go.

"Tell me." Elenor prompted.

"They will ride out to make contact with a group of Saxon rebels who inhabit the forest about Fernrean. Gerard is a fool in this, for he raped the Saxon's woman and in her shame she took her own life. He is more likely, then, to kill my lord rather than help him in this."

"Where? Do you know where - and when?

"William arrives here the day after tomorrow. They will wait for him on the road from the south as it enters the forest. It will be coming dusk and the King's men will be tired and in haste to reach Fernrean safely to rest and eat in comfort. Erland, the Saxon, is reputed to have over one hundred men with him, plus some Danish support, while the King rides here with only fifty men, the main band of his army continuing north towards York. He expects to leave here with Gerard and the two knights de Wulfe and de Grace, and a large portion of Fernrean's soldiers."

Elenor was dumbfounded. "How do you know all this?"

Joan avoided her eyes, uncharacteristically embarrassed.

"He thought I slept - that I had drunk too much. I was in his bed, and who could I betray him to? I am only a serving maid and no-one would listen to me. But you, lady. They would listen to you"

Elenor swung away and began pacing to and fro. It was a wonder there was not a path worn in the floor she had paced these boards so often. "We must get away from here to warn the King but we can do nothing until Gerard leaves to meet up with the rebels."

"He goes at first light."

"Then we must be ready to leave straight after."

Elenor was fully in command now and Joan regarded her with something approaching respect.

"You must say I am a cousin, here to stay after losing my husband and family. I know no-one outside this keep so there will be no danger of being recognised."

"You are right. You could be any serving wench in this castle" Elenor winced at that, although she knew it to be true.

"I know the paths well through the forest, for we hunted there as children before the Normans came." Joan's Saxon blood was obvious in her wheat-blond hair and blue eyes and Elenor realised that Joan's words earlier were the truth. They all did what they could to survive.

And Joan?

Had she been lucky to take Gerard's fancy?

She wanted to ask Joan if she had had a man, a lover, before Gerard had brought her here, but for now more urgent thoughts occupied her mind.

"How long will it take us to reach William on foot?" "If we leave as soon as possible after Gerard, we can be through the forest and as far as the river ford by nightfall. William should reach the ford at mid - morning I think, the day after tomorrow. That means we can find a secure place to camp through the night and be alert next morning for William's arrival."

Elenor's stomach growled loudly and protestingly and Elenor remembered that she had eaten nothing all day.

"I shall bring you some food.

He will not miss you tonight at the table, he will be too busy plotting."

There was a sudden warmth between the two women and Elenor felt the prick of tears at the thought that she had such an unexpected ally.

Joan left the room and Elenor sat down in the chair by the empty fireplace.

What they were about to do held such danger, such peril that only someone pushed to the brink as she was would contemplate it. For two women to journey alone as they planned held untold risks, not to say the chance that they may be caught out as they tried to leave Fernrean. But then the alternatives she faced were not to be considered.

To wait and see Gerard succeed in killing the King, then to be murdered herself so that he could replace her with another, or for Gerard to fail and she to be left as the widow of a traitor, if William did not order them all to be executed.

No! At least she would be taking some sort of control of her life if she did this - whatever the risks.

Joan re-entered the room with a tray of steaming food and a small flask of wine.

"Eat well my lady. We shall need all our strength on the morrow, for when we leave here there will be no turning back."

The two women stared at each other, blue eyes holding brown for several seconds. Joan was the first to look away.

"My lady... what I've done in the past - I've hurt you grievously in many ways..."

Elenor interrupted her,"You said it yourself. We all do what we must to survive. Now we must both survive this, and to do that we must trust each other. You understand this.?"

"Aye, my lady."

"Very well then. Until the morning."

"Goodnight my lady."

Strangely, Elenor had slept peacefully and well. She had not been disturbed by Gerard or any of his followers and she had heard no sounds from his room as she readied herself for bed. It was as though her mind had switched off for she had found herself attending to small tasks around her chamber in an automatic, unthinking fashion before finally climbing into bed and allowing her body to relax. Vaguely she had wondered if Joan was keeping him occupied and a sense of gratitude had stolen over her. Without the maid to help she knew there would be no chance at all of escape from Fernrean, for even if she should escape from the stronghold, she had no idea of where she might go or what she should do. She would fall easy prey to rebels or wild animals.

The song of the birds woke her at dawn and she wondered for a moment why she should have this feeling of excitement and anticipation. She was so used to waking afraid and unhappy that her brain, at first, was confused.

When she remembered what was afoot she had to force herself to lie still -

- not to leap out of bed and start that agitated pacing with which she normally worked off her anxieties.

Rest was essential, for once they set their plans into action their minds and bodies must be able to cope with the great demands they would ask of them.

The hardest part was trusting Joan. In spite of what she had said to the maid, all that had gone before was not easily forgotten. Still, she could not do this alone, and Joan's terror of William had been very real.

She must rest.

It was easier said than done.

Suppose they succeeded in escaping Fernrean and reaching William before Gerard, what would they say? "Pardon me , my lord King, but my husband plots to kill you."

And Joan was right - she did look like a serving wench - but she spoke Norman and could recite her lineage by heart. Then there was the state of her face. She could easily be trying to revenge herself on her husband for his treatment of her. Fortunately William's reputation with women was good. Elenor had never heard of him treating a woman badly - and his fidelity to his wife Mathilda was legendary.

She sighed. Whichever way this turned out it was better than waiting meekly for Gerard to kill her.

She must have dozed a little for when Joan knocked, the sun was shining directly into her chamber and as Joan carried the tray of food to the table, Elenor panicked.

"Gerard! Has he left? Are we too late?"

Joan nodded towards the window. "He leaves now..."

Elenor leaped from her bed and flattened her back to the wall beside her window glancing carefully out. Mounted on a scrawny brown steed which bore no resemblance to his usual prancing warhorse, Gerard was dressed in the leather gambeson of a common soldier. She watched him snarling and cursing at his men before they were finally ready, and they bunched together and rode out of Fernrean, heading east.

"My lady, come and eat, we must be ready to leave soon for we need to allow ourselves plenty of time for our journey."

Elenor shivered, then she washed herself quickly and dressed, curiously eyeing the bundle which Joan was unwrapping.

"Cloaks, my lady, heavy and warm, and these boots which I hope will fit you."

The short leather boots were a little bit big but Joan tore up one of Elenor's robes into strips to bind her feet. "It will also protect your feet from blistering. The journey is long and hard and you are not used to walking so far."

"Where did you get all this?"

Joan grinned, totally transforming her features. "Ask no questions, lady..."

Elenor found herself smiling back at her unexpected ally, then she turned to the food and they set to with a will. The good Lord knew when they would have a chance to eat again.

An hour later they were ready.

Elenor adjusted a fold of the cloak across her face. "How is this?"

"It will do. Come my lady. If we can escape Fernrean, then we stand a small chance of success."

A leather water bottle hung at each of their waists and a small bundle held bread and cheese.

"We cannot carry too much for we must not arouse suspicion." Joan opened Elenor's door and peered out. "Come." She beckoned and slipped out, her mistress close behind her.

Elenor's heart was thundering wildly in her breast, yet she felt more alive, more invigorated and more determined than she had ever felt in her life. They encountered no-one as they made their way through the keep. Even the hunting dogs were snoring peacefully in front of the fire and Elenor felt one strange brief moment of envy. Then they were through the great doors, down the small flight of steps and crossing the bailey.

At the gates they were stopped.

"Well now, who have we here? A new face I'll warrant."

"My cousin, Albrec. A grieving widow, you understand." Joan's voice was teasing and Elenor wondered how she could do it. She herself, was petrified.

"Grieving widow you say. Is she as comely as you Joan, my sweet?" The guard's hand plucked at Elenor's cloak, then dropped away at sight of her damaged face.

"Sweet Jesus! What happened to you?"

"It was an accident.

The cart overturned killing her husband and baby son and leaving my cousin in this parlous state."

"I'm sorry for you woman. Perhaps when you are recovered you'll come and see Albrec - see if we can lighten your sorrow."

"We would like that. I'm sure my cousin will show her appreciation for your concern."

The guard, Albrec, seemed not to notice that Elenor had not spoken a word. Her voice would certainly have betrayed her. Joan laughed into Albrec's face and the guard grinned back at her before he swung wide the gate and let the two women pass through.

Elenor forced herself on although her legs were trembling and she found herself envying Joan's easy way with the guards at the lower gate. They all knew her and were obviously used to flirting with her and Elenor wondered if she, herself, would ever flirt with a man. She dismissed the thought completely. If she survived this desperate plan she knew not what the future might hold for her afterwards, although she hoped that William would be grateful enough to be kind to her - to them both.

They were pushing on into the fringe of the forest now, beyond the village which they had skirted by mutual agreement.

The fewer people who saw them the better. Elenor was short of breath. Her incarceration for so long had taken its toll and she struggled to keep up with Joan, who although older than her, was much fitter.

"Joan! Wait - I must rest!"

"No time, my lady - we must move as fast as we can."

Joan did not even turn around, and Elenor bent her head and harnessed the iron will and determination she had used these past two years to survive, to her desire to reach William.

It was late into the afternoon before Joan finally stopped.

Elenor was exhausted. The stitch in her side was burning agony and her lungs heaved with the effort to catch her breath. Joan led her to a sheltered spot where the holly bushes formed a circular den at the base of some ancient oaks.

"A prickly bower!" Elenor's breathless comment made Joan laugh."Yet more welcome than your own these past years I think."

Elenor did not reply, thinking of Joan's part in much of her misery during that time. The woman glanced at her. "I asked your forgiveness. I tried to explain."

"It does not matter."

"I think it does. If not to you lady - then to me. Please."

Elenor plumped down, her back against the tree and closed her eyes.

She was hot, dusty and exhausted but if Joan wanted to clear her conscience then perhaps she owed her that - now.

"Very well - explain." Joan sat next to her and pulled out the leather water bottle from beneath her cloak, unstopping it and offering it to Elenor, who took several long grateful gulps. She gasped at the coldness of it yet it revived her a little. Joan took it back and drank from it herself.

"I lied to you last night."

Elenor gaped at her.

"Oh do not worry. It was not a great lie, merely a small change to someone's fate. You see it was I who was Erland's woman. We were to be married. Gerard laid eyes on me and that was the end of it. Erland took to the outlaw trail and swore to make the Normans pay. To him I was a dead woman."

There was a moment of silence, then Joan continued sadly.

"Erland and I had been companions since childhood. We went everywhere together and we always vowed to marry. He fought with Harold at Stamford and his wounds kept him from fighting the Normans. When William became King he would have accepted him. After all, with Harold dead, who else was there? Only the young atheling, and there would have been struggles between the earls to control him. No. William was strong and would keep the peace we thought."

Elenor grasped Joan's hand. "And then came Gerard."

"Aye. Then came Gerard. At first it was not so bad, although it was hard to change from ways we had always known. Unable to hunt for food, owning nothing of our own - but we survived. Until the day he saw me working on the land. It was hot and I wore only a simple shift. It was in shreds when he finished with me."

"Dear God, stop! I've heard enough!"

"No please - It helps to tell you. He brought me to Fernrean and to Erland I was dead.

Oh, he would still have had me.

He loved me. But I was kept locked up until I felt so dirty, so degraded I would not have gone to him if I had been released."

Elenor found her grip on Joan's hand was hurting even herself, and the imprint of her fingers could clearly be seen when she let go. Her arms went around her maid and the two women hugged close together as if to share each other's agony.

"What a coil this is. What will be the outcome? Come let us forge onward for in William is our only chance for life. We reach him or die!" Although the more exhausted of the two, it was Elenor who pulled the Saxon to her feet, and dusted off the twigs and leaves.

"We must stay to the path. This forest holds many dangers for such as us although I am prepared." Joan pulled from beneath her cloak a short, wicked - looking knife."This will sting sharp enough - at man or beast who try to halt us."

Elenor was impressed and wished that Joan had thought to arm her mistress also - but then perhaps she still did not trust her fully.

They pushed onward in a state of almost blind fatigue and they were certainly under divine protection, for they encountered none of those forest denizens who might have harmed them.

Dusk found them finally at the edge of the trees, not far from the point at which the road William must travel entered the forest. Elenor almost collapsed onto the ground.

"Thank God! I could go no further."

"Yet lady we must - for this is the ambush point.

We must reach William before he gets anywhere near this spot - further down, by the ford."

"How far?" Elenor used her hands to push herself up from the floor.

Joan was sympathetic."Not too far, my lady - a mile or two at most."

It was, in fact, much further but Joan had not wished to discourage her mistress for, in spite of the bindings around her feet, the blisters had risen and broken and Elenor could feel the blood inside her boots, sticky and warm. The sun had gone down and the cloaks they wore were most welcome against the late spring mists which ghosted eerily across their path. They hung thick and heavy over the waters of the stream which was made shallow by a narrow ford, the point at which William must cross to reach the road to Fernrean.

"We can fill the water bottles, for it will be mid-morning before William reaches here and we must take care that Gerard has not posted men near here to warn of the King's arrival.

We must stay hidden and rest."

Elenor nodded her heartfelt agreement with that and the two women made their way cautiously down to the edge of the stream.

"Joan - I must take off these boots, my feet are on fire..."

"No no lady. You will never be able to put them back on. Here - simply stand where the water can soak through the soles, not too deep or the boots will shrink and harden as they dry and you will be in a worse case than before."

Quickly they filled their water bottles before retreating into the bushes which bordered the banks of the stream, pushing their way through into the thickest part, hidden and sheltered. Joan trod down a thick bed of moss and fern then they spread out one cloak and wrapped the other closely around them both, huddling together for warmth. They shared the bread and cheese, washing it down with cold water then settling down for the night. In spite of their fear and the danger they were in, their exhaustion blotted out all thought and they were soon in a deep and dreamless sleep.

They almost missed him.

It was barely dawn and the two women were still deeply asleep as William and his men approached the ford much earlier than expected. It was fortunate that one of the horses decided that a dangerous beast was lurking on the other side of that sparkling ribbon of water and put his mind to convincing his rider and his companions that to set foot in the ford was to commit suicide. The ensuing commotion was enough to wake the dead. Horses whinnied and snorted, men cursed - "By the blood of Christ, Ragnor, that creature needs a knife through the heart. He'll be the death of you one day!"

The knight addressed as Ragnor was too busy to reply, clinging grimly to his rearing, half - demented mount.

William himself had already crossed the ford with several of his barons and was watching the performance with some amusement.

Fogged with sleep Elenor and Joan staggered to their feet and pushed their way desperately out from the bushes in a panic, terrified of missing their chance to speak to the King, and setting the hysterical horse once more into fits.

They were surrounded immediately by armed men, swords at the ready, held back only by William's shout."Hold! They are but women. Hold your swords!"

Elenor was sobbing in fear and desperation. Joan was white - faced but silent as her pitifully small knife was discovered and confiscated.

One of William's knights rapped out orders, quick and fierce and within seconds the immediate area around the ford was secured by a ring of steel.

They stood and faced their King. Dirty, bedraggled, still half asleep, terrified, Elenor drew herself up and tried to gather together what little dignity she had left.

William's blue eyes missed nothing. He frowned at the appalling state of Elenor's face and took note of the clothing they wore. No peasant women these in spite of their condition.

"Well now. What brings you here, scaring our horses and my warriors half to death? You!" He addressed Elenor, recognising her quality beneath the dirt and bruises. "Speak my lady!"

Elenor dropped to her knees in the dust pulling Joan down beside her.

"My lord King."

Her voice was trembling as was her body and she swallowed hard and took a breath to steady herself.

All their hopes, their lives depended on this moment. "Sire - we came to warn you of danger ahead..."

A grim ripple of laughter greeted her words and William held up his hand to still the sound.

"What danger my lady?" Although his tone was encouraging he did not tell her to rise.

"An ambush awaits you Sire - at the point where the road enters the forest."

"And how do you know this?"

This was the moment she had dreaded. She bit her lip."Because it is my husband who waits to ambush you."

William did not seem to react.

"And you are, my lady?"

"Elenor de Beauvrais Sire, of Fernrean. Gerard de Beauvrais is my husband."

"I see. Did he tell you that he intends to kill me?""No Sire. Joan, my maid..." She indicated the woman kneeling beside her,"overheard the whole plot. Although I already knew something was afoot - a plan to kill you, I did not know the details.""I see. How is it that your maid knew those details and you did not?" His questioning was merciless and Elenor's shame could not be avoided."She was occupying his bed Sire. He thought her asleep while he conferred with his men." She kept her face and her voice expressionless - an expert at self - control, yet did not miss William's flush of anger. A faithful husband himself, he deplored licentiousness in his men."'Tis only as we thought Sire. It is well that we brought more support than we intended. Shall we turn back?"

"No! I need Fernrean.

We shall stop here and decide what to do. We need someone who knows the area and we need to know more of de Beauvrais' plans."He looked questioningly at Elenor."My maid, Joan, Sire knows this countryside well. Indeed it is thanks to her that we are here at all, for I had never been outside Fernrean since the day I arrived... until yesterday."

William dismounted, his decision made, casting his reins to his squire and holding out his hand to Elenor to help her to rise. "Come my lady, join me and refresh yourself. When you feel better you - and your serving woman, can tell me everything."

His hand went to her chin and he turned her face from side to side, noting old scars, the split in her bottom lip, a thin thread of white scarring running down from her hairline where Gerard had near broken her skull with a faggot of firewood, as well as the new damage."Yes my lady, you can tell me everything."

His tone was deadly and Elenor almost felt a tinge of pity for her husband - almost!

William's men made a quick warriors' camp. No fires, two outer rings of guards and an inner cordon of dangerous - looking , iron faced men around King William.

"Allow me to make one or two introductions my lady..." William gestured around him to four men, obviously trusted companions and high - ranking lords...

"Lord Baldwin de Framois..."

A short, heavy man built like a bull but with
humorous brown eyes which twinkled at Elenor
as he kissed her hand.

"Delighted my lady."

She dipped a curtsey.

"Lord Edwin de Cercy..."

"My lady, enchanted." The young man smiled
charmingly and held her hand a little too long after
the formal kiss and Elenor felt herself blushing.
Blushing! After all she had suffered. The thought
made her smile back at him so warmly that he
was delighted and she was forced to pull her hand
away from him to be presented to the next
member of William's small company.

"Lord Ragnor de Louberon."

The gentleman with the hysterical horse...

"Forgive me for scaring your horse my lord,
but thanks to him for waking us - or we would
surely have slept on and missed you."

"I am honoured my lady." Lord Ragnor was
obviously embarrassed by his horse's behaviour
but was used to his companion - in - arms'
derision at the incident.

"Yes, I think for once we must all thank the
damned animal for saving us from death and
destruction."

William's comment roused laughter once more
and Lord Ragnor grimaced wryly making Elenor
laugh too, in spite of her state of exhaustion.

"And finally Lord Armand de Carrefour, in
command of my personal guard..."

"My Lady de Beauvrais."

The tone was clipped and cool.

He did not take her hand, merely inclined his head and Elenor felt unaccountably rebuffed.

Staring up at him she was suddenly very conscious of her unsightly bruises and broken nose and she thought those grey eyes beneath the conical helmet were unfairly critical.

"Now." William gestured to a fallen tree trunk. "If you will sit Lady Elenor we shall listen to your story.""Yes Sire."   Now that they had reached their goal Elenor felt sick and weak. The journey through the forest had taken its toll and Joan too was pale with exhaustion. Elenor pulled the maid down to sit beside her.

"Forgive me my lady..." William gestured to his squire and a goblet of wine was produced as if by magic. Elenor sipped slowly, feeling the liquor course quickly through her veins and settle the heaving in her empty stomach.

"Food Gilbert..." William snapped and a wooden trencher with bread and cheese was passed along.

Lord Ragnor, Lord Edwin and Lord Baldwin gathered around their King and the two women to hear the story, yet Elenor missed the other - the grey - eyed Norman in charge of William's guard.

Slowly she started her tale, from the moment she had left her home in France to travel to England in order to marry Gerard de Beauvrais.

She did not falter, nor did she miss a single detail of her existence with Gerard.

When she had finished, with the story of their escape from Fernrean, she looked up into the icy regard of Armand de Carrefour who had somehow joined them without her even realising it, and what she saw in his face made her blench with fear for there was murder to be read there and she thought for a moment that it was she who was the object of his rage.

"My lady we appreciate your honesty and your openness and we thank you for your courage in making such an arduous journey to warn us of our danger."

"This Saxon rebel, Sire. We need to know if he will make a pact with de Beauvrais or if he intends to betray him as revenge for taking his woman." Armand de Carrefour brought William back to the important question.

"My lord King..." Joan was unsure whether she should even address him. He turned to her politely and she took heart. "I could try to find him. To speak with him."

"We do not have much time Sire. They will realise something is amiss if we are not where they expect us to be when dusk falls."

Elenor heard the mistrust in his voice and strove to support her maid.

"If it were not for Joan, we would not be here my lord.

If she tries to find Erland she will place herself in great peril and if anyone can persuade him to our cause it would be Joan."

"And what reward in this for a Saxon woman who has shared her lord's bed, on her own admission, these last years.?"

"That was not of her will! You cannot know what it is like to be the plaything of such a beast! To be helpless, to survive God knows how. You! You are a man. A lord. A great warrior. If aught offends you can take up arms, call on knights and soldiers to aid you and thus no-one forces you to do anything against your will, things which sicken you, which make you wish to end your life. You, my lord, will never know how it is!"   Tears streamed unchecked down her bruised face. She trembled with fatigue and fear, yet she stood up and shook her fist at him as she spoke - a slight , half - starved girl whom this knight could kill with one blow.

It stunned them all. It silenced him. He inclined his head to her whether in admiration or mockery she could not decide and William stepped forward.

"It seems, Armand, that you had best call up your knights and soldiers to defend you from Lady Elenor."

The laughter took the tension from the moment and William bent towards Joan.

"Woman, if you can do this you will have the gratitude of your King."

"What more could I ask Sire?" Joan's answer made Elenor glance sideways at her for in spite of her defence of her maid she was only too aware of how good a survivor Joan was.

"Very well. Are you certain you are fit for such a task?"

"With the food and drink in my belly Sire it will not take me long to be ready."

"We can wait only until dusk, then we must make our move whether you have returned or not. You understand this?"

"I do Sire. I will do my best."

"I shall leave you then to rest and make your own farewells."

Both women curtseyed deeply as William and his lords, flanked by knights and captains moved away to hold their council of war.

The two women were silent, sharing the bread and cheese and what was left of the wine. Elenor felt a strange sense of unreality. They had achieved their goal it seemed, and yet their future was still uncertain.

"Do not worry, my lady, I shall find Erland and we shall be rid of Lord Gerard de Beauvrais - one way or the other."

"Be careful Joan. In William lies our future and I, for one, would not wish to cross him."

"Nor I lady, nor I. All will be well. And my thanks for defending me to that high - nosed Norman. I did not think you had the spirit."

"What? After all this time with Gerard? It makes me afraid of no man.

After all, what more could a man do to a woman than that which Gerard has done to us?"

"What indeed lady? What indeed?"

Elenor looked quickly at Joan yet the woman was munching on her bread and her face was bland so Elenor could read nothing more in that.

Joan washed herself at the stream and tidied herself, combing her fingers through her blonde hair and braiding it before tying her kerchief around her head.

She wrapped her cloak into a bundle and refilled her leather water bottle.

"Take some of this." Elenor tied up some of the bread into a cloth.

"Thank you my lady."

They stared at each other for a long moment, thinking of the past two years.

"God go with you Joan." Elenor put her arms around her maid and erstwhile tormentor and then Joan dipped her knee in a curtsey.

"You also, my lady. Take care."

"Is the woman ready?"

Elenor knew that voice immediately. It raised her hackles and she turned, chin in the air. "We are ready my lord." Her brown eyes challenged his hard grey regard yet he merely stood back and gestured to them to precede him.

The King stood alone and he straightened up at their approach. "Until dusk." He spoke the words directly to Joan.

"Until dusk Sire." She echoed him, then was away, trudging off across the sparse grass towards the tree line, watched by the whole company until she was out of sight.

"Get some rest." Armand de Carrefour was still at her side.

"Yes. I will." Now that Joan had left her, Elenor felt strangely alone and she swayed a little as she turned.

"My lady, steady..."

was all she heard as her ordeal and her injuries overtook her, and she plunged into a dark oblivion which remembered only strong arms enfolding her as she fell and a string of curses from Armand de Carrefour who found himself with an armful of woman as light and insubstantial as thistledown.

The look of confusion and helplessness on his face was comical and Baldwin de Framois could not help a grin as he moved to help the tall commander. "Here. She needs to rest. She will be comfortable here." A nest of heaped cloaks was quickly provided and Armand knelt to gently lay his burden down.

"Body of Christ - how could anyone do this?" Baldwin muttered as her face was fully exposed for the first time. Her eyes were not as swollen now, nor was her nose, but the bruises were yellow and her nose, which had been so straight, was badly bent out of shape.

Armand de Carrefour brushed back the wayward strands of hair from her face as gently as he could, then he covered her with his own cloak and sat back on his heels. He really had more to do than act as nursemaid to a bedraggled lady whose husband was a traitor to his King.

In spite of Gerard's belief that his various treasonable activities had gone unnoticed, William had long had his suspicions of Gerard, which was why he had taken this detour on his march no rth, in order to secure Fernrean. "The last thing I need is a stronghold full of traitors at my back," he had decided.

"Thomas!" Armand called to his squire.

"Yes lord?" The boy's face was eager.

"Thomas, watch over the Lady Elenor. When she wakes make sure she gets some food and something to drink."

He hesitated..."She will probably need a wash - and see if we have anything for those bruises."

"Yes my lord." The squire would rather have been listening in to the commanders' talk of battles but his lord was concerned about this lady it seemed and so he settled himself down to guard her.

Armand rejoined the King.

"How is the lady?"

"She is asleep Sire. Totally worn out. I have left Thomas to watch over her."

"Good. This matter could turn well to our advantage.

The Lady of Fernrean, beaten and starved or not, is one person we had not thought to have as a pawn in our game."

"Do you think the serving woman will be faithful Sire? After all she was de Beauvrais' bed mate."

"That is not to say it was her choice.

From what I understand it is the outlaw Erland who holds her loyalty. There may lie our difficulties I think."

"So long as she persuades him not to join Gerard, that is all the help we need from her. As to what happens after that?" Armand shrugged and looked questioningly at William. The King, however, gave nothing away.

"Come, my lord. We also need our rest. Our plans are made to cover all events we hope. The rest is in the hands of God."

Joan forced her weary legs to carry her onwards. Although she was much stronger and fitter than Elenor, their danger and the journey from Fernrean, even the meeting with William, had drained her. The only thing which kept her going now was the thought that she might save Erland and destroy Gerard.

God! How she had hated the Norman in the time he had kept her and used her! When Elenor had arrived Joan had rejoiced, thinking that surely he would let her go. But no! It seemed he preferred her to the slim young girl who came as his bride and he used his lust and sexual depravities to torture his wife, saving Joan for an easier kind of pleasure.

At first she had hated Elenor and despised her for the fact that she was Norman and married to Gerard. When she was forced to wait upon her as her maid she had been as surly and mean and insolent as possible, knowing that she would not complain to her husband.

As time had gone by, however, Gerard's cruelty had aroused Joan's pity, although she kept it very well hidden, putting her own survival first.

If she did not survive, how then could she take her revenge when the opportunity presented itself? And she had known her time would come.

She listened to every plan, every word which passed between Gerard and his co-conspirators when they did not even realise she was around.

She was nothing. A serving maid who served the lord better than she served his wife.

Joan tripped and fell bringing her mind back to the present. She lay for a moment, the sun burning her shoulders, then she rolled over and sat up. She unstoppered her water bottle and took a long drink, squinting at the sun which was now high in the sky. No time even to snatch a bite of the bread Elenor had given her. She must find Erland!

Suddenly she was alert! A sound - a whisper of movement at the edge of her senses.

She rolled back onto her stomach and wormed her way carefully through the long grass towards the edge of the forest. When she finally crouched in the cover of some bushes she caught the movement, a flash of someone within the shade of the trees.

Her heart was pounding and her emotions ran the gamut between hope and fear.

The group of men were almost upon her before she could be safely sure of who they were, then she rose from her hiding place like the goddess Diana, hands on hips, a challenging smile on her mouth and a defiant tilt to her chin.

Who would know that her insides were churning like a mill race and her heart was beating fit to burst?

Erland stared at her with total shock and disbelief on his face.

"Joan?" The word was a gasp. He almost ran towards her gripping her shoulders and staring hungrily into her face. "Joan what are you doing here? Are you alright? Joan, Joan. Dear God!" And she was swept into his hard embrace, his mouth capturing hers before she could protest and his men looking on, grinning like fools.

That kiss. That longed-for, dreamed of, hungry kiss was a life-giving balm to her starving soul and she could no more have denied him than she could have stopped breathing.

When he lifted his head, she tried to speak. "Erland!" He kissed her again."Erland!" And again. She drummed her fists on his chest. "Will you listen you great oaf? This is life or death and I need to talk to you."

She finally got through to him. He sighed.

"You are right, we do need to talk." His deep blue eyes were soft as they roamed her face and he kept his arms about her as if afraid she might leave him again.

"Have you seen Gerard?"

He frowned. "He is at my camp. Why?"

"If you let me go I'll explain."

"Very well." His mood had changed and his expression was guarded as he led her further into the forest to sit down.

When she was finally sitting facing him, she hardly knew how to start and it did not help that he was stern and unsmiling now.

"Tell me, Erland, have you agreed to help Gerard to ambush the King?"

He frowned. "The King? You mean that Norman bastard who slaughtered our people, who is still murdering them and who set this pig over us free men to plunder and rape? Is that who you mean?"

Joan reached out and grabbed the front of his jerkin. "Stop it! No! I mean the man who was crowned King at Westminster. The man against whom it is treason to plot and rebel. You will lose your head my love, and after all I have been through to survive, to make sure Gerard dies and we do not! I will not allow you to commit suicide."

They glared at each other while Erland's men made every effort to become invisible.

"Erland. Oh Erland. If you knew how I've suffered. If you realised what a chance for us this could be. That is... If you still want me."

"Want you? If I still want you? I dream of you. I hear your voice in the breeze. I think I see you in the village and risk my life to chase after you when you are not there. I want you so much it is like a wound in my heart." Raggedly he finished and his pain and misery made her weep.

"Then listen to me. William will owe me his life if we turn against Gerard and I will ask him to pardon you. Then we will be free. Free of Gerard. Free to marry if you wish. Please Erland!"

Her tear-stained face was upturned to his and he gently cupped it in his hands, wiping away the tears with his thumbs.

"What is your plan?"

So relieved that she felt faint, Joan rested her head against his breast." Have you agreed to help Gerard?"

"Yes. I do not know how he had the gall to come to me. The only reason I did not kill him on the spot was because I was curious."

"He places no value on women. He would not understand your love for me for he sees females only as playthings, creatures to be used and despised."

"What of his wife? I hear she is a weak and pitiful female who is not long for this world."

Joan smiled wryly. "Oh I would not say so. She may seem frail but her spirit is as strong as yours or mine, possibly stronger, for if he had done to me the things he has done to her, I would certainly have taken my own life."

"So! When can I kill him?" His expression turned wolfish.

"William knows of the ambush. He has more fighting men with him than Gerard thinks.

All you have to do is to pretend to go along with Gerard, then when he has committed himself ... change sides!"

He gaped at her. "But will William understand what is happening?"

"He will be prepared for it. He will not know for certain whether I have reached you, for he needs to enter the forest when Gerard expects him, more or less, so I have no time to return and let him know I have found you. We must trust in God and in William's ability to read the situation right."

"And what of you? Where will you be? I cannot take you back with me for he might see you. You must go to the village with Erik and stay out of sight until it is over."

"No. I must try and return to my lady. She is with William and she may need me there."

"The Lady de Beauvrais came with you?" He was incredulous.

"If she had not I could not have persuaded William. Would he have listened to a Saxon serving wench? No. I needed her and she needed to escape Gerard, so we helped each other."

Erland sighed and rose to his feet pulling her up into his embrace. "You have suffered so much. I am afraid to let you go lest I never see you again."

"I am set upon this course. Gerard signed his own death warrant when he took me and whether that death is from the hand of the King, the hand of the man I love or even my own hand, I care not so long as he dies!

'Tis you who must take care for you are within Gerard's reach and he is master of the game of a knife in the back."

He bent his head, his shock of blonde hair falling forward as a curtain for his kiss, tender and possessive.

"I shall send Erik with you as far as the road and, God willing, we shall be together again when this business is finished."

"Farewell my love." Joan lifted her hand to his face then left him, accompanied by Erik, a huge great giant of a man who would give his life for his leader.

Erland stood watching until she was out of sight, then he signalled to his men and they slid silently back into the forest and headed for their camp - and the Lord Gerard de Beauvrais.

He was in a foul mood, the Norman lord, and Erland was forced to keep a tight rein on his anger and contempt, the thought of Joan and her plan for their future together, firmly in his mind.

"Where in the name of Christ have you been? It is near time and you're pissing around in the woods, probably dallying with a wench! That's all you peasants think about, just like that woman you had. Aye she's a fine one in the sack..."

"Shut your mouth Norman!" Erland exuded menace as he thrust his face at Gerard "You need us - don't forget it. Now gather your men and we'll be off to meet this King of yours."

Gerard fumed eye to eye with the Saxon outlaw for a long moment then inwardly promising the insolent peasant a slow and lingering death when this was all over, he cursed foully and turned away shouting to his men. Erland watched him, a grim smile hovering at his lips.

Darkness was falling as they took up position just where the road to Fernrean entered the forest.

They were only just in time, for William's force could be heard and vaguely seen approaching the ambush which awaited them.

Erland's scouts had reported directly to him and the Saxon leader knew that William was with only a small portion of his men. If he had not spoken to Joan, Erland would have been worried. As it was he had made his own plans.

Gerard had not wanted to commit his small force to the front of the fighting, saying he preferred to keep his more experienced men in reserve in the event that something went wrong. In reality Erland and everybody else knew that he wanted a clear road to escape if something went wrong!

"You know what to do Ulf?"

"No need to worry Erland, we'll watch the Norman pig, and if he tries to flee we'll have him!"

"Good. Now make this convincing. Let's hope this King knows what part to play."

William and his men appeared to suspect nothing as they rode into the darkness of the forest and their conversation was all of Fernrean and their desire for hot food and a goblet of wine.

The attack seemed to be a complete surprise as Erland's band swooped down from the trees with battle cries fit to curdle the blood.

The Normans rallied round their King, swords whirling and shields edge to edge.

The noise was deafening and it appeared that a fierce battle was in progress as Gerard eventually ventured forth with his handful of men.

It seemed that the King would easily be defeated, for many of his guards were lying on the floor, grievously wounded and the King himself had fallen back, protected by only a few of his knights.

"Yield, my lord King." Gerard screamed, almost hysterically triumphant."Yield and your life will be spared."

In his eagerness he spurred his horse forward, not realising how quickly a path was cleared for him. His sword was out yet it met no other steel until he was almost face to face with the King he wished to betray. Then he was stopped. He was stopped by a tall grey-eyed knight who parried his wild blows with ease, playing with him, taunting him with the speed of his swordplay.

Gerard started to sweat. His eyes darted from side to side, his alarm growing as he realised that the fighting had suddenly ceased, that the only sound now was that of his own sword ringing against the steel of this devil who faced him.

His men! Where were his men? Disarmed and helpless they stood, surrounded not by the king's warriors but by Saxon outlaws.

Treachery! By the Christ, Saxon treachery! Yet he had no time to think for he was hard put to keep the deadly point of his opponent's sword from his throat.

Over-indulgence had taken its toll. His body sagged, his muscles screamed for rest, his arm could scarce lift his sword to defend himself.

It was almost pitiful as he tried to fight on - not courage but sheer terror driving his body to obey him. Finally he could take no more, and he threw down his sword and sobbed for mercy, falling to his knees and appealing to the King.

"I yield Sire, I yield! Mercy. For Christ's sake mercy!" He grovelled on the floor arousing contempt even in the breasts of his own men.

His opponent leaned down and in a voice which was no more than a whisper yet which made his blood run cold murmured,"And did your lady cry for mercy, you cur? When she screamed did you feel pity?"

Then William stepped forward and laid his hand on the sword arm of Armand de Carrefour feeling the shuddering desire to kill in every muscle of his commander's body.

"We need the information he can give us, my friend. After he has spilled his guts - why then you may spill his guts- more literally perhaps."

Reluctantly Armand backed away and Gerard was dragged to his feet, his arms tied behind him and a noose of rope placed around his neck. It was only then that the remainder of William's men came out from the trees around them, swords drawn, shields at the ready.

The 'wounded' rose from the ground, grinning, and joined their comrades around the King.

Erland now faced William.

For a moment blue Saxon eyes stared into Norman eyes as blue as his own and surprise was their main emotion. Then slowly he knelt before his King proffering his sword across his arm. William reached out briefly and touched the hilt then gestured to Erland to rise.

"Come. We ride to Fernrean. Then we shall decide how this toil will end."

They pushed on side by side to the stronghold of Fernrean, Norman and Saxon riding together, uncomfortable and suspicious, yes, but together.

Gerard was mounted on his horse with the rope still tight about his throat and men set to guard him under pain of death should he escape.

Erland searched the company desperately for sight of Joan and his man, Erik, but the darkness and confusion about them defeated him, and he would not ask.

When finally they came to Fernrean they encountered an unforeseen problem.

The place was closed against them.

"Open in the name of the King," roared Baldwin de Framois. No reply. No movement. The drawbridge stayed stubbornly raised.

"Fetch de Beauvrais."

Gerard was hustled forward.

"Order your men to let us in." William told his erstwhile liegeman, and Gerard made the mistake of trying to bargain.

"If you untie me I shall do so Sire. I am sure we can come to some agreement. I am prepared to co-operate fully...."

A blow in the mouth silenced him, and that same soft snarl which had questioned him about mercy and pity for his wife advised him to do as he was told.

Gerard's voice was a croak. "Open up. 'Tis I de Beauvrais. Open to the King you fools!"

They obeyed him, but slowly, and when the drawbridge touched the ground it echoed to the thunder of horses' feet as King William and his men made haste to secure Fernrean castle for the crown.

When Elenor awoke she was warm and comfortable and really did not want to move.

"My lady! My lady, please you must rouse yourself. The King is making ready to leave. My lady!"

She did not recognise the boy's voice but it was urgent enough to alert that sense of survival which had been developed so fully these last two years.

Her rush to get to her feet startled Thomas the squire into tumbling backwards.

"Oh! I'm sorry. Are you hurt?" Once on her feet she knew where she was and why she was here and a surge of energy and excitement shook her. The squire was scrambling up, brushing off the twigs and leaves and grinning.

"No my lady, I am well. I have brought food and drink for we leave here very shortly and my lord has asked me to take care of you."

"And you are?"

"Oh! Forgive me my lady. Thomas du Loupin, squire to Lord Armand de Carrefour."

He bowed before her and she acknowledged him gravely, enjoying his polite attention.

"Now where is this food, Thomas? I am starving!"

Indeed she was, and Thomas watched with satisfaction as she tucked into the bread and cold meat he had brought her.

"I shall bring you some water to wash with my lady, and then we must be ready to move out."

"I'll be ready, Thomas, have no worries about that." The grim satisfaction in her tone made him stare at her, unaware of exactly who she was and why she was there then his eyes moved away to a point above and behind her.

"We are almost ready, my lord."

"Good!"

Elenor turned to look up at the Lord de Carrefour, squinting against the rays of the sun and seeing in him only a tall dark shape which exuded power and confidence.

"I find myself in your debt my lord for providing me with a protector." She was not sure of him, remembering how she had shouted and shaken her fist at him. If he had been Gerard, she would, no doubt, have been dead by now.

"We did the best we could my lady, but you understand we were not prepared for female company." He was polite yet still reserved with her, and she could not make out his expression for he was wearing his coif and helm, the nosepiece obscuring much of his face.

"Are you able to ride? For we are ready to leave and one of the baggage animals has been brought along for you."

She was longing for the promised water to wash with but she did not want to hold up the advance on Fernrean so she merely nodded.

"Is there any sign of my maid?"

"No my lady, but we did not really expect her to return..."

"You think she will betray us!" It was not a question and Elenor found herself firing up again for an argument with him.

"You did not let me finish. We did not expect her to return before we left. There is the chance that she will meet us further along the road." There was amusement now deepening his voice, but it was still difficult to see his face, to see if he was smiling.

What on earth was the matter with her? She was ready to do battle with him for no reason at all. Surely all the fight should have been beaten out of her by Gerard?

"Now, if you are ready, your horse is here." He gestured to her and she fell into step beside him, leaving Thomas to pack away her makeshift bed of cloaks.

The animal provided for her seemed a placid enough beast and Elenor looped her skirts up, ready to put her foot in the stirrup, then gasped as two strong hands caught her round her waist and swung her with ease up into the saddle.

She gripped the saddle bow and looked down at him, not far because he was so tall and she could see now a shadow of a smile on that stern mouth, soft amusement in his grey eyes.

"You need some flesh on those bones, lady, for you weigh no more than a child."

"I shall turn my mind to it for you my lord, once this is all over."

He smiled and suddenly she was breathless, a bubble of anticipation closing her throat and a shiver tingling her spine.

"Thomas will stay with you. You will ride with the baggage animals - safe and sound - and I shall see you in Fernrean."

Why was that a promise?

He slapped her horse's rump and it surged forward to where his squire was waiting, disappointed at missing the fighting but pleased with his responsibility.

They waited as William and part of his force moved off along the road to Fernrean and other groups of his men drifted off in ones and twos to take up positions out of sight on the flanks of the main party. When they had grown small in the distance the order was given to the supply train to start out.

Elenor found herself worrying about Joan. If she had not found Erland, or if she had found him but been unable to persuade him to their cause, or worse, if she had been captured by Gerard or his men, then what would be their fate?

One thing she promised herself - she or Gerard would die before she allowed herself to be forced back into the fearful hell of an existence she had known before.

Some of her thoughts must have shown in her face for Thomas rode close beside her and tried to reassure her.

"My lady have no fear of failure in this for all the lords who ride with the King are seasoned fighting men who have defeated far more fearsome a foe than these outlaws they face this evening."

"I am worried about my maid, Joan, for she has been entrusted with persuading the Saxons to our side. If she fails to find them or if they will not listen to her, then the King will face a considerable force."

"Hah! My lord will make easy work of it. He is a doughty warrior and it is not for nothing that the King entrusts him with his personal safety."

"And what of my maid, a woman alone in these woods where men are waiting in ambush? She could be raped and killed and her body never found."

Elenor was working herself into a lather again for having found an ally in Joan, she could not bear to lose her now.

Thomas was silent a moment then brightened."Why , my lady, if she was resourceful enough to bring you both safely here from the castle of Fernrean then I doubt if this forest and a few ragged outlaws would defeat her. What say you?"

"Oh I suppose you are right Thomas for she is very clever and most courageous." Elenor sighed. "I wish I had half her spirit!"

"My lady, I know nought of how you came by your injuries, but it seems to me that only a woman of spirit could carry herself as you do after such an ordeal as that must have been."

Elenor smiled at him and he felt mightily pleased to have cheered her up a little.

She fell to wondering about his master - if he had a wife and children waiting in some stronghold for his return. Did he love his wife? Was he a kind and gentle husband? That smile he had given her had had a strange effect on her senses and she found herself envying the woman who might be his wife.

"Does my Lord de Carrefour hold land from William here in England?"

"No my lady. As yet the King has preferred to keep my lord with him for he trusts no-one as much as he to guard his back while he makes his throne secure."

"I see. So he has left his family in Normandy?" She wondered if he thought her questions strange or even bold.

"No my lady. He has no wife for he is the youngest son of his father and has spent his life fighting for King William, first to secure the Dukedom, and now here in England."

The boy was glad that he had been able to distract the lady from her worries and chattered happily on about his lord's virtues and feats in battle.

He obviously hero-worshipped his master and it was easy to catch some of his enthusiasm for the man.

A shouted challenge from the knight who led their small group made Elenor unconsciously tighten her grip on the reins, causing her mount to sidle nervously.

"Who is it Thomas? Do you think it could be Joan?"

"It is two people my lady, a man and a woman. At least I think it is a man. It could be a bear by his size."

Worried, in case it was Joan and she was not recognised, Elenor kneed her mount to the front, Thomas close behind her. When she saw that it was indeed her maid she could scarce contain her relief and gladness.

"Joan! Joan how went it? Did you find your Erland?"

The Norman who had challenged them leaned forward. "My lady we must move on. If you vouch for this man as well as your maid then make sure he stays with you until we reach the castle."

"Certainly sir, of course. Forgive me."

He acknowledged her and signalled for the small column to go on.

"Thomas, could you mount Joan pillion behind you? She cannot possibly walk all the way back to Fernrean. Look at her!"

Joan had travelled God knows how far since leaving Fernrean and now she swayed unsteadily and Eric bent and lifted her to a seat behind Thomas where she wrapped her arms around his waist and turned her cheek to rest against his back.

Elenor was burning with questions but she knew Joan was not capable of answering right now. She turned instead to the hulking bear of a man who had accompanied her.

"You are Erland's man?"

"Yes lady." he stared at her guardedly, not willing to give anything away.

They were travelling forward again slowly and he fell in beside her close to her stirrup. Thomas watched suspiciously from her other side.

"Did Joan speak to Erland?"

"Yes lady."

"Is he with us?"

He turned his head, such a towering mountain of a man that even on horseback she looked him in the eye.

"You are the Lady de Beauvrais?"

"Yes. Your name?"

"Erik, my lady. Erland will take his chance for revenge on your lord." He had the plaits and beard of Viking ancestors and she almost missed his answer, fascinated as she was by his barbaric appearance, then as the meaning of his words sank into her brain, she gave a whoop of victory. It startled everyone, including her horse, and it woke Joan who smiled wearily at her mistress' delight.

Erik allowed himself to look taken aback at her reaction and Elenor brought her horse back under control and told him confidentially.

"I hate him so much that to see him disembowelled while still alive would only give me a small measure of satisfaction."

"I see." Then he said no more but settled his long stride to the pace of her horse as they headed for Fernrean.

They heard the din of the battle as dusk deepened into night and the commander of their small group growled an order to close their ranks and keep silent.

Joan came fully awake on her pillion seat and Elenor peered into the darkness anxiously as they approached the forest and halted. They seemed to wait an eternity before all became quiet again but their commander still would not let them move forward until he was certain it was safe.

It was so dark within the forest that Elenor could scarce see even her horse's ears. She wondered how those at the front could see the path and she was strangely glad of the reassuring presence of the huge barbarian at her right stirrup. They pushed onwards through the night for nigh on three more hours before the glare of Fernrean's torches could be glimpsed ahead of them. Elenor was suffering the terrors of the damned as they drew closer to her former prison for she would not believe that Gerard might have been defeated, even killed in the confrontation with William. As they reached the drawbridge she pulled her horse to a halt, staring through into the torchlit bailey.

Erik looked up at her. "Have no fear, lady, your husband will not have survived this battle, or if he has he will most certainly be a prisoner of the King"

She swallowed hard and nodded. "You are right, Erik. If Erland kept faith with Joan then Gerard could not possibly have been the victor." Allowing her horse to move forward once more, she shuddered as they passed beneath the heavy timbers of the outer gate, feeling a little more confident as she realised that those on guard were most certainly not her husband's men.

They dismounted in the lower bailey and their horses were taken from them, Elenor giving Joan her shoulder to lean on for the maid was stiff and unsteady when Erik helped her down from Thomas's horse.

"Well my lady, this may be our moment of truth. If only Erland and William have called a truce. Even if Erland is a prisoner, I can plead his cause to the King."

Elenor heard clearly the strain and anxiety in Joan's voice and attempted to reassure her, although she knew her own future was uncertain for after all she was the wife of a traitor.

"Have no fear. I see Saxon men standing free here in the bailey and surely that would not be so if William had not come to some arrangement with Erland?"

True enough there were members of Erland's band helping with horses and supplies and they called a welcome to Erik.

"I shall join my comrades my lady, and discover what happened at the ambush. Will you be alright?"

"I can look to my lady, Saxon. Have no fear of that." Thomas's voice was truculent and Erik hid a smile from the boy.

"Of that I have no doubt sir squire." He bowed and turned away leaving Elenor, Joan and Thomas to make their way up towards the keep.

It seemed to take forever for the steps of both women were heavy and reluctant. Finally they stood in the doorway of the hall their eyes blinking at the bright torchlight, desperately trying to seek out a familiar face.

"Joan!" It was Erland and he swept his love into his arms and hugged her fiercely, burying his face in her hair and murmuring undying devotion into her eager ears.

Elenor stood alone.

Shivering now, not only from cold, she felt a sob rise into her throat. The anti - climax was too much for her and her fear and uncertainty almost overwhelmed her. Then a warm cloak was suddenly draped about her shoulders and the iron strength of a supporting arm rescued her from her nightmare of loneliness and despair.

"Come my lady. Your chamber awaits with a warm fire and hot water to end your ordeal. We have secured everything within these walls and your husband is where he can do you no harm. You can rest easy this night."

Elenor was in a daze and Armand de Carrefour found himself acting as lady's maid once more as he supported her up the stone steps towards her chamber.

It was a chamber transformed. The fire was blazing brightly and the fearful dark shadows were banished by a multitude of candles. A tub of hot water stood before the fire and clean linen not only dressed her bed but awaited her on a stool by the tub for her to dry herself when she had finished.

She turned to thank him but he had gone. No doubt on the business of the King and Elenor hastily stripped off her filthy clothes and climbed with a moan of delight into the tub of hot water. It was paradise.

As she scrubbed at her hair and skin she felt as if she was scrubbing away the degrading touch of Gerard de Beauvrais and she ducked her head again and again beneath the surface to rid herself of the years of terror and humiliation. She left the tub only when the water started to cool and she sat before the fire allowing her long hair to dry into soft curling tendrils which caught the light of the wavering candles.

She still did not know what had happened to Gerard. He was still alive. She knew that from what Armand de Carrefour had said and she could only hope that she would not be forced to face him ever again. How William would deal with her and with her maid Joan was another matter, although it seemed that Erland was still free and that seemed a good omen.

Wearily she slid between clean linen covers and snuggled down with a sense of safety and well-being which she had never before felt within these walls of Fernrean.

Elenor awoke slowly and luxuriously, still half dreaming of her home in Normandy and her mother's soft voice singing as she wove the bright tapestries which had adorned their hall. All gone now. Gerard had plundered everything.

The thought brought her wide awake. Gerard!

Quickly she threw back the covers and slid from her bed. The tub and dirty linen from her bath the night before had all been cleared away and fresh water was gently steaming in a bowl set by the fire.

She wondered at such efficiency as she washed and dressed, thinking of Joan and Erland, envying them. The knock at her door brought that involuntary tightening of her nerves and she told herself not to be such a fool.

"Come in!"

It was Joan of course.

"My lady." The maid curtseyed low and Elenor grasped her hand to raise her.

"How goes it Joan? Have you seen William? What has happened to Gerard?... And Erland? What is happening?"

The questions tumbled almost incoherently from her tongue and Elenor found herself shivering once more with uncertainty, anticipation, she knew not what.

"Steady lady, calm down. Sit and eat and I shall tell you what I know."

The bread was fresh and there was honey to spread, warm milk to drink. It was definitely a sign that Gerard was no longer in charge.

"Gerard and his men are imprisoned below. William has been in close conference with his men since first light."

"And Erland?"

"Is a free man so far. His men are confined to the lower bailey but there are no restrictions on his own movements."

Elenor was silent, munching on the bread and honey, yet her mind was busy with conjecture.

"The King will not be able to leave Fernrean without someone he can trust in charge. The rebellion in the North makes his departure urgent so he must make a decision today. Gerard's fate is surely sealed but as to myself, what lies in store for me?"

The thought took away her appetite and Joan watched with concern as her mistress rose and started her old familiar pacing of the boards.

"You must not forget that the King will be grateful for our part in warning him of Gerard's ambush and his sympathy already lies with you because of Gerard's vile treatment."

"But what can he do with me?"

"You never know, my lady, he may find you a new husband."

"Oh my God! I had not thought of that."

"Well you had best turn your mind to it, for it seems to me to be the most logical conclusion."

Elenor was horrified - and afraid.

Her experiences with Gerard had left scars, not only physical, which would be long in healing.

A sharp rap at the door and the two women glanced apprehensively at each other.   Joan crossed quickly to open it, smiling with relief as she saw Erland looming there.

"The King has sent me to fetch your lady. We are to attend her."

Elenor was at Joan's shoulder. "What of my husband? What has happened to him?"

It was the first time she had met him properly and Erland bowed slightly to her. Her face still bore the marks of Gerard's abuse and although the Saxon was well aware of the hated lord's treatment of his wife, even so he was shocked. The woman was so thin and the signs of her most recent beating disfigured her face badly.

"He has been questioned throughout the night and he stands now under sentence of death as a traitor to his King." He frowned with concern as her eyes closed and she swayed slightly.

"Come my lady, pull yourself together. We must face the King."

Joan's briskness steadied her and she descended to the hall with her head held high.

They were all seated, maps spread out on the table, armed men at every corner.

William watched, expressionless, as the Lady Elenor de Beauvrais, flanked by her maid and the Saxon outlaw Erland, knelt before him.

"We find ourselves constantly beset by traitors, thieves and murderers. Men, and women, who would stab us in the back for the sake of a gold coin or raise up our realm against us for the sake of more land or more power." He paused and the men about him were silent, one or two nodding their agreement. "Sometimes the tools we are forced to use are not what we would wish and we finish by breaking them or discarding them. Gerard de Beauvrais is all of these things; a tool I was forced to use in taking this realm of England, and also a traitor, a thief and a murderer. You, as three of my loyal subjects..." he laid heavy stress on that word 'loyal',"... have been most desperately abused in one way or another by this treacherous villain and I find myself in your debt for your timely intervention on my behalf."

There was a pause while the King spoke quietly to Baldwin de Framois, then Erland took a breath as William called him by name.

"Erland. Step up and receive the thanks of your King." William used the words deliberately and Elenor heard a small sound from Joan as her lover hesitated for one brief unbearable moment before rising and approaching the King.

He knelt and placed his hands between William's and took the oath of fealty, stumbling over the latin words, red - faced and sweating when he had finished.

"Now you have sworn to me, you are no man's man but mine."

"Yes Sire." Erland stood back, holding himself with pride and Joan found herself the object of William's attention.

"Joan, maid to the Lady Elenor."

"Sire." She stepped forward.

"Your courage and fortitude are more than I might expect from one of my knights. You are a free woman who has but to name her reward."

Joan could not speak for a moment, for her dreams and desires seemed to lie at last within her grasp. Hesitantly she explained to William.

"Sire. All I have ever wanted is this man..." she indicated Erland who made a convulsive movement towards her. "...To marry him and bear his children in peace and love. When Gerard de Beauvrais came here, he destroyed our lives and I admit that everything I have done, I have done for revenge on him. Now you offer me my heart's desire once more and I swear I shall be your liege woman as my man is your liege man and our lives will be yours to do with as you will."

She knelt and placed her hands between the King's then he raised her and gave her the kiss of peace before she sought the haven of Erland's strong arms.

Elenor was almost faint with suspense and uncertainty. She was, at the same time, happy for Joan and Erland yet full of envy for the love they shared, while she; she held value for no-one. Who would care whether she lived or died?

Stumbling, she rose to her feet when William spoke her name.

"My Lady de Beauvrais. Sorely abused and afraid as you were, yet you placed yourself in untold danger to warn us of your husband's treachery. Most women would have been destroyed by the cruelty and humiliation you have endured. Gerard de Beauvrais life is forfeit for his deeds, which leaves you a woman alone, easy prey for another such as he. I cannot leave this holding at my back, vulnerable and undefended yet I am not prepared to force on you a husband not of your own choosing. Therefore I leave you still Lady of Fernrean until such time as you find a man to your taste, subject of course to my approval."

Elenor could scarcely take in what he was saying. It was unheard of for a lady in her position to choose a husband. Fernrean in truth belonged to William and whoever was lord there, held it from the King.

"However, I must be certain that you are secure here until such time as a new lord takes command."

That was the sting in the tail.

There was a shuffling and a murmuring amongst William's lords and Elenor looked at each of them consideringly:

Baldwin de Framois, clearly a man with a sense of humour.

Ragnor de Louberon, shy and easily embarrassed, yet a competent fighter or he would not be so close to the King.

Edwin de Cercy, a ladies' man, yet inoffensive in his admiration.

Armand de Carrefour. She was not so sure of him. A hard man. Tough, enigmatic and cool. She could not fathom his depths.

"My Lord de Carrefour has agreed to stay and garrison Fernrean with his own men. I shall miss him sorely yet I know I can safely leave you in his care, my lady, as no-one could· accuse him of being a womaniser!"

The laughter at this remark raised the spirits of the gathering and only Elenor noticed the faint stain of colour on the hard planes of de Carrefour's face.

William held out his hand to Elenor and guided her to a seat beside him. She could not help glancing up at the man who was to be her castellan for the foreseeable future but he refused to meet her eyes, staring straight ahead, his face expressionless.

"And now let us deal with de Beauvrais!"

Elenor made a sound of protest. She had no wish ever to see Gerard again but the great doors were opening and the unsteady bulk of her husband, chained hand and foot and surrounded by grim-faced guards, appeared and was shoved forward to fall before the King he had betrayed.

Elenor shuddered and shrank back into her seat, hoping Gerard would not see her and unable to control the hate and fear which gripped her.

Then there was the reassuring grasp of strong fingers on her shoulder and a lethal whisper - "Have no fear lady, the scum will never lay a hand on you again. Not while there is breath in my body and you are in my charge."

His touch burned, the breath of his whisper raised the hairs on her neck and she was so busy dealing with this run of reaction to him that she missed what William was saying.

If you had not known what he was, Gerard may have aroused your pity. Filthy and beaten he grovelled before the King. Muceous streamed from his nose, tears from his eyes. He bore the marks of the questioning he had undergone through the night and he seemed to Elenor to have shrunk before her very gaze.

"They threatened me Sire. They swore they would kill me and everyone at Fernrean - my wife, my men, my servants. I had no choice." His voice quivered and broke.

"Your wife? They threatened your wife?"

"Yes Sire."

"Tell me, de Beauvrais. Is this your wife? The woman you are so concerned about?"

"She was not well Sire.....an invalid confined to..." His mouth gaped open as he saw her and for a moment his expression was almost comical then his face twisted with fury. "You bitch! You conniving betraying bitch! It was you... How did you do it? How did you get out of here?

I'll kill you..."

His voice rose to a strangled shout and his rage forced him to his feet, the chains clanking about him as he lunged towards her.

Petrified she fought for breath, whimpering with terror as she frantically tried to push back the chair and escape from him. She was rescued by the man who had been standing behind her. He hurtled across the table in one vaulting leap and before Gerard could escape, Armand de Carrefour had looped a length of the shackles about his throat and bent him backwards, throttling the life from him with the chains. Gerard heaved and roared, throwing himself about to escape that deadly grip, but to no avail and slowly his face turned purple and his hands fell limply to his sides. He hung unconscious, before William calmly gave the order to his commander.

"Armand! I have use for him still. Let him go."

The disgust was plain on the face of the tall knight as he released his prey to fall in a grotesque heap to the floor.

William signalled to the men at arms to take Gerard away then turned with a smile to the Lady de Beauvrais. She, however, was staring with those huge soft brown eyes up at the man whom he had assigned to her protection. William's smile deepened in satisfaction and he cleared his throat to attract her attention. She gave a little hiccup and guiltily transferred her gaze to the King.

"My lady we are almost finished here. Your husband will accompany us north, and when I have all the traitors in my hand..."

He held out his hand, palm up."

I shall pluck them all and send them to their damnation..." and he closed his fist hard making Elenor jump. He beckoned to Erland.

"You and your Saxon band will have a chance to prove yourselves. You march with us in the morning to join the main part of my army. I am sorry to tear you away from your sweetheart, so if a priest can be found and you are willing then what better time to celebrate a wedding?"

A cheer went up from William's men, his lords banging approval on the table, and Joan· was covered in confusion, swung laughing and protesting up into Erland's arms.

Elenor was totally bewildered. The strain of the past days was taking its toll and she found herself struggling to control a rush of tears. Everything had happened too fast and William and his men seemed suddenly much larger than life.

She fought to pull herself together for it would not do to be weeping and sniffling when she should be as happy as everyone else seemed to be.

Once again he was there.

A goblet of wine was pushed into her hands.

"We need a little celebration just now. William knows this. He has driven his men hard and he is wise enough to know they deserve some reward.

You also, I think, need to realise that there is some pleasure in life, still."

Elenor sipped gratefully at the wine, wondering at his kindness. But then William had ordered him to look after her, had he not?

And if there was one thing she knew of Armand de Carrefour, it was that he was totally loyal and obedient to his King.

She smiled up at him, the wine doing its work, warming her, relaxing her, loosening her tongue.

"I am in your debt, my lord, both for your kindness and your defence of me."

His gesture was deprecating,"You are in my charge lady, I have told you, you need have no fear while I am here."

He was so tall and his broad shoulders seemed able to take the weight of the world. It was the first time she had seen him without his helm and with the mail coif pushed back and she noticed that his cropped dark hair held a glint of silver.

"You have followed William since he fought for his birthright in Normandy, I am told."

He laughed suddenly and she was amazed at how it transformed his features, banishing the grimness.

"Has Thomas been regaling you with my life story?"

Fascinated by his smile and worried because the wine seemed to be causing her legs to tremble - at least she thought it might be the wine - Elenor stammered," Oh no. It was not that way. I was asking him if you were married... I mean if you had a wife in Normandy...oh!" She was completely flustered by her own big mouth and all Armand de Carrefour could do was laugh at her."I just wondered if any woman could put up with your arrogance!"

In her determination to stop him laughing she shouted the last words, then was horrified to realise that they were the centre of attention. The whole company looked on, thoroughly enjoying the little scene.

"To arms! My lord shall I send for your men?"

William choked, and his commander spread his hands in dismay. "I merely offered the lady my protection Sire, and thought to make her smile... and she attacks me for no reason."

"If you will all excuse me?" Elenor gathered her sorely abused dignity about her. "Joan, if you are to be wed so suddenly, we have plenty to do. Some fresh meat would not go amiss if a certain great oaf could stop laughing long enough to hunt!"

They made way for her as she swept past, nose in the air, bowing low and trying to stifle their amusement. Joan followed close behind her mistress, joy and happiness in her heart, and it was only when they reached Elenor's chamber and had closed the door behind them that she realised her mistress was crying.

The sobs shook her fragile frame and the tears streamed unchecked from her eyes.

Throwing up her arms she wailed in distress, the delayed shock of her ordeals being finally allowed its way.

"My lady, my lady, hush! Calm down please." Joan pulled her into her arms and soothed her as a mother soothes a distraught child.

Elenor, however, could not stop for it was as though a dam had burst and the years of terror, pain and degradation took their full toll. Rocking her gently to and fro and murmuring consolation, Joan let the storm have its way, wisely knowing that Elenor needed this emotional cleansing before she could ever begin to contemplate a new beginning.

Gradually, slowly, she calmed, and she was a sorry sight at the end for her eyelids were red and swollen and her face was blotched and ravaged.

Joan shook her head."Sweet Lord did you ever see such a face? You will scare all the wedding guests away."

"Oh Joan I am sorry. In my self - pity I ignored your good news."

Weak and trembling with the chaos of her emotions, the Lady de Beauvrais, nevertheless, made a stern effort to gather her wits about her.

"My lady it is a new beginning for us both. Erland is all I ever wanted and without your help I would not now be within reach of my heart's desire. I can never repay you. For you too, life will change, for you are under the King's protection and you may choose your own man, an opportunity granted to few women of your rank."

"Gerard is not dead yet." Her tone held a faint note of dread.

"As good as, my lady. William will not lightly allow his escape, never fear."

"And where will I meet a suitable husband? I know of no-one outside these walls."

A brief image of her new castellan intruded into her mind but she shook it impatiently away. Distracted now, as her maid had intended, Elenor forced herself to dismiss all thoughts of herself and concentrate on Joan's happiness. For once the mistress turned maid, and Joan was bathed, her long blonde hair washed and brushed out then braided and coiled around her head. "For I am no longer a maiden, surely." A sadness edged her voice."My man must take soiled goods."

Now it was Elenor's turn to admonish -'"Tis rubbish you talk. Erland is desperate for your love and whatever happened with Gerard must be put aside. You talk to me of a new life, well you are right - so let us enjoy this wedding as a fresh start for us both."

There was not much in the way of wedding clothes in Elenor's chests so for the first time since that terrible moment when she had eavesdropped Gerard's plans to ambush William, she opened the door which led through to Gerard's chamber.

She had actually never been in her husband's room and she was wary, even though she knew he was safely imprisoned below and the very scent of the man made her hackles rise.

In fact the room had been cleaned out and as they entered from the connecting chamber, Thomas, Armand de Carrefour's squire, came in through the outer door.

"Oh! I am sorry my lady. My lord told me to prepare this room for him. I did not realise you were here."

"No matter Thomas. We merely seek some of my husband's belongings." She thought that may have sounded a little mercenary."He had many of my personal things in his safe - keeping..."

"I have put everything that was in here in the small room my lady, for your attention."

"Oh. Very well, thank you Thomas."

The two women retired hastily, closing the door firmly behind them.

"He is certainly ready to take full charge, this commander William has left you."

Elenor's heart was fluttering strangely at the thought of Armand de Carrefour sleeping only yards away and she hurriedly distracted herself by throwing open the lids of the various chests Thomas had stacked neatly around the small closet.

With a cry she discovered a large old chest containing many of her mother's belongings and between them they carried it through to Elenor's room.

It had obviously not been opened since it had been brought from Normandy, probably because the style of clothing was a little out of date and Gerard had not bothered to search through it. Elenor found herself on the verge of tears again, but made a determined effort and kept her sadness at bay.

The materials were soft and rich for her father had not been a mean man, and although the waistlines, for the most part were a little generous, it only took a few quick stitches to make the linen shifts and low waisted over - dresses fit well. When she was ready, Joan looked very much the glowing bride. Elenor pounced on a copper hand - mirror.

"Here's a prize! Look at yourself in this. Erland will be dazzled."

Joan was laughing with excitement as she turned the mirror to see as much of herself as she could. "Now you, my lady. Let me do your hair and see if we can find something to fit you."

"A difficult task, I think." Elenor's mouth turned down wryly, but Joan would not be gainsaid and soon Elenor too was arrayed in an over-gown of soft gold with an intricately embroidered girdle to catch in the loose material. Joan left Elenor's long silken tresses loose but for narrow braids caught back and pinned beneath a soft coif. The folds of the coif served to hide much of the now rapidly fading bruises and her mistress's flushed cheeks and bright eyes could well attract an admiring glance.

Finally they were both ready and with their hearts in an excited flutter, they left the room to descend to the hall below.

Gerard de Beauvrais held black, bitter hatred in his heart. Hatred for William. Hatred for Erland, that outlaw bastard. Hatred for Armand de Carrefour, but most of all, a killing, tearing, perverse hatred for his wife, Elenor de Beauvrais. The puling bitch had brought him nothing but bad luck since he had bribed de Vere into marrying her off to him. The trouble was that he had thought she had far more wealth than she did. His disappointment and rage at what he saw as de Vere's deliberate deception had been taken out in full measure on the helpless female who was now his wife

And now this. The cow-eyed little slut had betrayed him to William. He would have his revenge. Oh yes. He would have his revenge.

He groaned.

There was not a part of his body that did not hurt.

His throat was so badly bruised and swollen where that thrice -- damned son of Satan, de Carrefour had strangled him, that he could hardly breathe, let alone swallow the spittle which bubbled in his throat.

Swearing foully he pulled at the chains which bound him to the wall causing the guard to peer through the barred door curiously. De Beauvrais hunched away, muttering.

If only he could get out of here. What had William said? He needed him. If he needed him, that meant he had to keep him alive.

At least for now. And all were agreed, where there was life, there was hope.

He grinned evilly to himself. Let them enjoy their petty victory for now and when the time was ripe, then would he strike!

The hunting had been good. Armand de Carrefour tipped the leather water bottle to allow a gush of clear fresh water to take the dust from his throat. He had with him a half dozen of Erland's Saxons as well as ten of his own men. Communication had been a little difficult at first because of the language barrier, but the excitement of the chase and the enforced team work had soon created a bond which needed few words.

'A great oaf ' she had called him.

Well maybe she was right. He was not polished where women were concerned for he had had little to do with the fairer sex, preferring to follow the warrior's road. He had been William's liegeman since the days when William had fought for his Dukedom in Normandy. When the invasion of England had been completed there had been even more to do with guarding William's back once he was King.

"A fine result my lord."

Armand did not bother to hide his surprise.

The barbaric Erik had insisted on accompanying them and his comment now, in a fair Norman tongue, was obviously well calculated.

"Aye Viking. My lady orders and I obey."

The two men grinned at each other.

"It seems to me that you make her angry at the slightest thing."

A slight shrug from the Norman lord and a perplexed frown."I admit I have no skills where women are concerned, and she is not used to courtesy from a man, I think."

"A gross understatement lord." Erik watched the angry tide of colour and the tightening of the grip on the heavy battle sword.

"That piece of dung! William should have let me kill him. Twice I have been thwarted."

"Well you know what they say. Third time...."

"True! Let us hope that is the case."

"You have been with the King a long time." It was not a question.

"Since I was a youth of sixteen. My father had so many mouths to feed that I was forced to make my own way at an early age."

"You have never married?"

"I have never had the time! Courtship takes so long and as a landless knight I was not the best catch."

Erik laughed. "I should have thought William would have amply rewarded you by now."

The grey eyes narrowed thoughtfully. "Perhaps it is time to settle down.

I shall discharge my duty here with the Lady de Beauvrais and when William has seen to these rebels, perhaps there will be a holding left vacant for me."

"You have no ambitions then for Fernrean?"

"You insult me. The lady is under my protection and I am not one to take advantage of a helpless female!"

Erik raised his hands placatingly."My apologies lord. I mistook your mettle."

"Here. We are home." Armand de Carrefour shrugged off the matter and the hunting party answered the challenge from Fernrean and entered the bailey to whoops of congratulation.

Scenes of chaos and hilarity met their eyes as they crowded through the gates with their spoils. Servants hurried to carry away the deer and young boar they had killed which, along with a few dozen rabbits and a score of fat wood pigeons, would make a fine wedding feast.

Erland was being scrubbed to within an inch of his life. There was water everywhere as they doused him thoroughly where he stood, naked and shivering, in front of the stables. The Saxons had taken command of the stables and cow byre where there was plenty of clean straw and hay still left from the winter forage to make warm beds for outlaws used to the rigours of the forest.

Armand removed his helmet and pushed back his coif. He was not dressed for hunting and the sweat he had worked up in the chase was making him itch. He desperately needed to bathe also.

"Hey Saxon! Is there room for me?"

"Welcome my lord! And Erik you stinking barbarian, you are not invited to my wedding unless you wash first."

There were hoots and catcalls as Armand and Erik dismounted and started to strip.

Then as William's commander stood naked, waiting for the pails of water to be poured over him, they fell silent. The hard years of fighting were there on his body for all to see, not only in the scars of past wounds, but in the iron hard muscle which banded every inch of his lean frame. It was no wonder he had found it so easy to overcome Gerard de Beauvrais.

"Well..." he growled,"Are you all man-lovers that you stare so? I shall freeze to death if you don't get started."

Galvanised once more into action, it was not long before his skin was smarting with their enthusiastic cleansing. When they had finished he was gasping and he shook his dark cropped head to rid himself of the excess water. Thomas had arrived with clean undershirt and leggings and the squire collected the cast off clothing and his master's mail shirt and weapons with care.

"That had best be checked while we have the chance Thomas."

"Yes lord."

"Your helm my lord. " Erland held the conical helmet out to him and the two men stood eye to eye, assessing each other.

"My wife will be in your charge while I am away. I lost her once and I could not bear to lose her again."

"You will not lose her through any neglect of mine, I swear."

"Well then." Erland slapped the Norman's back.

"Let us get to it and enjoy the celebrations and if aught should happen to me while I fight for William, I trust you to see to my woman for me."

The two men walked together up towards the keep, shoulder to shoulder.

It was late evening by the time all was ready.

Erland stood nervously before the little, flustered priest whom they had found hiding in the village. With Gerard as lord he had discovered that to survive, it was best to stay out of the way.

Norman and Saxon mingled easily together and William watched complacently.

The wedding had been a good idea. It gave the erstwhile outlaws something tangible to fight for and from past experience he knew they would be loyal, hardy warriors.

There was a hush as the two women descended the stairway. Joan's head was high and she never took her eyes from Erland. The vows did not take too long and when Erland took his new wife in his arms to kiss her, the cheers nigh raised the roof. The celebrations included the villagers from Fernrean, all of whom had known both Joan and Erland from childhood and the merrymaking in the courtyards easily rivalled that of the King and his men within the hall. The music and laughter, the huge bonfires outside and the flickering torches in the hall and the whole happy scene seemed like a fairy tale to the Lady de Beauvrais.

William's barons made the most of this respite from their world of fighting and Elenor found herself entertained on every hand as they boasted and joked and even sang. Armand de Carrefour was politely attentive, nursing the same cup of wine throughout the evening, aware of his responsibilities even so.

Elenor finally plucked up the courage to speak to him.

"My apologies, my lord, for my behaviour this morning. I don't know why I was such a shrew. You have provided a fine feast here and I thank you."

"My pleasure my lady. I admit I enjoyed the hunt and it gave me an opportunity to inspect the lie of the land. This holding is well built and easily defended. Your husband at least seemed to know what he was doing in that quarter."

Elenor shuddered and he found himself placing his hand on hers. Those pansy brown eyes did something strange to his stomach and he swallowed hard as she gazed up at him.

"He must have been insane to treat you so." He murmured softly and she flinched then shrugged.

"He was cruel and perverted by nature, yet I admit he seemed to hate me and take pleasure in my pain more so than with anyone else. I gave him no reason. I was not a shrew whatever it may seem to you." She smiled trying to make a joke of it and when he smiled back at her, her legs turned to jelly.

The dancing had begun with the villagers and soldiers outside and the great doors were opened for those within the hall to join them.

Joan and Erland led the whirling laughing throng and Elenor too was swung away from de Carrefour, protesting and giggling in the arms of Edwin de Cercy. As she whirled about in the young knight's arms she caught kaleidoscope glimpses of her castellan standing with William in the doorway at the top of the steps watching the dancers. She could not see his expression but his arms were folded and he leaned almost broodingly there.

Watching.

Just watching.

Her partner gave her up reluctantly to Baldwin de Framois who slowed down the pace of the dance somewhat.

"I am not built for this, my lady, but I could not resist a turn or two. You look very much better this evening."

"I feel almost human Sir, thank you."

"You are content with William's dealings, my lady?"

That glimpse once more of de Carrefour.

"Aye, my lord. I consider myself most fortunate."

"You may trust de Carrefour completely. William could not have chosen better. Even myself, I could not claim to be so honourable."

"It will be a long time before I put my trust completely in a man."

The dancers were tiring now. Several couples had slipped away in the dark and soft whispering and sweet kisses were exchanged, vows made. Tomorrow would see many a parting and there was a bitter tenderness in each touch.

She sensed him there before she saw him and Baldwin stepped back with a wry, knowing smile.

"My lady?"

Her lashes fluttered down to hide the faint sense of panic which touched her, then his hand took hers, his arm slid lightly about her waist and he swirled her about so fast her head spun.

Their bodies did not touch yet she could feel his warmth, and the latent strength of his hold was almost terrifying. She kept her gaze fixed firmly on his breast and wondered at the grace and power of the man as they danced. When the music ended she spoke softly and he bent his head to hear her.

"I thought you were not a lady's man, my lord, yet you dance most expertly."

"All a question of balance lady, and rhythm, and they are two of the things required of a successful warrior."

She knew he was smiling and was determined not to rise to the desire to argue with him.

She suddenly realised that the musicians had stopped playing and slipped away with their own partners and she and the tall lord were left standing together.

He still held her hand, her waist was still in his embrace and there was barely an inch of space between them.

Desperately she felt the urge to rest her forehead on his chest, to feel the roughness of his cheek, perhaps, against hers. But she was afraid. Oh how she was afraid!

Armand felt her trembling like a small terrified bird within his grasp and he wanted to pull her into his arms and protect her, reassure her, murmur consolation into her ear. But he knew he could not. He cursed de Beauvrais for his satanic brutality, and he cursed William for laying this obligation upon his honour.   Then with iron determination he stepped back.   Stepped away from the bruised and beaten lady whom he was assigned to protect.

"Come my lady. It is getting late and William leaves at first light. Joan and Erland have gone to their marriage bed and Thomas has readied your chamber for you. I hope you can manage alone this night."

She laughed ironically. "You jest my lord. There have been many nights when I have managed alone, but I thank you for your concern."

As they re-entered the hall together, William and his barons were standing before the embers of the fire, finishing their wine, in a sombre mood. They watched Armand escort Elenor to the bottom of the stairs and bend to kiss her hand, then stand until she was out of sight. Baldwin and William exchanged knowing glances.

"De Carrefour is ensnared although he does not know it."

William shrugged.

"The lady deserves a good man. I know of few better than de Carrefour, and it seems he will never settle down unless pushed to it.

I need someone I can trust here at Fernrean yet I would not wish to force a man upon her, however honourable I know him to be. She has suffered enough."

"And de Beauvrais?"

"Oh he will die. Make no mistake, but it suits my purpose to keep him alive just now. He will turn against de Touron and the others, thinking to save his own skin."

Armand de Carrefour joined them. "Everything is ready Sire for your departure."

"Good. We shall see how these Saxons handle themselves in full battle. Erland fought at Stamford with Harold so we know that he, at least, is a seasoned warrior."

"Those who hunted with me today are good marksmen. Never a shaft went astray."

"Better, then, that they fight for me rather than having to hang them for poaching my deer."

That raised a grin or two, then Edwin de Cercy yawned and stretched. "If you have no further need of me Sire, I shall go to my bed.,"

"We had all best retire. Armand, I know you understand the importance of Fernrean in this conflict. Beware. Watch your back for there is treason all about us."

"What of de Beauvrais' men?"

"His two knights will share his fate. The foot soldiers will be given the opportunity to swear loyalty to you.

We will split them. Some I shall leave here and the rest will come with us where there are plenty of eyes to watch them. So. Until the morning."

They all bid him goodnight and Fernrean fell silent.

The Lord de Beauvrais brooded bitterly on his hatred deep in the cellars of Fernrean.

The Lady de Beauvrais slept peacefully, a smile faintly touching her lips.

Armand de Carrefour stretched out his lean frame in the room next door to her, optimistic now about the future at Fernrean.

Erland and Joan, worn out with their passion, lay replete in each other's arms.

William, the King, needed little sleep and he pondered on a little into the night planning his strategy for the forthcoming march on York.

The hunting dogs before the fire dreamed on, unaware and uncaring of the change of lordship at Fernrean.

Although it seemed as if all was total chaos and confusion throughout Fernrean when dawn broke the next day, in truth there was an order and purpose beneath it all which spoke of years of experience in putting an army on the road.

Elenor had woken early and washed and dressed quickly, although it was still dark. She found her way down to the kitchens for the first time since she had entered Fernrean as Gerard's wife. Grimacing at the grease and smoke, she found herself a kitchen boy and ordered him to bring her some breakfast. With her hip hitched up onto a stool, she watched as the cooks laboured to provide bread for William's force to take with them. There were large rounds of cheese and smoked ham, all packed in hessian sacks to be loaded onto the provision wains. Enjoyment lay in all the bustle and hustle around her and in the respect and deference shown to her by those who sweated in the heat of the great fires.

The kitchen boy brought her a bowl of oat porage sweetened with honey and she spooned it hungrily into her mouth.

She seemed to be eating rather a lot of late, but then she had lost time to catch up on. When she had finally finished her breakfast with a satisfied sigh, she decided to explore a little.

Unbelievable as it was, in the two years she had lived at Fernrean, she had seen only her own room and the great hall. The only time she had seen or breathed fresh air was when she had hung from her window on those occasions when she was sure Gerard was safely out of the holding, and yearned after the larks carolling high in the sky.

Briskly now, she set off on her tour of inspection. The kitchens, built of stone as was the main keep, formed part of the semi-circular wall of the upper bailey and she went out through the double kitchen doors, set wide this morning to allow the cool air to circulate. It had rained in the night and a thousand scents and odours mingled as the sun came up and steam started to rise all about, giving an eerie, half hidden quality to the sights and sounds about her. Dodging the sunlight-sparked puddles, Elenor made her way out of the gate and down into the lower bailey. Here lay the stables, cow byre, pig pens, and quarters for the men at arms. Here lay also the greater part of the noise and confusion which was slowly resolving itself into a disciplined column of fighting men.

Elenor clung to the doorway of the stables as the knights destriers, those great valuable warhorses, were led respectfully out.

Eyes wide and excitement bubbling she saw William swing up to the saddle, closely followed by Baldwin de Framois, Edward de Cercy and Ragnor de Louberon, the latter letting fly numerous curses as his horse performed its usual hysterical antics clearing a wide circle around him. In the ensuing commotion Elenor failed to notice that they had brought Gerard from his prison and heaved him onto a horse, tying him hand and foot. He, however, saw her!

His face twisted with hate, his lips drew back in a snarl and with a mighty kick he forced his horse to surge towards her, intent on mowing her down beneath his mount's steel shod hooves. Elenor was totally oblivious to him for she had spotted Joan and Erland and was seeking a way through the crowd to reach them. It was only as the shouts of alarm grew closer that she realised her danger. She spun round, her eyes widening with shock and fear, then desperately she sought a way of escape. Gerard was so totally obsessed with getting to her that he flattened everyone who tried to stop him and there were cries of agony as his horse trampled regardless over man, woman and child.

The entrance to the stables was behind her and she reached it with a sob of thankfulness, then unexpectedly rage swept over her. She had had enough.

Enough of fear, enough of tears and enough of the black - hearted swine who was Gerard de Beauvrais.

A hay fork stood against the wall of the stall.

It took only a second to snatch it up and whirl back through the doorway to face him with the fork held like a spear, the sun glinting on the wicked sharp tines and a shout of defiance on her lips. Armand de Carrefour was almost impaled on her makeshift weapon and he threw up his arm to deflect the stabbing blow, taking one of the tines through the muscle of his shoulder.   Elenor's shout turned to a shriek and she dropped the hay fork as if it were red hot, bringing a curse of pain to the lips of her castellan.

"Christ, lady, if you wish to be rid of me, you have only to say so. There is no need to kill me."

"Forgive me, oh my lord, forgive me. I thought it was... I meant to kill... that is..."   Armand grasped his shoulder, the blood seeping slowly, bright red, through his fingers.

"I know my lady. Calm down. I was joking."

Joking! The man was joking, when she had just near killed him. She could not believe it!

"Please, you must let me attend to the wound. It is bleeding badly."

"I do know this." He gritted his teeth. "Yet lady, I have suffered far worse wounds than this pin-prick, so do not bother yourself..."

"Bother myself? Come. Do as I say."

She took his sound arm and towed him along determinedly towards the keep.

He glanced helplessly around but was met only by the bland, deliberately straight-faced expressions of the King and his barons.

Gerard was on the floor bound and gagged and suffering from a sound beating.

Erik, Erland's barbarian, stood astride him, a spear at de Beauvrais' throat and a grin on his lips as he watched the Norman warrior, protesting and embarrassed, being hauled away by the slip of a girl who was the Lady de Beauvrais.

She could not believe she had done it. In all the years of cruelty she had not been able to strike back and she had become conditioned to acceptance. Her actions now filled her with elation and she was only mortified at the fact that she had speared the wrong man! Sliding a sideways glance at him she almost smiled to see the look of long-suffering patience on his face. Still grasping his shoulder he accompanied her docilely until they reached his bedchamber.

"Really, my lady, Thomas can attend to this scratch, you have no need to concern yourself."

"If you go in and remove your mailshirt my lord, and leave me to my job, I shall judge what attention is needed. Now. Two minutes and I shall be there."

Before he could say more she had whisked away and he sighed and opened his door to go inside and do as she bid.

Thomas had seen what had happened and was waiting for him.

"My lord, my lord, sit down. Let me help you."

"For Jesus' sweet sake, Thomas, don't fuss! 'Tis bad enough being speared by a chit of a girl without all this. I am a warrior not a lady's maid. This is nothing!"

Nevertheless his breath hissed between his teeth as his squire carefully pulled the mailshirt over his master's head. The tine of the fork had gone cleanly through the muscle but had torn downwards when she had dropped the fork in shock. Armand was surprised at the pain for the wound was a mere pinprick compared to some of the damage he had suffered in his years fighting alongside William. It was bleeding profusely and the padded jerkin and soft shirt he wore beneath his mail were soaked with his blood.

A light knock heralded Elenor's arrival and he saw her pale at the sight of the stained clothing in a heap on the floor.

"Do not panic. It looks much worse than it is, truly." He was quick to reassure her.

The tray she was carrying held a bowl of water, a jar of salt and some cloths and needles and thread. Placing it on the table by his bed she turned determinedly, lips pressed together, to inspect the wound.

He was sitting on the edge of the bed, stripped to the waist and Elenor suddenly found she was trembling.

The long smooth ridges of muscle, even now he was relaxed, gave evidence of the tough life which was his and a brief vision of Gerard's loose and flaccid flesh pinning her body beneath it came into her mind.

She swallowed hard on the thought of what it would be like with this man. Trapped between the triangle of the bed, the table and the long stretch of his thighs, she was so close to him that her nostrils flared at the scent of him. Clean and fresh, the sweat beaded his muscles and she forced herself to concentrate on adding salt to the water and dipping a cloth to clean his wound.

"I'm sorry. This will sting." The salt would fight any infection, and precious though it was she did not spare it for his sake.

"I know, my lady, I know." He smiled at her and once again she was ensnared by the light and warmth of the grey eyes. Fascinated, she was so close to him now she could see the darker ring around the pupil and the thick black eyelashes which made his eyes seem brighter.

"Thomas." Although he spoke to the squire his gaze never left hers."Go down and make my apologies and farewells to the King."

"Yes my lord."

There was a deep silence when Thomas left, a silence which seemed to enfold the two of them. Elenor broke it finally, her voice a thread of sound.

"It will not need stitching. If I bind it tightly it will do. Rest it but do not let it stiffen."

She was bent forward slightly at her task and it took only that half turn of her head towards him.

Their breath mingled, his mouth touched hers, lightly, oh so lightly, hardly a kiss, more a caress and her heart almost stopped.

He did not touch her.

Only their lips met but that searing tender contact raced through her blood like fire and she whimpered. Hardly a sound at all really, yet he heard it and jumped up and away with a curse.

"Dear God! Forgive me. I am not made of iron and you must think me an animal to take advantage of you."

Bewildered and longing for that kiss, Elenor stammered "No. No, my lord, please. It was my fault. Gerard was right and you must think me a slut."

"Never! That bastard would be dead 'ere this, if I had my way. To treat you so..." His wound had started bleeding again and she implored him to return and sit. "Please, just let me bind it. Then I shall go and we shall forget this."

"I dare not come near you now. William has laid a heavy charge on me in this and my honour will not allow me to betray him or you."

She could not believe what he was saying. Although the bruising on her face was fading rapidly, her nose was still crooked and her bottom lip still split. That he could find her so irresistible that he must force himself to stay away from her, was a shock which left her weak.

"I shall merely bind the wound. I shall stand away from you... I beg you let me attend to you."

He ran his hands over his short cropped dark hair.

What on earth was the matter with him? Just the smell of her had fired him up so much that he would take her here and now if he could.

And they were to be alone here for God knew how long.

Constantly together. He sighed. Better to get used to it then for he was damned if he would dishonour her.

"Very well. I am sorry if I insulted you."

"It was no insult my lord. Believe me." She smiled gently and gestured to him to sit.

"I shall sit here." He pulled out the heavy chair by the fireplace and she collected her bowl and the linen to bind his wound.

The task was completed in silence. He gazed stonily ahead and did not even flinch when she pulled the bindings tight. When she finally finished and stood with the tray in her hands once more to leave, he tried to explain.

"I have no soft ways with a woman and I know not why I did what I did. But your safety and well-being have been entrusted to me and I would not wish you to think that I was a man such as your husband. I will not betray my trust even though my body may demand it. I hope you forgive me."

She did not know how to answer him.

She had never felt anything so much as the trembling fear and anticipation his kiss had aroused in her and she had never had to deal with any man before who would put his honour before his own desires.

From the sudden increase in commotion outside, it was clear that William and his force were moving out. It saved her from replying for he got up and went to the door to shout for Thomas.

Bending her head she ducked under his arm to make her escape and when he turned back to her, she was gone.

Elenor sought her room as though the devil himself pursued her and she almost threw the tray and what it held to the floor when she reached its sanctuary. Breathless and shaking she leaned her back against the door and closed her eyes, feeling again that feather light brush of his mouth on hers. With trembling fingers she touched her lips wondering if they showed some sign of that brief burning contact then bowing her head she pictured him standing there, half stripped, powerful in his strength, yet gentle in his dealings with her. 'Sweet Jesus why could Gerard not have been one such as he?' Bitterly her heart and mind craved the thought. Her favourite pacing helped to calm her.

The slamming of his door stopped her and she crossed over to her window to watch for him as he erupted into the courtyard below. He was in a blistering mood, setting his men to jumping to their tasks with an unusual alacrity, surprised at his unreasoning temper.

He disturbed Joan, dreaming at her vantage point on the walls of the upper bailey, watching the tail end of William's force carrying her husband with it as it disappeared into the forest.

A worried frown creased her brow and she glanced up at her mistress's window catching a faint movement there and leaving her post to hurry anxiously inside and upstairs.

The command to enter when she knocked was so faint she barely heard it and her concern increased.

She went in and hurried over to where Elenor leaned, chin on hands, on the windowsill, watching him as he prowled the keep and she did not even turn to see who had entered.

"My lady are you alright? Do you need anything?"

Elenor's reaction amazed her.

"Need anything? Oh yes Joan, I need something but it seems I am not to have it." She sounded bitter and at the same time sad.

Joan leaned next to her as she watched the commander's tall form and at that moment any remaining doubts or tension between the two women dissolved as the salt had dissolved in the water Elenor had used to bathe Armand de Carrefour's wound.

"He seems a fine man. A good hunter and warrior Erland says. You know he almost killed Gerard in the ambush? It was only the King who stopped him."

There was no reply at first and Joan cast an anxious glance at her.

"He is certainly an honourable man." Elenor laughed a little hysterically." I never thought I would want a man to forget about his honour..." and she turned into Joan's waiting arms and cried out her frustration and uncertainty.

Joan would not allow it this time.

"Come now, my lady. None of this. Where is your courage? Where is the woman who survived two years of Gerard de Beauvrais?

You are made of finer steel than this. Come now - tell me what happened."

Still sniffling and weepy Elenor allowed herself to be persuaded away from the window to sit and tell her maid all that had transpired between herself and de Carrefour when she had simply wanted to attend to his wound.

When she had finished she glanced at her maid to see her reaction. Joan was thoughtful, then matter-of-fact.

"It seems to me that we have been presented with a perfect solution. This commander is not only a brave warrior, he is gentle with women, he is close to the King and you find him attractive. What more could we ask in a lord for Fernrean?"

"Oh no Joan, you go too fast. Just because he seems to desire me does not mean he would wish to marry me. If he did, why is he so worried about his honour? It would be perfectly honourable to offer for me, I should think."

"Perhaps not. Perhaps he feels that he would be taking advantage of a position of trust. It is so hard to read some men."

Elenor was suddenly contrite."Joan, what a selfish thing you must think me. The last I saw, you were bidding your Erland farewell."

Joan actually blushed - a delightful sight.

"All is well with me my lady. My only worry now is that he returns safely."

"Hah! You surely do not believe he will allow anything to happen to stop him coming back to you?

And William is no inexperienced youth in these matters of war. No. He will come home, never fear."

Joan was glad to talk of Erland. Glad she had distracted Elenor from her distress. She was so happy herself that she felt she wanted everyone around her to share her joy. Allowing herself to think of de Carrefour she made up her mind. If it was possible to gain him as a husband for Elenor de Beauvrais then she would do everything she could to achieve that end. Yes. He would make a perfect lord for Fernrean.

Unaware of that plotting and scheming going on upstairs, Armand finally completed his devastating tour of inspection in the stables. His destrier whickered to him from its roomy stall at the end and he smiled self - mockingly.

"Renard, old friend, have I neglected you? I think you and I need to talk."

He picked up a grooming glove from its box and moved over to the great roan warhorse, murmuring softly to it as he checked its mouth and eyes, its legs and feet.

The animal relaxed, its eyes drooping as the man started the long rhythmic sweeps of the glove over its glossy hide.

"Curse William for putting me in this position. That devil knows I have no way with women, especially one who has been so abused."

He turned his attention to the horse's feet, picking out the muck and loose stones with his dagger.

"And yet she did not reject me. She did not scream or run or strike at me. Care must be taken in choosing her husband for although William has the veto she would be easy prey for any soft spoken villain who treated her kindly."

He sighed and rubbed Renard's ears. The horse butted at him playfully, making him laugh.

"Aye. 'Tis an easy matter with horses. The gentle word, the firm hand. More complicated with womenfolk. Those soft eyes of hers remind me of a fawn, wondering and shy. Curse that bastard de Beauvrais! Would I could kill him with my own hands, I would make sure he suffered. He does not deserve an easy death."

"My lord?" Thomas was cautious, looking around to see who his master was talking to.

Armand was embarrassed but covered it with sternness. "Yes Thomas. Where is the groom? This horse needs more care. My life could depend on him."

"I know not lord. I shall attend to it. You are ready for some food my lord?"

Armand had not even broken his fast for there had been so much to do that morning and subsequent events had pushed all thought of eating from his mind. Now he was suddenly ravenous.

"Lead on Thomas. I'm starving!"

Thomas grinned, pleased at his master's change of mood.

As Armand followed his squire up to the keep he felt a sense of satisfaction at the state of the stronghold.

It was well built and organised and he found himself coveting it in spite of his proud words to Erik the barbarian the day before.

At least William knew he could trust him and at least if the Lady Elenor was married to him she would be sure to be treated well.

He shrugged. He would play the dice as they rolled for him and if the lady was willing?

His stomach contracted at the thought and he was amazed at the effect she had on him when he had barely met her but three days ago. Well they had ample time now to get to know each other and this time the thought brought with it a good measure of delight.

Once they had left Fernrean behind William
started to push them hard. They could accomplish
twenty-five miles in a day with no problem but
from dawn to dusk they marched with only short
breaks to rest the horses and they almost doubled
their daily rate of travel.

"Why the devil is he in such a hurry?"
grumbled Erland. "The rebels will not go away
and he'll be arriving with an army that's half dead
from exhaustion."

Baldwin de Framois ranged alongside him and
smiled sympathetically. "The garrison at York
castle is holding out against the rebels. Robert of
Comines and his men have been massacred at
Durham and William does not intend the same
thing to happen to his men at York. He means to
teach these rebels a fine lesson this time."

They had rejoined the main army two days after leaving Fernrean and William had left Erland with his erstwhile outlaws and some of the men at arms from Fernrean and they had joined with some of the English forces giving their dues to William in armed support for lands they held in the south.

Gerard de Beauvrais was under a heavy guard of mercenaries, men who had been employed by William many times, both in his struggles for the Duchy in Normandy and in the taking of England. Erland was glad to see the last of him.

"By rights he should be dead now. I won't rest easy until he's safely under the ground."

"I could always put paid to him in the night. With no-one the wiser." Erik grinned and fingered his knife but Erland shook his head.

"I would not want to lose you over that God-forsaken bastard. No. The King will deal with him I have no doubt."

"What? No revenge for what he did to your Joan?"

Erland ran a hand through his wayward English locks and sighed. "I would that I could have taken him apart inch by inch. Set the dogs on him and watched him torn to pieces - but I have sworn to William now, and as my overlord his is the right to mete out justice." He threw a branch on the fire, his face moody in the flickering light. "And Joan has made me swear to stay out of it. So - as long as he dies - I shall be content."

Gerard de Beauvrais sweated in front of his King.

"Truly Sire, that is all I know. The only contact I had was de Touron and he was in league with the Atheling and the English earls."

William's lip curled in disgust and he nodded to the guards to take him away.

"Shall I kill him now Sire?"

Baldwin fingered his dagger.

William considered it. "No. We have not the time to bury him and I do not want wolves on my tail."

William Fitz Osbern, in command of the main part of the army in the King's absence, drew out the maps once more.

"One more day Sire, at this rate. They know we are coming. They know the ambush at Fernrean did not succeed."

William cursed."I had hoped to avoid all this, but it seems to me I must teach these rebel northerners a lesson they will not forget."

"And shall we hang them Sire?"

"It goes against my will but I must make an example." He frowned. "De Beauvrais is as good a start as any. When we reach York he is a dead man."

"What of the Saxons of Fernrean?"

"I think Erland is a man of honour. A good warrior also. If he proves himself we shall find ample reward for him."

"I am glad de Carrefour guards our back." Baldwin took a long draught from a water bottle.

"Let us hope he guards the lady's back also..."

The remark by one of Fitz Osbern's knights caused Edwin de Cercy and Ragnor de Louberon both to grope for their swords their faces flushed with anger.

"You insult the lady Sir!"

"How dare you speak so..."

"My lords, please. Save your zeal for the rebels. De Carrefour has no need of you to defend his honour. All know he is beyond reproach."

Fitz Osbern's man bowed. "Of course that is so. I apologise my lords - a bad joke."

The two young lords still bristled but were forced to subside before William, and their anger was as much for the Lady of Fernrean as for their comrade de Carrefour.

Gerard de Beauvrais fell on his face as his guards pushed him contemptuously into the tent he occupied with his two knights, also held prisoner, chained and beaten into spilling what little information they had.

His blood boiled with the rage and hate that consumed him and, coward that he was, he was so eaten up with the desire for revenge that he would take any risk, face any danger to escape and return to wreak his vengeance on Fernrean and all within, most especially that whimpering bitch of a wife. He cursed the day he had thought to take her, deceived by de Vere into thinking she was a rich heiress.

Stiffly he rolled over and pushed himself to a sitting position.

The enforced marching had made him lose weight and the flesh hung in loose folds about his body.

His beetle-browed eyes were red-veined and bulbous, his nose ran continuously so that now he did not even bother to wipe it clean. His clothes were stained with sweat and blood and his greasy hair hung in reeking lank coils. Even his own men found him repulsive.

He did not sleep, brooding on his hatred, and when camp was struck before dawn he was standing waiting for the guards to take him to his horse.

The early spring mists covered the ground and it was impossible to see front or tail of William's army. Gerard's horse skittered and ran, sideways and in circles, and the guards cursed it for crows' bait. In the confusion Gerard spotted a knife - to be sure an eating knife, yet sharp and deadly still, lying forgotten by the embers of the fire. Deliberately he got in the way of the shying horse, allowing himself to be knocked off his feet, rolling as if unable to help himself towards the dying fire and over the knife which was his objective. Sly and unseen his scrabbling fingers found it and in a trice he had slipped the prized weapon inside his sleeve.

It took several minutes to calm his mount, and in that time he had made sure the blade was secure.

Evil satisfaction coursed through him and he made none of his usual bad-tempered grumbling protest when they heaved him up into the saddle.

Pre-occupied with moving out, his guards noticed nothing, only his two knights glanced meaningfully at each other, then allowed their horses to fall in behind him.

When they camped that night they were within a few hours march of York. What small resistance they had met so far had been easily and contemptuously dealt with. William was confident of success.

"The Danes have deserted them already. They will not stand and fight and I shall make sure that there is nothing left in this region after this to support them should they wish to try their hand again at rebellion."

His barons looked at him, surprised. They knew he had lost patience with the constant uprisings. He had not expected such grumblings and petty rebellions within his new realm and unlike his predecessors, who had ruled England before him, he was not prepared to tolerate such challenges to his authority. The Normans within his following, like Gerard, who had joined the rebels for gain, William could not forgive and he showed them no mercy.

Erland and Erik shared a rabbit, one of several bagged by Erland's outlaws.

"Well, tomorrow should see the worst of it. With luck it will be over by nightfall."

"How long, I wonder, will the King want to keep us with him?"

"Until it is finished. He needs all the good men he can get.

These mercenaries are all very well, but they grumble so, they lack commitment, they do not fight for hearth and home, merely for money. It makes a difference."

Erland sighed, thinking of Joan, her softness, her passion, her courage. He longed to return to her, but he also needed to prove himself and his men to the Norman King, to show that Saxons could be steadfast and honourable.

A sound in the night alerted him.

A cry.

He listened intently but it was not repeated. A wolf perhaps, or a nightbird.

Erik glanced at him curiously but Erland shrugged. "'Tis nothing. I thought I heard a shout."

"Probably one of the guards."

Nevertheless a shiver of uneasiness fingered Erland's spine and he found it impossible to settle again.

"I think I'll take a look around."

Erik moved his hand to his war axe. "I'll come with you."

"No. Stay. Finish the food. I shall be alright. I think I am past the need of a nursemaid."

Erik grinned and Erland stood and hitched his sword in its scabbard so that he might draw it out easily should he need it, then he melted into the night as he had so often done in his outlaw days when to become a shadow was to survive.

Erik heaved a satisfied sigh as he sucked at the last bones of the rabbit they had shared, and tipped up his water bottle to clean the grease from his fingers. Erland was a lucky man, he thought, glad that life seemed to have taken a turn for the better for his friend.

As for himself; a full belly, comrades around a campfire, a trusty weapon and the prospect of a good battle on the morrow.

These were all the pleasures he needed for now, and when his body clamoured for a woman, well there were many only too eager to share the huge barbarian's sleeping place.

A yawn startled him from his thoughts and he shrugged his cloak closer about his shoulders, throwing more wood on the fire and glancing around a little uneasily for his comrade. Only he remained awake now. The rest of their Saxon band had rolled themselves in their cloaks and were snoring, or muttering and snuffling in their sleep. It should not have taken Erland long to check out the perimeters of their camp unless he had met with trouble on the way.

As time went by, and the fire started to die, Erik could stand it no longer and he stood up and hefted his war axe, pushing the embers of the fire together with his foot. He made an awesome sight in the dying glow of the fire. Huge and warlike with the studded bosses of his leather war gear and the bands of his helmet catching the ruddy gleam of the burning wood he resembled Thor, the war god of his forbears.

Warily he moved into the surrounding trees, every sense alert for trouble, becoming more certain with every step that something had gone awry for Erland. He worked his way steadily around the camp, taking his time, searching every inch of the way Erland may have taken.

William's guards were totally oblivious to his passage in the night and he smiled grimly to think of the throats he could have cut were he the enemy. When he was almost at the point where lay the group of tents housing the King and his lords, he became still, frozen, listening, straining to hear something, a sound on the edge of his senses. A breath, a groan --- there! Urgently, forgetting caution, he pushed through the heavy undergrowth until his feet hit something, something which flinched away and drew in a gasp of pain.

"Erland...!" Frantically Erik bent to the body of his comrade and as gentle as a woman his fingers sought for wounds, sought the source of the blood which flowed, hot and sticky. He cursed the darkness which blinded him and raised his great voice in an appeal for light.

" 'Ware the camp! To me Normans, move your carcasses, there's enemies in the night while you sleep!"

Within seconds he was surrounded, torchlight flooding about him, weapons bared, voices raised in consternation.

Erland lay in a pool of blood and Erik's howl of anguish and rage reached even the ears of the fugitive who had committed the deed, as he fled into the night on a stolen horse heading for York and safety.

Gerard threw back his head and laughed triumphantly. He had not expected to have one of his enemies practically walk straight into his hands.

He whirled Erland's sword over his head and whooped like a madman and his two knights were hard put to keep up with him as he urged his horse onward.

Challenged at the rebel lines they were quickly surrounded and led off towards de Touron's encampment.

"Are you a complete imbecile? Could you not even carry out a simple ambush? All the planning had been done for you and all you had to do was lie in wait and kill the Bastard."

"I was betrayed, not only by my wife, but by the Saxons I thought were my allies. I should have known better than to trust them. At least I've taken some small revenge and believe me I shall have dealt with all of them by the time I have finished."

De Touron looked at Gerard, his lip curled with distaste and regretted that they had had to use this piece of filth. Now, however, they had not much use for him.

"So now, what do you want here?"

Gerard snorted. "Men. I need some men. I intend to go back and recapture Fernrean.

They have only a small garrison and many of them are my men anyway. It will be easy, and then we'll have William between us once more. You should have done as I said in the first place and left me trusted and quiet in my holding until you had engaged William here, then I could have taken him in the rear and he would have been caught like a rat in a trap!"

"You're a fool! William suspected you all along. Why do you think he was on his way to Fernrean in the first place? And who has he left in command there now?"

Gerard quivered with his hatred. "De Carrefour. That whoreson..."

With a bark of laughter de Touron cut him short."De Carrefour? ...And you expect to retake the place from that wolf? Now I know you are insane."

"He will not expect me. He will think I am dead by now and that he is safe. I know of ways into the keep which I have kept secret from everyone. Even those who planned and built them are dead."

"Hmm. I can imagine." In a world which was hard and merciless, nevertheless de Touron and his kind had a certain honour which was totally lacking in Gerard de Beauvrais, depraved and satanic as he was. In spite of this the rebel commander considered his options.

"I cannot spare too many men. You will have to rely on whatever help you can get from within your walls. And for God's sake don't foul this up or I'll kill you myself if need be."

Gerard grinned and sniffed, wiping his sleeve across his nose. "Don't worry. This will be easy I promise and you will thank me at the end of it."

"I doubt that. Still, we can be in no worse case because of it." And De Touron turned away effectively dismissing Gerard de Beauvrais.

Within the hour they were sneaking back through William's encircling army, their horses' hooves and their weapons padded and their cloaks pulled close against detection.

"Twenty men, by Christ! What can I do with twenty men? Even then he would not have given me this many had I not protested."

"With the element of surprise, my lord, and if we can join forces with our men inside..." De Wulfe was whispering. They had filled their bellies with hot food and drink and replenished their weapons but if they were caught by any of William's men they would not stand a chance.

"Aye." Gerard chuckled, low and evil. "What a fine surprise it will be too. I shall enjoy this. Oh yes how I shall enjoy it."

When they were clear of William's army they mounted and pressed forward into the night heading gleefully towards an unsuspecting Fernrean.

In William's camp Erland lay unconscious. Grievously wounded as he was, there were not many who gave much for his chances. William lay a commiserating hand on Erik's shoulder as he sat watch over his friend.

"It is easy to say I should have killed de Beauvrais when first we captured him, and looking back I would not have hesitated if I had foreseen this. The devil must have obtained a weapon from somewhere, God knows how. I have six good men lying dead, their throats cut from behind. How he did not finish Erland off is a miracle."

"He probably thinks him dead but Erland is not an easy man to kill. He will fight to survive even if only to disembowel that spawn of Satan."

"I hope so for I need men such as you and Erland. De Beauvrais will have fled to the rebel camp and when we defeat them tomorrow we shall find him, most likely cowering like a dog in some filthy corner."

Erik's fingers caressed the handle of his beloved war axe. "I shall be at the forefront. I shall pray to my gods that I find him first."

Elenor had to force herself to go down to the hall in the morning to face Armand and when she did finally get up enough nerve to do it, her courage was wasted. He had been up with the sun and had left the holding to go hunting, using the opportunity to familiarise himself with the area around Fernrean and to accustom both those ex-outlaws of Erland's who had been left behind and Gerard's former men at arms, to his command.

Spring had definitely arrived. The sun sent its welcome golden fingers to warm every nook and cranny of buildings, beasts and men. The feathered denizens of the forest almost deafened the Norman lord with their sweet song and he found that the light chestnut horse he had had brought from the stables for his use was under the illusion that it was a warhorse.

Dancing and sidling, it took all his skill to calm it, and the damnable ache in his shoulder did not help matters.

The thought brought with it a vision of Elenor's face, so close to his when their lips had met and he could have sworn that he could feel the silken caress of those few, endearing loose strands of hair which had come undone when she had struggled, first to escape Gerard and then, as she had thought, to dispose of him.

His grim mouth relaxed into a smile as he remembered her dismay and confusion when she had drawn his blood instead of Gerard's.

That must be the only time a wound had been known to give a measure of pleasure as well as pain. Thinking of pleasure turned his mind back to the feelings she aroused in him and he reminded himself that he had stirred himself early on purpose to avoid her, to find sanity in those everyday pursuits which were vital for their survival. Thinking of her like this defeated his objective.

Suddenly the hounds set up a herd of deer and in the heat of the chase he was able to find relief from the torment of his unfamiliar agonising.

Elenor felt deflated when she realised he was not in the stronghold, and when Joan brought her something to eat, she hardly tasted it.

"He has gone hunting." Her voice was gloomy.

"Good. That means fresh meat tonight. More than we had when Gerard was here."

Elenor cast her maid a jaundiced glance.

"He cannot be so smitten, then, to make himself scarce 'ere I have awoken."

"My lady, gather your wits.

Mooning about will have no effect whatsoever on this man for if you have set your heart on him, then you must make an effort to make yourself attractive."

Elenor laughed at that.

"Oh yes. Well enough for you to say that with your blonde hair and a figure a man would die for. Even Gerard was smitten, more than he would like to admit I'd say for he never treated you so cruelly."

"You can believe that I never did anything to attract that monster..."

"I know. That is my point." Elenor sighed and picked up her mother's hand mirror, staring at herself forlornly. "What could he see in me?" She gently touched her crooked nose and then the split in her lip.

"Enough of this self - pity. Your eyes are definitely your best feature - and your hair, so soft and silky. You need to put on some weight but that is easily done now. I have never seen such long curling eyelashes, you need only put them to the proper use."

Joan pushed and pulled and twirled her around, keeping up a running commentary which verged on the bawdy and soon Elenor was giggling and squeaking in protest until the challenge from the gates and the clatter of horses' hooves stopped them in their tracks, breathless.

They flew, as one, to the window to watch de Carrefour dismounting in the lower bailey and accepting congratulations on the success of the hunt before striding up towards the keep.

The two women looked at each other.

"I'm afraid." whispered Elenor.

"No time for that," answered her maid and she grabbed her mistress's hand and dragged her towards the door, out, and down the stairs to meet the commander as he came in.

He stopped and surveyed them suspiciously, removing his helm and rubbing his nose where the nosepiece had chafed the skin.

"My lady. Joan." He nodded to them.

Elenor did not know what to say. Just the sight of him so close again set her knees trembling. Joan nudged her sharply.

"Er.... My lord. How... how was the hunting?"

He smiled and she swallowed the tightness in her throat.

"Excellent. I have not enjoyed myself so much for a long time, and we are well stocked now with fresh meat."   There was a boyish pride in his voice and as he spoke he walked across to the table, pulling off his gauntlets and pushing back his mail coif. It was damnably hot hunting in full mail but he dared not take the risk of being attacked by rebels or outlaws.

Joan gestured silently and comically to Elenor.

"A drink my lord?"

Elenor slipped forward and lifting the jug of cold ale poured some of the foaming liquid for him, desperately forcing her hand to stay steady.

Sitting on the edge of the table, one leg swinging,   he quaffed it in a single draught, exposing the strong brown throat to their admiring eyes.

He set down the empty cup and wiped away the froth with the back of his hand, growing a little uncomfortable under their concerted gaze.

"How is your shoulder my lord?" Joan took the initiative but Elenor wished she had not asked the question, bringing back as it did the memory of what had followed the attention to his wound yesterday. It was obvious that the same thought had occurred to him for his grey eyes immediately found Elenor.

"It is nothing, thank you, although my mount tried his best to do further damage this morning."

She was close to him before he had finished speaking, her fears forgotten in her concern.

"Let me see. It may be bleeding and you would not know beneath your mail."

His hand went up to grasp at her probing fingers and her eyes caught in the steel grey mesh of his as he pleaded low. "Please, my lady. Leave it. It is fine believe me."

She could see the pulse in his throat beating fast and hard and his grip on her hands was almost painful, then she knew that he was not afraid she would cause him pain by seeing to his wound but that he could not trust himself so close to her in that situation again.

She looked down, with difficulty, for she could have drowned in the bright trap of his regard. "Very well. I'm sorry."

Her whisper was only for him and he smiled yet they did not move away from each other for it was as though their bodies had a will of their own, needing to be close, needing each the other.

Joan watched with satisfaction.

She was coming to hold a high regard for Armand de Carrefour and the more she saw of him, the more she was certain that he would be perfect for Elenor.   Still, there were many obstacles in the way, not the least of these the pride and honour of the man himself.

"My lady, did you not wish to speak to the cooks and arrange the meal for this evening?"

"Oh! Yes. I'll come now. Excuse me my lord."

He watched moodily as she turned and walked away from him, Joan following on behind her after a bob of the knee.

He eased his shoulder, knowing full well it had started to bleed, yet desperate at all costs to avoid being in so intimate a situation with her again.

"Thomas!" The squire came at the double.

"You will have to help me sort this shoulder out Thomas.   That idiot of a horse had no consideration for a wounded man."

In his chamber Thomas fussed over him and did a fair job of re-binding the wound, but Armand found himself snarling at the boy over the slightest clumsiness and by the time he was dressed again in a soft surcoat to replace the heavy chainmail, poor Thomas was a bundle of nerves.

Armand was contrite.

"Go Thomas. I am not fit company just now, you must forgive me."

The boy's face brightened. "It is no bother, my lord. You are tired after hunting."

"Thomas... Just go!"

"Yes my lord." He retreated in haste leaving Armand to grapple with the unfamiliarity of the soft warring emotions roused in him by the Lady de Beauvrais. Finally he left his room to attend to the business of Fernrean, forcing himself to concentrate on the tasks in hand and to stop mooning like some callow youth over an unattainable prize.

Elenor was enjoying herself about the stronghold as Joan introduced everyone from the huge bearded Saxon in charge of the kitchens, a man who could not hide his delight at the change of overlord, to the lowliest stable boy. Elenor had been raised and trained well by her mother to one day have charge of her own demesne but no-one could have foreseen that her lord would be one such as Gerard, a tyrant who treated her worse than a despised slave rather than as his lady wife.

It was familiar territory, therefore, as Elenor took over the general duties of Lady of Fernrean and when she and Joan took advantage of the fine weather to eat some fresh venison pasties washed down with a light wine, in a private corner of the battlemented upper bailey, she felt a sweet surge of joy and contentment take hold of her.

"I feel as though I have been re-born. Everything about life now is so exciting."

"Aye my lady. Not least our new commander." Joan tilted her chin down to where they had a view of the lower bailey and Elenor's heart skipped its beat as she could see him standing there, arms folded over his chest, watching the farrier shoeing his war-horse.

He fussed over the massive animal, arguing congenially with the man on whose ability rested the soundness of the valuable destrier, yet he did not lose his temper nor threaten as Gerard would, no doubt, have done, and when the job was finished and the horse trotted up beneath his critical eye, he pronounced himself satisfied. Elenor saw him slip the farrier a coin and the man seemed most appreciative.   Armand gentled his horse for a moment and she found herself envying the animal his caresses, then he took the lead rope from the stable boy and led the animal inside and out of her sight.

Elenor knew that she must soon face the prospect of choosing another husband, for although William had said that he would not force a man on her, still she knew that Fernrean could not be left long without a lord.

Even if Armand de Carrefour was willing to stay as castellan, there would be bound to be some hint of scandal implicit in that situation. Although she found that she trusted him completely, it was apparent that he did not trust himself.

What bothered her most was that Gerard's cruelty and abuse had made her so afraid of the sexual obligations which she would face in any marriage she made. Common sense told her that what she had suffered was not something she should expect in a normal marriage, nevertheless any man who wanted her must have patience and an understanding of all she had been through.

Sighing softly she turned to question her maid almost shyly.

"Joan I need to ask you some questions. They are personal and you need not answer me..."

Joan smiled softly. "I know what you need to ask." The maid hunched forward and looked earnestly into her mistress's face.

"What Gerard did to you, and oftentimes to me, was depraved and obscene. Unnatural even. The act of love between a man and a woman is a beautiful thing with feelings and emotions beyond imagination, especially when true love and passion spark between them.

I cannot describe how I feel when I am with Erland but I tell you that if you think you can find that with a man, then take him! Grasp the opportunity with both hands and let nothing stand between you."

When she had finished, her face was barely inches from Elenor's and her expression and voice were so intense that tears came to Elenor's eyes and she stood agitatedly to pace the battlements.

"If you knew how I envy you. How I wish with all my heart that such a love could be mine."

"Lady, if there is one thing I have learned these last years, it is that if you want something badly enough, then you must go out and fight for it. Whatever it takes... you must have a brave heart and just do it! Take control of your life. You have an opportunity granted to few women, so put aside your doubts and fears, lady. If this man, this Armand de Carrefour, is the one you want go after him wholeheartedly."

Elenor stared at her maid, knowing she was right.

If she wasted this chance the King had given to her, then she was worse than a fool. She walked to where she could see the entrance to the stables.

"You are right. You did it, I can do it. But once more I may need your help."

"Lady, you do not even have to ask."

They watched as he came out of the stables.

It had obviously been hot work in there grooming the great horse for he had stripped down to chausses and shirt, open to the waist, giving just a glimpse of the binding Thomas had used on his wounded shoulder.

He wiped the sweat from his brow and then something made him glance up towards them, shading his eyes against the sun.

He could not have realised who stood there for they must only have been silhouettes against the sky, yet there came a tension and stillness to his body for a moment before he strode forward towards the gates to the keep.

"I am not sure I have the trick of it. I was not brought up to flirt, to enchant a man, merely to be a good wife." She was panicking now.

Joan giggled."'Tis easy lady. Just do what comes naturally."

He was suddenly there. His dark hair was spiked with sweat and the sun reflected the silver brightness of his eyes. He exuded total power, total confidence, the soft linen shirt merely emphasising the breadth and strength of him. Looking from one to the other he was perplexed.

"Have I interrupted something my lady?"

Her air of suppressed nervous excitement gave a sparkling animation to her features which made her appear young and vulnerable and, to him, totally irresistible.

Elenor took a breath to commence this first attempt at flirtation when Joan forestalled her;

"My Lady Elenor was just saying my lord, that to ride out one morning in this fine spring weather would be a most delightful change after being cooped up in Fernrean for so long."

He looked surprised, then he frowned, thinking about it. "You must forgive me. The pleasure I had hunting early this morning should have made me realise that perhaps you would enjoy an excursion.

It should be safe enough with adequate escort, so... In the morning, my lady, if this weather holds we shall do our best to give you an outing to remember." His smile did those usual strange things to her stomach then he turned away, excusing himself, his mind on tomorrow's arrangements.

When he had gone bedlam broke out.

"Oh sweet Jesus, Joan, what shall I wear? I have nothing suitable for riding out - nothing attractive, everything hangs on me like rags. How could he possibly be attracted to such a scarecrow?"

Joan was laughing at her. "My lady, you know what they say - love is blind."

"He would have to be blind for certain, and I can only thank the Lord that I may be able to turn my skill with a needle to my own advantage for a change."

Once again Lady Elenor's mother provided the bounty for her daughter. It did not take long for Elenor, with her clever fingers, to take in the soft wool of a forest green overgown gathered up to reveal the short leather boots she had worn when she and Joan had escaped from Fernrean.

These had been softened and water-proofed with a mixture of grease and tallow and they fitted Elenor much better now than when they were new.

Finally happy with her garb for the following day, Elenor started to prepare herself to face Armand at the evening meal.

It would be the first time they had sat and eaten together, just the two of them with no other guests present, for yester eve Elenor had pleaded fatigue and taken her meal in her own chamber, leaving him in solitary charge of Fernrean hall.

She had been unable to face him then, uncertain and afraid of her own emotions.

That was not to say she was any the clearer now about how she felt, but she had set her mind upon her course and she would deal with her wayward heart and its sly surprises as and when there was the need.

Dressed in the amber gown she had worn for Joan and Erland's wedding, she left her room and descended to the hall with a fair amount of trepidation in her breast.

He was already seated, waiting for her, and he rose politely, taking her hand to seat her next to him with a smile.

Her stomach was turning somersaults at the mere touch of his fingers and she silently scolded herself for being such a goose.

"My lady, you look well this evening."

- Christ's wounds man, can't you do better than that? he cursed himself.

The radiance of her smile made him blink and her obvious pleasure at the small compliment reminded him that she could scarce have heard even such a simple pleasantry from that bastard Gerard.

"Thank you my lord. You are so kind. How is your shoulder this evening?"

God she was so sweet in her concern!

"A little stiff that is all. It will not take long to mend, I assure you."   - Pour her some wine, you dolt!

"Some wine my lady?" He felt all fingers and thumbs.

"Thank you." Elenor was starting to relax and enjoy this polite attention. He was not wearing his mail this evening, but a deep red surcoat which suited his dark features and she found herself unable to look away from the lean good looks of him. She cast about for some suitable conversation.

"I wonder how William is..."

"The King should be well advanced..."

They both spoke together then laughed to cover their embarrassment.

"I am sorry Lady Elenor, you were saying?"

Elenor took a determined gulp of her wine.

"I was thinking of our men with William, particularly Erland. I hope they are finding it easy to fit in with the ranks of those with whom they were so recently at odds."

"Erland is a brave man who also has a sensible head on his shoulders. He will manage very well never fear. I only hope he and his men can keep up, for when William has a mind to move quickly, there is no rest for man nor beast."

The wine was having the desired effect, its warmth relaxing her and making conversation easier and they continued to talk of the King and his march on York, then went on to more mundane matters of life at Fernrean.

It was with a shock that Elenor finally realised that the meal was over and that they had been discoursing amiably and at times, merrily, like long - wed husband and wife. It seemed the thought too had occurred to Armand for he fell silent and started fiddling with his knife.

"It grows late, my lord, and I should like to be fresh for our ride out in the morning, so if you will excuse me?"

Elenor was a little unsteady as she rose and he reached out to grasp her elbow.

She was growing used to the burning sensation his touch aroused but still she drew in her breath as it coursed through her and his hand dropped away, his expression uncertain - a warrior on unknown territory in this game of courtship.

"Until the morning then, Lady Elenor."

"Until the morning."

Her voice was soft, almost caressing and the fierce leap of elation he felt had him grinning like a fool. He watched as she walked away from him and he found himself looking forward to tomorrow with eager anticipation.

It had taken Elenor a long time to get to sleep. Excitement, fear, anticipation - all these feelings roiled around inside her, raising her to a fever pitch of anxiety.

Eventually, of course, she drifted off without even realising it and when Joan woke her in the morning her head was still full of dreams, dreams of Armand de Carrefour.

She hardly spoke as she washed and dressed and Joan watched her worriedly, laying out bread and honey for Elenor's breakfast.

"Are you alright, lady?"

Elenor essayed a brief laugh. "Well, Joan, my stomach feels as if there are twenty serpents fighting inside it, and my knees are knocking so badly that I feel sure that you can hear them, but if we ignore that - then I am well. Better than I have been for a long time."

"Lady, he is only a man, and I would say a good man. You will come to no harm with him, I am sure of it."

A knock at the door made them jump.

"Enter." Elenor's voice gave no sign that the serpents were gnawing her insides and to Thomas's eyes she appeared cool and calm and attractive in the forest green gown.

"If you are ready, my lady, my lord awaits."

The two women looked at each other before Elenor stepped forward to accompany the squire down to where his master waited in the outer bailey.

Joan felt much as she thought a mother hen must feel with only one chick and she watched from the window as the slender figure in green followed the boy Thomas down to the lower bailey where Armand de Carrefour awaited her. Joan saw them pause for a moment, close to each other, before he put his hands about her waist to lift her to the saddle of the patient grey palfrey which stood for her.

Elenor's heart was thundering like a drum as she was lifted easily onto her mount by Armand. He seemed reluctant to let her go once she was up there and it was only as her palfrey started to fidget that he stepped back and looked round for his own horse.

Once in the saddle he gave the order to move out, before reining his mount back next to Elenor as they rode towards the village.

"I thought that we would ride in a large circle around the village and towards the river. We have some food with us, my lady, although I am not certain that the weather will not break this afternoon."

He glanced up at the sky, and indeed there were some darker clouds visible on the edge of the horizon.

"Well then, my lord, let us enjoy this sunshine while we can."

Elenor kneed her mount forward leaving the commander to canter to catch up with her. She smiled across at him, trying to remember to flutter her eyelashes as Joan had instructed her. It seemed to have the required effect for that devastating smile of his nigh drew her heart from her breast.

As they rode through the forest, her mind roved back to that nightmare journey when she and Joan had escaped Fernrean and were desperately trying to reach William. Her fear and terror had pushed her onward then but her feelings now were so totally different. She felt a joy and excitement in her heart which was like nothing she had ever known before. It was as if he sensed it in her for he laughed like a boy at her side, then suddenly pulled up his horse and pointed. "Look! There!"

They had startled a herd of deer; hinds with fawns at foot and he remembered his earlier impression of her - fawnlike, graceful - those huge brown eyes wary, alert for danger. How anyone could hurt her was beyond his comprehension.

"My lord do we hunt?"

"No!" He threw up his hand, preventing the men from pursuing the deer. "We have meat a - plenty. We do not need to kill more."

Elenor could not believe his words and she turned wondering eyes on this lord, this man who seemed of a different species to the kind of man she was used to.

He turned his head and caught her staring at him and there was one of those moments when everything about them seemed to fade into insignificance. There was only the two of them suspended in time, caught in a web of undeniable and powerful attraction.

Their horses were close, his chestnut for once standing quiet, and Armand leaned towards her, drawn like a magnet, in spite of himself, to her mouth, those lips soft and parted slightly on a breath.

"Elenor..." Her name was whispered like a prayer, desire clogging his throat.

Elenor's eyelids fluttered closed and she waited, hardly daring to breathe, for his kiss.

A loud cough startled them apart and shocked realisation that they had almost embraced in front of a dozen of de Carrefour's grinning soldiers forced a rush of colour to mantle Elenor's cheeks and throat. Armand covered his embarrassment with the strained order to move on and Elenor looked determinedly ahead, her back ramrod - straight, her ears burning.

Armand had never before had to cope with such a jumble of emotions.

Life for him had always been a straight-forward matter of survival, both on the battlefield and, often, in William's court.

This woman at his side aroused in him such a powerful desire to protect as well as to possess that he could not think straight.

One thing he was now determined on.

In spite of all his honourable intentions not to take advantage of her, he knew he would ask William for her hand. A horrible thought suddenly occurred to him, causing him to glance quickly at her. What if she refused him? William had promised her the choice and for the first time in his life Armand de Carrefour knew fear. Not fear of death but fear of rejection. He had never wanted a woman so desperately before. In fact females had played so small a part in his life that apart from the odd whore his experience was severely limited.

He was so quiet, so totally wrapped up in his doubts and speculations that Elenor began to think she had done something wrong. Had she been too forward? Too easily wooed?

Did he think her a light - skirt on the look - out for any man who would be kind to her? Dear God she would go mad with the worry of it all for she knew now for certain that this man, this honourable, gentle warrior was the only man for her. Her problem was that she did not wish to make a fool of herself by asking William for Armand de Carrefour as her lord, only to discover that he did not want her! What a humiliation that would be.

"My lord. Did you not plan to stop here to eat? For it is noon sure enough and this is as far as we can go if you wish to return before dark."

Armand had not realised that they had come so far. They had reached a small tributary stream of the river they had forded when Elenor had waited to warn them of the ambush that day. It seemed so long ago... He nodded to the serjent who had spoken to him.

"Right. We stop here. Water the horses and tell the men to break out the supplies." He turned to Elenor. "The cook has packed a picnic for us my lady. I hope it is to your taste."

Oh dear! How formal he sounded. Elenor smiled politely. "I am sure it will be very good my lord. I have not done anything like this since I was a child. You are very kind."

He cursed silently as his lack of familiarity with women and their feelings made him feel a bumbling fool.

He turned away to his men, excusing himself almost gladly to return to that which was familiar to him. Within minutes a small camp was made and the soldiers were hungrily devouring the food provided for them. Something more tasty then they were accustomed to eating for the cook had excelled himself in honour of Lady Elenor.

Elenor herself sought for a topic of conversation with her castellan. She thought the weather should be safe enough. He leaned across to pour her some wine and she found herself stammering like an idiot again. "The - the weather - has been fine. That is to say for the time of year we are having pleasant sunshine."

He took his cue from her. "Aye, my lady.

At least William's army will not be awash with spring floods.

There is nothing worse than struggling with war - horses in the mud and trying to keep mail and weapons dry!"

"I wonder how Lord Ragnor is coping with his horse."

That remark brought mutual amusement and Armand grinned at her. "He should be receiving payment as a jester instead of a warrior. Still I should not like to bestride such an unreliable beast in the midst of a battle."

"Your war - horse is the roan?"

"Aye. Renard. As wily as the fox for which he is named. I have had him from a foal and he has saved my life many a time."

His voice held an enthusiasm and affection which found her once more envying the horse his master's regard. She felt on safe ground, however, talking of horses for her father had been an avid collector and breeder of the great destriers required by the knights in battle. She wondered what had become of the brood mares left behind on the lands in Normandy.

If she was truly mistress of Fernrean, then it followed that she was once again mistress of her family lands which she had brought to Gerard on their marriage. She must remember to ask the King about the matter.

"More of this pie, my lady?"

"No. Thank you, but I fear I have already eaten far too much. I must remember to thank the cook for such an excellent picnic."

"You need more flesh on those bones. A strong wind could blow you away."

She grimaced. "I know I am too thin and I think that great Saxon in the kitchens has every intention of fattening me up."

Involuntarily his eyes caressed her ˉbody, making out the soft curves beneath the forest green gown. There was a moment of silence before a great fat raindrop splashed onto Elenor's cheek.

"Oh no!" The clouds which had seemed but a line on the horizon that morning had gathered and thickened, becoming black and heavy with the promise of rain. Armand de Carrefour looked up.

"Serjent! Pack everything away. We're in for a storm - curse it!" He should have realised that the good weather could not last and now for this to spoil the day he had planned for Elenor's pleasure.

He boosted her up onto the grey palfrey, steady as a rock, thank God, in spite of the rumble of thunder.

"Here it comes my lord. We'll be soaked 'ere we reach Fernrean."

Elenor was chilled suddenly, the darkening skies seeming a bad omen.

"Do not worry lady. We'll soon be home."

"Not before the rain my lord." In spite of herself she laughed at him, feeling a surge of recklessness drive away the sense of doom.

With a whoop the soldiers were all about her and the band of men and horses surged together onto the narrow trail through the forest.

The lashing rain caught up with them, almost blinding them as they struggled along the path homeward.

"We must find shelter my lord, until the squall passes." The serjent was shouting above the sound of the rain.

"Look. There. The ruins!"

The outline of the crumbling buildings from whence Gerard had plundered the stone for Fernrean loomed through the sheets of rain and they headed gladly for its shelter.

Breathless they fell from their horses and sought the dry musty stillness of the ancient walls. Soaked and shivering Elenor, nevertheless, felt still the tantalising excitement his presence aroused.

"It will be on for some time. Serjent!"

"Yes my lord?"

"A fire. To warm my lady and dry our clothes."

"No problem my lord."

Dry leaves and withered branches soon conjured a fierce crackling blaze at which Elenor was glad to warm her chilled fingers.

"I am sorry. I had planned such an enjoyable day and now this..." He gestured helplessly.

"Oh please! How could you expect to predict the weather. I mean - I have great faith in your abilities my lord, but controlling the skies could be a little too much to ask I think."

He looked at her sparkling eyes, her flushed cheeks, the dripping wet tendrils of hair curling about her temples and with a groan he swept her close into his arms.

He breathed in the wet scent of her, every sense in his body absorbed her trembling slim form as he embraced her, tenderly, achingly.

He did not know how he had held back for so long as his mouth searched desperately for hers.

Elenor felt one brief moment of fear, then as his lips commanded her surrender, she wrapped her arms about his neck and gave him back kiss for kiss. He turned, lifting her bodily in his arms to press her against the ancient stone and he raised his head, his hard fingers gripping her jaw, his grey eyes, smoky now with passion, devouring her features as if he feared she was unreal.

"Elenor..." His whisper was fervent, shaky and she sobbed, pulling him closer, cursing the chainmail which came between them, preventing more satisfactory contact. His hands slid down her body as though memorising every curve, every line, lingering at her waist, her hips and finally cupping her buttocks to lift her higher against him.

Elenor's fingers tangled in the sleek wetness of his dark cropped hair and her mouth lingered hungrily on the strongly etched planes of his face, then down his throat, frowning as his mail prevented further exploration.

The fire leaped higher, casting weird dancing shadows on the walls of their haven and they were brought shatteringly down to earth by the embarrassed bulk of Armand's serjent bringing more fuel. Hastily the man retreated, but hard reality had intruded into their world of passion and Armand released Elenor slowly, reluctantly, struggling to control his clamouring body.

Elenor felt sick with desire and she sank down onto a huge stone plinth tumbled at some time in the past from the roof, her legs unable to hold her.

His hand brushed her cheek and she flinched from the burning contact.

"Forgive me. I lost my reason then..."

"There is no need to ask forgiveness my lord, for my desire was as great as yours." She turned her head to look up at him and gulped as tears welled into her eyes.

"No. Don't. Elenor I could not bear to see you weep sweet heart."   He was close to her, gathering her once more into his arms, this time to console her, to soothe her, although the touch and scent of her once more set his blood to racing.

"Why do you weep? You have no cause to be sad for my intentions are truly honourable."

"You do not understand," she gulped,"I am afraid."

"Of me?" He was incredulous.

"Yes. In a way."

He could not believe it and he held her away from him trying to make her look at him.

"Why? I have given you no cause. I do not understand."

The hurt in his voice wounded her.

"You have done nothing. It is not that. It is what others have done. Gerard..."

She could not carry on.

"Curse that bastard! Lady you must know all men are not like that. We were all appalled by what he had done to you. Indeed every man of William's company was sickened."

"It was not the beatings. It was... It was... other things."   She could not look at him, could not explain, she was too ashamed.

He cradled her close to his breast, his lips against her forehead, his fingers gentling her hair, soothing her as he would his horse, the only experience he had of calming a distraught creature.

"We have all the time we need to get to know each other. I want you to trust me. I want you to want me as I want you. I would never hurt you nor allow you to be hurt you must believe that."

The gentle touch of his fingers in her hair was having the opposite effect to that which was intended and Elenor tried desperately to ignore the melting heat of her thighs, clamping her knees together tightly in an attempt at self-control. How she could be so wanton after all Gerard had put her through she did not know. All she did know was that Armand de Carrefour aroused such sweet desire in her at his lightest touch. She pushed away from him although he was reluctant to let her go.

"You are right my lord.

We have time enough to become well acquainted, thanks to William. ...And I do trust you." With that she escaped him and reached the entrance to the ruins before he could detain her.

"The rain has stopped and I can see blue sky. I think the sunshine is returning."

He came to stand behind her, looking out, reluctant to leave their cosy den yet anticipating the return to Fernrean, anticipating also the courtship which lay ahead.

He stretched, easing the tension from his muscles and rubbing his fingers through his hair feeling the promise of love and a passion which snatched the breath from his throat.

"Do we ride out my lord?"

The sergeant's beaming face was evidence of approval and as they gathered their horses' reins and made ready to ride, the atmosphere amongst Armand's men was almost avuncular.

The troop dropped back as they wound their way homeward, displaying a tactfulness quite amazing in such a hard-bitten crew, leaving the two riding side by side to talk quietly but easily now. Their minds free from doubt, they were set on a course which seemed heaven to them both and Armand and Elenor returned leisurely to Fernrean.

Joan had been watching anxiously for their return. The storm had doused Fernrean thoroughly and she was worried already about how Elenor was faring with the Lord de Carrefour. When she heard the guard shout from the gates she almost broke her neck in her haste to reach the courtyard.

"My lady you are soaked! Come inside quickly before you catch a chill. I have ordered hot water for your bath."

Elenor was laughing and her cheeks were flushed as Armand walked around to lift her from the grey palfrey. She was held by him for a moment, easily, effortlessly in spite of his still aching shoulder and she squeaked at him."Please, my lord, everyone is watching!"

"Let them. I care not if the whole world knows how I feel." But to spare her blushes he set her down and stepped back to allow Joan to fuss forward and escort Elenor up to her chamber and pamper her in a hot bath before the fire.

"Well? How did you fare with the lord out there? He was most attentive on your return."

Elenor leaned back dreamily, luxuriating in the hot scented water.

"I have never met a man like him. Even my father who was certainly fond of my mother was never so courteous or so - so - passionate!"

"Passionate? My lady what happened?" Joan was agog with curiosity and excitement and because Elenor could not view her simply as her maid after all they had been through together, she confided in her without reserve.

"It was his kiss. It seemed as though he drew forth my very soul. If he had wanted to take me there and then I could not have resisted!" And she closed her eyes, reliving the demanding touch of his mouth, the overwhelming trembling pleasure of his body pressed hard against her.

"The important question, my lady, is whether he has mentioned marriage?"

Joan held out the linen cloths for Elenor to be dried when she stepped from her bath. Elenor frowned. "To be honest, he did not actually ask me. He did not use the word 'marriage'" Then she finished in a confidential rush"But he said his intentions are truly honourable and surely that is the same thing?"

"Hmm. With this man you are probably right."

The two of them giggled together like young maidens instead of women who had been through the degrading hell of life with Gerard de Beauvrais.

As the evening drew in they worked on some more of the gowns from Elenor's mother's box until there were three with which they were satisfied.

They were both light-hearted and happy and when Elenor went down to join Armand for the evening meal she gave a silent prayer of thanks for God's mercy in sending Armand de Carrefour to Fernrean.

She paused in the bend of the stairway, to watch him unseen for a moment as he quaffed a goblet of wine.

Thinking of Gerard and his constant drunkenness, she was unworried about the possibility of Armand following that same path. It was true what she had said to him that morning in the old ruins. She trusted him. And that was little short of a miracle after all she had been through.

He looked up towards the stairs as if sensing that she was hidden there and she descended quickly to be met by his outstretched, eager hand.

"You look delightful, lady. The fresh air agrees with you, I think."

She looked up and smiled, responding to the teasing innuendo in his words.

"Perhaps we can ride out again soon, my lord, for I have not had so happy a day since I was a child, although I think I shall be a little stiff and sore in certain areas tomorrow," and she grimaced, rubbing her backside ruefully.

It made him laugh and their shared merriment drew them closer, forging a bond which was stronger even than their mutual physical desire.

He made a great show of pulling out her chair and shouting for a cushion to ease the hardness of the heavy oak seat.

"Thank you my lord."   She was still giggling and he snatched her hand to his lips turning it palm upwards to press a tantalising, sensual kiss in that tender spot. She felt as though every nerve end in her body was centred on that one burning kiss and her lips parted, her tongue peeping out to moisten them.

"Dear God, I cannot stand it. To be so close to you, so intimate, is torture lady. Make   no mistake - I have never hungered for a woman as I hunger for you. We had best decide on our course and obtain William's permission to wed or I swear it will kill me to wait."

There! He had said it! He did wish to have her as wife. Elenor was so thrilled she thought her heart would burst. She took so long to answer him that he turned pale, thinking she would refuse him. His relief when finally she spoke made him feel weak.

"I suppose we could send a messenger after the King, or would that be unseemly haste my lord?"

"I care not. The sooner the better and to hell with what anyone thinks."

She loved his impetuosity and watched, totally enthralled by him as he signalled to the serjent who had accompanied them that day.

A few murmured orders and then Armand turned back to Elenor.

"I shall prepare a letter to William for us both to sign, if you agree, and a messenger can leave at first light." She nodded."Certainly. How..."she did not wish to seem too forward"..how long will it take?"

"On a fast horse? A few days there, a few days back - and however long it takes William to decide."

The same awful thought occurred to them both.

"What if he refuses?" she whispered.

"He will not!" His face turned grim, his tone a threat. "And if he does we shall marry anyway. What can he do about it?"

"He can shut you out. Take away his favour and impose harsh conditions for your tenure."

Armand shrugged his broad shoulders. "What does that matter? So long as I have you."

His words melted her bones and her hand shook as she reached out to take a drink of her wine, aware of where they were and how many eyes were upon them.

"You honour me, my lord." She whispered the words.

"Not true. 'Tis you who do me honour. I am a younger son with no lands of my own to bring to this marriage.   You could have anyone you wanted."

She interrupted him. "I want you! And if that seems too bold then I am sorry."

Grey eyes met brown and held fast in a pledge that would not be broken.

Two hearts, two minds as one in that moment.

The meal passed in a dream for Elenor after that.

Armand de Carrefour belied the impression she had had of him that day at the ford when first they had met.

He entertained her with stories and anecdotes of his days as a youth, when he had followed William in his fight for the Dukedom of Normandy. Stories and scandals of the court had her wide - eyed with shock at times especially where the stories touched on those she knew, the Lords de Louberon and de Cercy. Those two young men seemed to have had more than a fair share of scrapes.

It was only the quietness of the hall which at last made them realise how late the hour. They were virtually alone save for one or two servants who hovered, waiting to clear away the table but unwilling to disturb Elenor and Armand.

Elenor stood in confusion not wanting the evening to end, yet aware of how tired she was after a day which had held so much for her, not only physically but emotionally.

"You are tired and I have kept you here listening to my foolish talk." His hand came up to caress her cheek, tenderly almost wonderingly. "You have enchanted me my lady. Time holds no meaning it seems." He laughed at himself.

"'Tis true I am tired.

Even so I would this moment could never end for I feel as though I stand on the edge of life and what lies ahead of me is unknown yet dangerously desirable."

Her hands were clasped beneath her breast and she was not sure that she understood, even herself, what she was saying.

Then impulsively, daringly, before she could think and regret it, she leaned up and pressed a kiss - a fleeting , trembling kiss, to that hard mouth. Before he could catch her, before he could hold her, she had fled, her feelings a mixture of soaring elation, excitement and horror at what she had done.

He stood, stunned, watching her, the imprint of her kiss still on his mouth, until she was gone from his sight.

For several seconds after she had gone he stayed there before, like a man awaking from a dream, he moved away from the table and made his way out of the hall.

It was his habit to check every inch of Fernrean before retiring at night and he set off now to do just that, although he found it well nigh impossible to keep his mind on what he was doing. Eventually, of course, on his final stop before seeking his bed, he turned to his usual friend and confidante.

"Renard. How goes it?"

The stallion turned his head and whickered to him in welcome.

Armand collected some oats from the feed bin, sniffing them before feeding them to the destrier, to make sure they were free from dust or mildew and then the huge animal tucked in happily when the grain was poured into his manger.

Armand leaned on the side of the stall.

"Well old friend, get used to this place for it seems we may finally be settling down." His usually stern mouth relaxed into a smile.

"Who knows? We may even purchase one or two wives for you also. How would you like that?"

Renard snorted into the manger as if in reply and Armand laughed and patted the great crest. "Well if it's good enough for me, it's good enough for you."

Satisfied that all was secure he made his way up to his room, passing her door quickly although those grey eyes missed nothing of the damage to the lock hanging there. Mentally he made a note to have it repaired first thing. It was important to him that she should feel safe and secure now that Gerard was gone and she had put her trust in him.

Thomas had dozed off in the chair by the fire and Armand hesitated to disturb him. A falling log did the job for him and the squire jumped to his feet, rubbing at his eyes and yawning hugely.

"I'm sorry my lord. I did not mean to fall asleep..."

"Do not worry Thomas. I've a mind to be alone, so get to your bed. I can manage well enough."

"But my lord..."

"Thomas!"

"Yes my lord." Another yawn split the boy's features although he struggled against it and Armand grasped his squire by the shoulders, whirled him around and pushed him from the room, closing the door firmly behind him.

Alone, he stretched cramped muscles, wincing slightly as his shoulder reminded him it was still not healed, then he stood before the embers of the fire to undress.

In the next door room, he thought, she would probably be asleep by now and he wondered if she would dream about him. Her goodnight kiss had shocked and delighted him for he knew that she would never have done such a thing had she truly not trusted him.

The jug with the water to wash in was warm by the fire, and he poured it into the bowl and splashed it onto his face and body gratefully , rubbing damp hands through his hair to flatten the short, spiky ends. A sense of peace and well - being enfolded him as he dried himself and wrapped his cloak around him to keep the chill from his naked body. The spiced wine was cool but he sipped at it slowly, staring into the glowing embers of the dying logs, and finding himself planning some changes to the defences of Fernrean.

The stone tower was basically sound with its steps up to a massive doorway, and dungeons and storage below.

The kitchens and the well were within the stone walls of the upper bailey which was topped by a timber palisade to add height and provide cover for the archers. Armand wondered why Gerard had not taken the stone to full height, but then he thought perhaps he had run out of suitable blocks.

Thinking of the stonework took his mind to the ruins where they had sheltered that day and remembering the softness of Elenor's body in his arms caused his loins to react alarmingly.

He had never had the fierce carnal appetites of some of his fellow barons and he had never, never forced a woman, even in the heat and triumph of a sacked town or city. Such things did not fire his blood. Finishing his wine quickly, he sought his bed and he could not remember a time when he had looked forward to the next day with such eagerness. Sleep claimed him almost as soon as he had stretched his lean strength into repose.

On the upper and lower battlements of Fernrean they kept a good watch. Although the main uprising was to the north, Fernrean was so strategically well located to William's rear that some might find it a good idea to take it. They felt secure in this stronghold built partly of stone and never dreamed that the Roman ruins had provided more than just materials for building. The secret entrance to Gerard's hidden tunnel lay not inches from where Armand and Elenor had pledged themselves that day.

The detailed scale drawing of Fernrean keep was a masterpiece which fascinated Armand de Carrefour. It had taken his serjent at arms, Gyrth, three days of measurements and sketching to produce the plan for his lord and as Armand pored over it he shook his head. "Gyrth, you are wasted. You should have entered the church, man, you have such talent."

The grizzled veteran laughed. "Not a life for which I'd have been suited, my lord, I thank you."

Armand grinned in return for he knew how Gyrth enjoyed his ale and his food, not to mention the company of any pretty maid who might be willing. They bent once more over the drawing and Armand frowned   "You say you had some problems with the measurements around the keep?" "Aye my lord. The outside did not tally up with the apparent thickness of the wall here." His stubby finger jabbed down onto the parchment. "The storerooms should be bigger unless he has added an extra row of stone to that wall."

"Why do that?

When he could have used more stone to raise the height of the encircling walls of the bailey?"

Gyrth shrugged.

"From what I hear, lord, reason was not one of the great talents of the Lord de Beauvrais."

The serjent was being tactful. Stories of Gerard de Beauvrais and his exploits were circulating like wildfire now that the folk of Fernrean realised that he had truly gone for good. Even the hardened troops who had followed Armand de Carrefour for many a year and who had seen rape and murder a - plenty, were sickened by some of his deeds. Armand had heard enough to make him realise why Elenor was so reluctant to talk of her former life with Gerard. Body of Christ! What pleasure it would have given him could it have been he who had sent Gerard's soul on its way to hell!"

"The only thing lacking to make Fernrean impregnable is stone for the outer defences. Perhaps another trip to the ruins in the forest would yield enough material for that."

Armand glanced sharply at his serjent for it had been Gyrth who had accompanied him and Elenor that day when the storm had forced them to run for shelter.

The man's face was innocent, however, so Armand let the matter go. He found he was reluctant to tear down any more of that ancient Roman villa even to strengthen Fernrean and somehow he knew Elenor would feel the same.

As if his thoughts had conjured her, the Lady de Beauvrais appeared, flushed and smiling, in the great doorway to the hall.

She was carrying a huge basket filled to the brim with sweet - smelling herbs and an enormous variety of medicinal plants and berries. Her air of triumph made him smile.

"My lord, success! I did not dream that we had such an abundance of healing plants so close at hand, and so early in the year."

Bustling into the hall, closely followed by an apple - cheeked Joan, she chattered on happily. "That great Saxon in the kitchens is in for a surprise also - and he can make no more excuses for ill - flavoured food."

It was marvellous to see the change which had been wrought in the Lady of Fernrean but a scant week since she had seen the last of Gerard de Beauvrais. Her soft curves were fulfilling their promise, her gentle brown eyes had lost that haunted shadow of terror and her smile was ever ready to beguile the onlooker. Every time he was close to her Armand de Carrefour felt as though a giant fist had a grip on his stomach and he wished his messenger to William could have been gifted with wings so that his swift return could hasten their marriage. As it was he found sweet torture in sleeping each night not yards away from her.

"I hope the escort you took was adequate.?"

He looked over enquiringly at Gyrth who nodded emphatically. Elenor giggled. "Oh more than adequate my lord. I have never seen such nimble gatherers of flowers."

A sudden vision of his best men tripping about at the beck and call of the ladies, picking flowers at their command forced Armand to choke down a surge of laughter.

Luckily he avoided his sergeant's eye or he would have cracked and been lost in mirth.

Elenor placed her basket on the table and glanced curiously at the parchment laid out there. A closer examination brought a gasp of admiration. "My lord, where did you get this?" She leaned to trace the outlines of the buildings with her finger.

"Gyrth prepared it for me."

Those huge brown eyes turned an admiring gaze on the serjent which almost made him blush. "'Tis truly an amazing piece of work serjent. How clever you are."

"'Twas nothing my lady."

"Three days work!" Armand would have none of his modesty.

"How did you do it?   It is so precise." She could not move away from it. It was as though that piece of parchment with its painted lines and numbers held something of great importance to her.   Frowning she studied it, a tingle of presentiment tightening her skin, then Armand's presence behind her as he moved close worried at the change in her, distracted her and she turned around to face her castellan.

He wanted to talk to her, to be alone with her and cast about for some excuse in his mind which would rid them of Joan and Gyrth and even the servants about them.

"I shall take the herbs to the kitchens, my lady, and see about drying them. Serjent if you could help me here?"

My God - was the woman a witch?

Joan almost laughed aloud at the lord's expression. It was so obvious that he wanted Elenor to himself that he may as well have shouted it to the roof top and she took pity on him with her chivvying out of the serjent, Gyrth, and her few quick commands to send servants scurrying on unnecessary errands.

As Joan closed the door behind her, her last glimpse was of Elenor and Armand close together, rapt in each other's gaze.

Inevitably her thoughts turned to Erland and she sighed on the memory of their one night together before he had left with William to fight, possibly against men of Saxon blood. Her prayers each evening and morning held desperate pleas for his safety for she did not think she could survive if he was taken from her now after all she had suffered.

"Can you manage?" Gyrth's gruff voice startled her from her thoughts.

"Certainly serjent. Can you?" She teased him, knowing he liked her and seeking to distract herself from her gloomy pondering.

"That depends on what I have to manage." The clumsy innuendo made her raise her brows and she put him sharply in his place. "At the moment all you are asked to do is carry that basket without spilling my lady's gatherings... no more than that.

He grimaced in resignation and followed her obediently to the kitchens, fascinated in spite of his telling off, by the curve of hip and buttock which swayed before him.

"Three days the messenger has been gone."

"It seems like three months."

"He should be with the King by now."

"'Tis torture to be so near you, not even knowing if we shall eventually be together."

"You said it did not matter how he replied."

"And I meant it!"

"If you do not, then I shall die. Whatever Gerard did to me I could survive for I hated him so much, that hate kept me alive. But you - I do not hate you. No my lord -- I love you!"

Armand de Carrefour swallowed hard on what, in another man, may have been mistaken for a sob, then Elenor de Beauvrais was swept into an embrace which threatened to break every bone in her body.

It gave her what she so desperately needed - reassurance.

The reassurance that this man was not about to let her go, whatever the future may hold for them both.

She revelled in the iron strength of the arms that held her, knowing no fear now only the growing heat of desire as she tilted back her head for his kiss.

When his mouth took hers she wrapped her arms about his neck and responded with such a seeking fire that he groaned, bending her backwards over the long table, every nerve clamouring that he should make wild, passionate love to her.

Elenor was stunned by the onslaught of desperate, uncaring hunger which his kiss aroused in her

She breathed in his need as she was crushed by his strength, then when he raised his head briefly she cried out, low and soft. "No! No please." She meant her denial for him not to stop but he mistook her and thought she rejected him. His grey eyes were confused and not a little hurt, his breathing harsh and ragged and he shook like a man with the ague.

"Elenor, this cannot go on. I cannot sleep, I cannot eat, I think of you constantly when my mind should be concentrating on the defences of this keep."

She gulped, her body crying out for his, yet not knowing how to respond to his need.

"I - I - c - cannot - I do not know..." Her head drooped."My lord if your need cannot await the marriage vows... I shall... I am w- willing."

She could not go on and he swore, feeling like the lowest cur on earth.

The trouble was that he had never had to cope with such demands from his body before. Tenderly, carefully, with that iron control for which he was so famous on the battlefield he cradled her softly to his breast, his lips against the sensuous silk of her hair.

"My love, what you offer is beyond value indeed. Yet I would not take advantage of your sweetness so. No. We shall wait. It should not be long now and I swear   -   I shall not starve to death!"

She giggled, achieving the end he desired and he dropped a swift kiss to her brow before moving determinedly away.

Elenor felt cold without his arms about her and also slightly ashamed at what she had offered him even though he had made her laugh. The memories of the things Gerard had done to her made her feel unclean, tainted and she hoped Armand would never discover any of the gory details of her life as the wife of Gerard de Beauvrais.

Picking up the plan of Fernrean, Armand studied it again, frowning, trying hard to concentrate on his plans for the defences. He was still puzzled by the inconsistencies of the measurements Gyrth had taken. His body was slowly coming back under control yet he wanted to keep her with him. "Will you accompany me? I need to look again at those storerooms beneath the keep."

She smiled up at him and it took all his self control not to snatch her back into his arms

"I can think of nothing more delightful than inspecting storerooms with you my lord."

Laughing together Armand and Elenor left the hall. A chill breeze had sprung up outside, the blue skies vanishing beneath a tide of black clouds.

"It seems we should expect another downpour."

Armand glanced upward. "At least this time we do not have to run for shelter."

Their eyes met and held on a memory.

"What a pity my lord."

His soft laugh at her remark strengthened the bond of intimacy which enfolded them then he was concerned as she shivered suddenly.

"You are cold. Here."

Before she could protest his cloak was about her, enveloping her completely in its heavy folds.

"Oh no! You will need it yourself."

His laugh this time was full and deep. "Not I, lady. I have stood many a cold and lonely watch on freezing battlefields before I even owned a cloak. Have no worries about me."

Indeed he seemed invincible in his strength and power as he towered over her and once again Elenor could only be immeasurably grateful that he had come into her life and that he seemed to want her so desperately.

Armand held her arm as they descended the winding steps into the dark nether regions of Fernrean keep.

In his other hand he carried a torch which flared and sputtered spasmodically in the damp and draughty gloom of the underworld created by Gerard de Beauvrais as storerooms and dungeons for his stronghold.

Elenor did not know why, but as they emerged into the open space which was directly below the great hall, she was seized by fear, a fear which clutched at her vitals, a fear which could only be engendered in her by one person - her former husband Gerard.

Armand de Carrefour felt her trembling.

"Is it too cold for you down here my lady? You need not stay if you do not wish."

"No. No it is not that my lord.

This cloak is well enough to keep out the cold and damp.

'Tis just a feeling - evil - I know not what."

She attempted a laugh."Considering the fact that these were built as storerooms, there is not a great deal stored here, I think."

It was true. There were half a dozen rooms off the central space and although it was obvious by chains dangling here and there that some were used as dungeons - indeed Gerard himself had been incarcerated here - the other rooms were almost empty, save for a few rusty weapons in a heap in one corner.

"There should be some siege provisions surely, even at this time of year."

Gyrth had followed them down with two men at arms also carrying torches, sending rats scurrying from the light.

Gyrth's comment made Armand frown, strangely aware that he was missing something - something important. He let go of Elenor's arm to unroll the plan which Gyrth had drawn and to spread it out on the damp floor, the corners held down by stones.

"'Tis here my lord. The wall is thicker here from the entrance to the third chamber, then in the fourth chamber it changes and the wall on the other side of the entrance is narrower..."

Elenor had wandered away from them and was inspecting the storerooms in question.

The slime on the walls made her shudder and she imagined what it must be like to be imprisoned down here, in the dark, perhaps awaiting death. She ventured no further in than the doorways for the fear was so heavy upon her she was finding it difficult to take a decent breath.

The third chamber.

This was the one they were discussing.

The torches behind her threw the length of her shadow across the floor and partway up the opposite wall.

This room lacked an opening at ground level and the air was therefore staler, more rank.

For one brief moment she thought she caught the stench of Gerard and she clasped her arms about her wondering if this was where William had imprisoned him, then she jumped as Armand came up behind her and took her reassuringly by the shoulders.

"He was not kept in here."

Uncanny how he seemed to read her thoughts

"My lord! My lord!" The shout from the top of the stairs whirled them all about, their expressions ludicrously the same - alarm, surprise.

"A horseman my lord. He requests entrance and he carries the King's colours."

Armand and Elenor looked at each other.

"The messenger?"

"Too soon, surely."

She followed him as fast as she could, cursing the hampering folds of skirt and cloak, yet blessedly relieved to feel the cool fresh air once more on her face. He had already reached the outer bailey by the time she emerged from below and as she made her way down to him she could see the outer gates opening to admit the King's messenger.

A dark premonition made her suddenly pause, her hand going out to steady herself on the post of the upper bailey gate.

"What is it my lady? That is the King's man is it not?"

Joan had come up behind her and her face was so pale, her blue eyes huge as she gazed down to the lower yard. Involuntarily Elenor's arm went about her maid's shoulders and the two women walked downwards together to where Armand de Carrefour listened to the exhausted man who had almost fallen from his lathered, near foundered mount.

They knew by his face that something was terribly wrong.

"What is it, my lord?"

He was silent, his eyes leaving Elenor to rest on Joan.

"Erland?" The whisper came through stiff white lips and at his nod Joan's eyes closed and she crumpled in a heap in the dirt at their feet.

Gerard had lost five of the men loaned to him by Humphrey de Touron.   The problem was that he had been unable to resist what seemed to him to be easy prey. With most able - bodied warriors either fighting for William or against him, the one or two holdings Gerard passed on his way to Fernrean were sadly under - manned and not as well fortified as Fernrean itself. Those left behind to defend the land fought fiercely yet to no avail for their resources were limited. Gerard, in his own inimitable way, showed no mercy. Especially not to the women.

It was as though each female he encountered held the features of Elenor and he treated them accordingly. Rape, murder, torture. It merely whetted his appetite for the attack on Fernrean. His men were deliberately avoiding him now, sensing his burning insanity, his inhuman cruelty and sadism.   It appalled even these hardened unsentimental soldiers, mercenaries every one who had fought from the land of the Viking Chieftains to the Norman holdings of Sicily and beyond.

The crazed mind of Gerard de Beauvrais was concentrated solely on his revenge and in their mad dash from York they had ridden three sets of horses into the ground. Picking up fresh mounts was easy enough as they murdered and plundered their way in a frenzy towards their goal.

Fernrean was dark and silent as Gerard and his two knights slipped silently through the trees to reconnoitre their position. The torches which lit the bailies of Fernrean gave the castle the appearance of floating in a sea of darkness and the eeriness of it all caused Gerard's men to cross themselves surreptitiously and whisper a prayer for protection although God knew they could not serve a more evil master than Gerard de Beauvrais. He hawked and spat wiping his chin with the back of his hand as he stared malevolently down at the sleeping Fernrean, then gesturing bad - temperedly to his men he grabbed at his horse's reins and swung to the saddle.

It was not far now to the ruins of the old Roman villa which guarded Gerard's secret in the depths of the forest. His men were tired, their horses exhausted and only Gerard, with his fierce obsession seemed to have endless energy, driving them on with kicks and curses and threats. They stayed with him not only out of fear but because they had nowhere else to go. Masterless men who had committed the deeds commanded by Gerard would find no place nor sympathy even in rebel - torn England.

They were glad to see the fallen, overgrown pillars of the villa.

Wet and cold and exhausted as they were they could not have put up much of a fight if they were discovered. The whole success of Gerard's plan lay with the secret passageway and his intention to steal in the night and cut as many throats as possible before the inmates of Fernrean even realised he was amongst them.

"Shall we light a fire my lord?" Hubert de Wulfe approached him hesitantly for Gerard was as likely to deal a blow as make a reply.

"Aye. Get some light in here."

"It seems someone has already camped here, lord."

The remains of the fire which had warmed Elenor and Armand drew Gerard's gaze and his rage. He exploded into the dead ashes like a lunatic, kicking them about, raising a dust to choke himself and his men.

"They've been here! What have they discovered? Are my plans brought to nothing?"

He grabbed a torch, freshly lit, from one of his men.

"Here. You. Move this pillar!"

They obeyed him quickly, three of them heaving and straining at the stone pillar which lay in the rubble. When finally they had pushed it aside Gerard fell eagerly to the floor, scrabbling at the broken paving with his hands until his fingernails were broken and bleeding.

"Help me here you fools!"

The stone he was trying to lift gave way beneath the concerted efforts of his soldiers and the cold whiff of foetid air, damp earth and rotting leaves made them turn away, coughing.

Gazing down into the gaping black emptiness before him, Gerard chortled low, rubbing his hands together. "Undisturbed! Secret still! Now I have them and I'll make them sorry they ever meddled with me. Right! You!" He stabbed his finger at one of his men. "Down with you. Take the torch, see if it's clear, then come back."

The man obviously did not want to go and he looked round at his comrades for support. They avoided his eyes however, and in the end he descended the rough wooden steps slowly and reluctantly.

They waited in silence.

They could hear the fall of loose earth and stones as he groped his way along the passageway which was supported by wooden stakes and broken stonework. The tunnel was, in fact, a brilliant example of Gerard's building skills and if he had not been of such a cruel and perverted nature, so evil and unscrupulous, his talents could have commanded a high price from princes and war lords far and wide.

The minutes ticked by and Gerard could stand it no longer. He lay on his great belly and shouted after his man.

"Hurry you fool! Is it clear? Can we get through?"

The intrepid scout had obviously gone too far to hear him for he gave no answer and Gerard cursed, jumping to his feet and pacing the ancient stones in a strange parody, did he but know it, of Elenor de Beauvrais.

The tunnel had taken weeks to construct for it ran beneath the forest directly in a line to Fernrean and the huge roots of the great trees above made digging a nightmare. Only a small number of men had known of it for Gerard had always intended to eliminate all witnesses to his secret. He used serfs from the village for his workforce, expendable flesh whose loved ones would not dare to question the lord were they to disappear.

He knew therefore, beneath his madness, that it would take a good few hours for his man to follow the length of the passage and return, so he finally curbed his impatience and squatted before the fire his men had lit.

Morose and silent again he ate what sparse fare they provided and took notice of none of them. Even his knights were excluded from his company by his attitude and preferred the rougher, but simpler camaraderie of the soldiers.

A rumble of thunder added to the doom laden atmosphere and the superstitious men - at -arms muttered uneasily amongst themselves.

The storm slowly, heavily, gathered force and the sudden flash of lightning heralded the onset of a spring storm which proved to be both awesome and malevolent.

Through the thick canopy of leaves crashed the rain, driving even into the broken crevices of their ancient den , spitting into the fires and lashing at the exposed flanks of the tethered horses. Two broke free in their terror and were away before anyone could catch them.

Gerard seemed not to notice the chaos about him. His knife flashed, carving slivers from a chunk of wood.

"Bitch, whore, bitch, whore, bitch, whore..." The litany went on, each word matching a flying splinter of wood. Christ how he longed to get his hands on her, how he would make her suffer. What he had done to her before would be nothing compared to what he had planned.

"My lord..." The gasping plea from the tunnel entrance galvanised Gerard into action and he almost fell in his haste to reach the man who was trying to heave himself out of that hellish hole.

Dragged by the scruff of his neck up and onto the floor, the soldier found himself hammered with questions. Confused and barely able to breathe from the lack of oxygen in that long and nightmarish journey underground, he fought to answer his lord.

"Is it clear? Is it safe? Can we get through?" Gerard had him by the throat shaking him as though he could more easily force answers from him that way.

"Yes!" Choking, frantic to escape. "Yes lord."

The answer that Gerard sought seemed to calm him a little and he let go, allowing his victim to fall to the floor and heave for breath.

The storm still raged and with the tumult caused by the wind and the thunder, it was hardly possible even to hear himself speak.

In spite of this, Gerard roared his orders at his men, grabbing them, pushing them even kicking at them to force them down into the gaping maw of the tunnel.

He seemed to think of nothing but getting inside Fernrean and they almost rebelled against him - almost.

Down in the stinking, stifling dark there was at least relief from the elements above but with their torches guttering and dying from the lack of air, they soon found themselves in total blackness, unable to turn around or go back with Gerard, his sword at the ready, behind them. No room to disobey him, to fight. Only room to die.

The tunnel had crumbled in places and the great roots of the trees seemed to reach out like the talons of some strange beast lurking in the dark, ready to tear at eyes and flesh.

De Wulfe, in the lead, felt the sweat stinging him as he groped his way forward, fear of being buried alive keeping him moving onward. The tunnel seemed endless and panic caught at the men who followed de Wulfe. They pushed at him, totally blind, convinced that they would never breathe fresh air again.

"Easy you fools or you'll have the whole lot down upon us!"

His snarled warning slowed them, steadied them but they were growing weaker.

The headlong journey from York, the various skirmishes on the way and now this. They would be lucky to be able to stand, much less attack a castle defended by de Carrefour.

De Wulfe's probing sword rang on stone and the man almost wept with relief.

Death in battle he could face with equanimity, but the thought of all that earth above him, a living grave, had totally unmanned him.

He dropped his weapon and began to feel around the edges of the stone wall in front of him. Steps lay to his left and there was open space around him, enough to allow him and the men immediately behind him to stand up.

Gradually they all fell forward from the tunnel and de Wulfe stooped to help Gerard as he emerged cackling with triumph even as he gasped for air. They all raised their faces gratefully to the down draft which spread its reviving blessing over their filthy sweat - slicked skin.

"We are beneath the keep. These steps will bring us out into the storerooms and from there we can steal through the whole of Fernrean until not a man is left alive."

In spite of themselves they were awed by his evil genius in constructing the passageway and as they sat on the steps resting and passing round the water bottles they began to believe that perhaps his plans would succeed after all.

Gyrth was the first to reach for Joan as she lay in the dirt. He lifted her in strong yet careful arms and Elenor dodged about him, smoothing Joan's dirt-draggled hair from her pale face.

"To my chamber, Gyrth, quickly."

He obeyed without a word, leaving Elenor hesitating behind him, torn between her concern for Joan and her need to find out more from Armand of what had happened to Erland. He noticed her anxious hovering.

"I shall come up shortly. I need to talk to the messenger to find out all I can. Go with Joan."

His face was dark and grim, frightening in its knowledge of things he did not wish to tell her. Staring up at him Elenor felt cold fingers of foreboding clutch at her spine, paralysing her for a few brief moments before she remembered Joan and her need for care and attention. Hastily then she turned to run and catch up with Gyrth as he made his way up towards the keep.

Armand de Carrefour watched her retreating back briefly, closing his eyes and cursing silently at the news that William's man had brought, then he swung around on the waiting messenger. "Come, tell me everything you know - every last detail. Our lives may depend on it."

Gyrth stood back to allow Elenor to open her chamber door with its newly mended lock.

"Here Gyrth." She indicated the bed and the burly serjent gingerly laid down his burden, a slowly reviving Joan.

Elenor poured some water into a cup and held her by the shoulders, supporting her as she drank.

The maid took a few gulps then pushed away the cup, covering her face and allowing the slow heaving sobs to rack her body.

"Thank you Gyrth. You may leave us now."

"Yes my lady." Obviously deeply concerned yet helpless in the face of Joan's distress, Gyrth backed out of the room, closing the door quietly behind him.

It was impossible for Elenor, faced with the depth of Joan's grief, to even consider what words of consolation she could offer. Nevertheless she tried her best.

"My Lord de Carrefour is questioning the messenger now. We must not think the worst, for you said yourself that Erland is a hard man to kill."

Joan just shook her head, unable to answer, rocking herself backwards and forwards, her arms clasped about her knees, her face buried in the folds of her skirt.

"Please, Joan, consider, he may only be wounded or captured."

It was hopeless. Joan was deaf and blind to all reason and when Armand's knock came at the door Elenor was praying that his news would hold out some hope for her maid, for this woman who had become more than a servant, this woman who had become her tight bound friend.

When she let him in, however, her heart sank with that strange foreboding of danger.

"The news?" Her voice quivered, her eyes wide and fearful. Behind her Joan raised a swollen desperate face, tendrils of blonde hair stuck to her tear streaked cheeks.

It seemed as though he searched for the right words."Erland still lived when the messenger left William's camp."

A whimper escaped Joan's throat and Elenor glanced quickly at her maid before her gaze was drawn back to de Carrefour. Something still bothered him. A grim expression almost of doom shuttered his face.

"What? What is it?" Standing so close to him that she could see that dark ring of grey around the edge of his pupil, so close that she could almost taste his tension, his unwillingness to pass on a knowledge he would rather was not his to impart.

He took Elenor's shoulders in a grip which hurt, but she did not flinch, needing to know as if her life depended on it, what it was he feared to tell her.

"Gerard..." still he hesitated.

"Oh dear God - what? What is it?"

"He has escaped.   'Twas he who did for Erland." he said it quickly now to get it over with.

A shriek of rage, fear, protest from Joan seemed to come from a great distance as his words penetrated Elenor's brain and only his grip on her shoulders steadied her as he had intended it should.

"How?"   She gasped the word, her chest constricted with shock. "Tell me how could it happen.?"

"He should be dead! Dead! " Joan's voice held hysteria. "Still he reaches out to hurt us. Satan is his master and the devil takes care of his own!"

"If he is foolish enough to come near Fernrean then I shall take care of him - and this time no-one will stop me!"   Fierce and dangerous he had suddenly become and his fingers dug so deeply into Elenor's flesh that she knew she would have bruises on the morrow.   Still she exulted in his strength needing to feel protected, safe from the nemesis that was Gerard de Beauvrais.

"Oh he will not be fool enough to come here! He will make good his escape to the north with the Atheling's forces. He is not known for his valour when his enemies are strong - he is brave only when his foes are weak - unable to defend themselves."   Joan's voice now held searing contempt for the man who had used her so callously over the years, then she begged for more news of her husband.

"You say Erland still lives. Please, tell me what happened, lord. Will he be coming home?"

Her voice had dulled now, her mind dismissing de Beauvrais and concentrating on the man she loved so deeply.

De Carrefour sighed, reluctantly relinquishing his hold on Elenor.

"Some wine is needed here, I think." He went over to Elenor's side table and poured wine for the three of them, handing the two women a cup each before crossing to the window and staring out, as though to watch for Gerard, as though to see where the enemy might be hiding.

"It seems that Erland left the camp to investigate sounds in the night. When he did not return after some time Erik became worried and searched for his comrade through the darkness of the forest. He discovered Erland sorely wounded.

He had come upon Gerard as he was making his escape and that evil swine obviously thought he had left Erland dead."

His broad shoulders almost blocked out the light and Elenor's fear receded a little. She knew that Gerard could be no match for Armand de Carrefour if he faced him in honest combat - but then that was not Gerard's way. No, not at all. His way was the knife in the back, the silent ambush, the poisoned cup and because Armand was so honest, so honourable in all his dealings, it was there where the danger lay.

Putting down the cup with the barely tasted wine, Elenor crossed to the window beside him.

Hesitantly she touched his arm.

"You must realise what kind of a serpent Gerard is - how evil, perverted and cowardly.

Do not watch for a direct attack but for the unexpected treachery. Please - do not underestimate him."

"Will Erland then be coming home lord?" Joan's voice held an appeal which he could not ignore.

"It seems he is too badly hurt to be moved. If he improves then he will certainly be coming here to Fernrean, but you must understand that they were all surprised that he had survived at all." Armand's tone was gentle for he did not wish to upset Joan again though he thought it was better that she did not build up too much false hope.

"Thank you my lord. Erland will fight hard for his life I know, even if only to avenge himself on Gerard de Beauvrais."

"He would have to take his place in line." Armand smiled wolfishly.

"Now I must leave you. If de Beauvrais comes anywhere near here we shall know about it and then... I shall have him!"

He swooped to Elenor, a burning kiss jerking her heartstrings then he was gone, leaving a heavy silence behind him.

Elenor collapsed on the bed next to Joan.

"I cannot believe it. I cannot believe it. He should be dead, yet still he comes back to threaten us. What will it take before we are truly rid of him?" Her voice held fear, disbelief and helplessness.

"If he ever comes near me again I shall kill him myself, one way or another, whatever the consequences." Joan's fists were clenched and her entire body quivered with her hatred.

"We can never allow ourselves to become his victims again and should he return here and by some chance regain control of Fernrean, you and I must stand together against him."

The two women stared into each other's eyes.

"Let us make a pact then. Between us we shall defeat him, whatever the danger, whatever the cost."

Joan gave one nod of assent and they hugged each other tightly to seal their pact.

A buoyant feeling of self - confidence kept Elenor's fear at bay for the rest of the day as she made herself busy in the kitchens showing the Saxon cook how to prepare sweetmeats to follow the evening meal.

"Your skill puts me to shame, my lady. With all you have taught me I could seek a place at court."

"I am sure William would not poach my servants Arnulf, and besides, I would miss your great bulk in my kitchens to keep order."

They grinned at each other, in one accord, and the threat of Gerard seemed to recede further. Surrounded as she was now by people who seemed to have a high regard for her, the ogre almost lost his power over her.

Crossing back to the keep Elenor felt a spot of rain on her face and glanced upwards.

Another spring storm seemed to be threatening and she shivered, wrapping her cloak more closely about her shoulders and ducking her head to avoid the great drops which blew into her face. Where was Armand? she wondered, suddenly longing for him.

The next second she cannoned into him. His arms came about her, his breath was warm on her brow. "Now, my lady, what have I done to deserve this attack? You come at me like a bull!" He laughed down at her, his grey eyes inviting her to laugh with him. The wind blew her hair and her cloak about her, pressing her against him and he suddenly whirled her around into the shelter of a wall pillar, out of the wind and out of sight of the casual observer.

"Gerard's escape alters my intentions not one whit. It is simply a case of how soon I can catch him and kill him."

His voice was husky, his mouth close to her ear, breath tickling her neck arousing goose bumps along her skin.

"I don't want to think about him. I cannot bear it."

The links of his mail were pressing hard against her but she did not care. She looked up at him with those great brown eyes and he kissed her.

Everything was blotted out save for that possession of her mouth and she urged him closer, her fingers joined behind his head, her lips parting beneath his. That soft flowering of passion burned him so that he was no longer master of his own actions.

He pulled at her cloak, at the shoulders of her dress, his kisses seeking the silken skin beneath. A course of desire made Elenor's legs buckle and her own kisses landed awry on any part of him that she could reach.

The rain grew suddenly heavier, soaking the pair of them and bringing some sense of their surroundings back to Armand.

"This is madness. Curse Gerard. How could William let that bastard escape?" He spat his frustration, banging his fist against the wall above her head, then pulling her against him under the shelter of his cloak to run with her into the keep. The great doors boomed shut behind them and they shook off the drops of scintillating rain before crossing to the ever present embers of the great fire to warm themselves.

"The messenger we sent to the King should have reached him by now. It should not take William long to secure the city of York and if Gerard is there William will deal with him. If he is not. If he is heading for Fernrean then the men I have out keeping watch will capture him. My problem will be to persuade. them to save him for me to kill."

Elenor sat in the chair, her chin on her hand, watching him dreamily as he talked. He could not be more of an opposite to Gerard, in looks, in manner and in spirit and she knew that no matter what happened he held her heart in his hand.

"Do not look at me so!" The abruptness of his tone startled her and she jerked upright.

"What?"

"If you look at me like that I shall be hard put to stay away from you and talk sensibly."

For one crazy moment she wanted to cry out. 'Do not be sensible.

Do not hold back but take me in your arms and show me what real love between a man and a woman is like.' She bit her tongue on the words, afraid that he would think less of her if she uttered the wanton thought. At least Joan had known the sweetness of Erland's love even if, God forbid, he should not survive. She, however, had known only cruelty and pain and the debauched, perverted desires of Gerard de Beauvrais.

Elenor sighed and rose dejectedly from the chair. "I think I shall go and see how Joan is faring..."

He caught her as she walked away from him but this time she resisted him. What was the use? It seemed she would never know the happiness of lying in love's embrace.

"Elenor! Elenor what is it?" He would not let her go and she was no match for his strength. When he held her cradled hard against his chest she pleaded with him.

"Please let me go my lord. Like you I am only flesh and blood, yet if a woman, unmarried, gives in to her desires then she is a whore, a harlot to be despised..."

She could not hold back a sob and his embrace tightened, robbing her of breath.

"You think too lightly of me lady. Nothing... Nothing could ever make me despise you.

How could you believe that of me? Marriage vows or not, my feelings will never change. I could never love you less, I give you my oath as a knight on it."

This time his kiss demanded her surrender.

He did not hold back and his hard embrace changed to a coaxing caress which burned the length of her back to her buttocks, filling her belly with fire and making her tremble for his possession. His mouth forced her lips apart, his tongue ravaging her sweetness with a hunger which could only convince her of the true depth of his love for her.

He raised his head at last to whisper "I am burning for you my love. If this matter is not settled soon I shall go mad."

His fingers caressed her soft cheek, traced the outline of her mouth, swollen with the fervour of his kisses. "You had best stay away from me for I cannot trust myself with you."

She sighed and rested her head against his shoulder still racked with the shudders of desire which his touch had aroused in her, then she made a determined effort and stood away from him, shivering as she lost the warmth of his embrace.

"I must go to Joan."

He nodded. "I hope for her sake that Erland survives to return to her."

"As do I. I can understand her love for him now, and I know how I would feel if it were you lying wounded and so far away."

He stepped forward and she fled before he could reach her, heading for the sanity of her room and the safety of Joan's company.

Thwarted he watched her go, wanting to follow her, to take her softness in his arms again, to taste the sweetness of her lips but he knew he could not allow himself to dwell on such things.

Not as long as Gerard de Beauvrais was still
on the loose. He picked up his cloak and swirled
it about his shoulders to venture out once more
into the rain and listen carefully to the reports
coming in from the scouting groups he had out
searching the area. They were all the same.
Nothing. No sight nor sign of Gerard de
Beauvrais.

Armand was weary and dispirited by the end of the day. His scouts had been returning, soaked and tired but without any information on the whereabouts of Gerard. He supposed he should be glad that de Beauvrais was obviously not coming back to cause trouble at Fernrean. William had probably caught up with him and it would not be long before they heard news that Gerard was dead. He would dearly have loved, though, to have got his own hands on him, to take in some measure, revenge for the terrible things he had done to Elenor.

"A hot bath my lord? It will revive you." Thomas indicated the wooden tub in front of the fire, steam rising invitingly from the hot water it contained.

Armand allowed a smile to lighten his grim features.

"Nothing could be more welcome Thomas."

It took only moments for him to strip off his sodden clothing, shivering as the chill air hit his damp skin, and climb into the tub.

The hot water made him groan with pleasure as it drew the tension from hard, tight muscles, the cascade from the pailful Thomas poured over his head making him gasp, then he relaxed back into the bath with a grateful sigh.

He lingered until the water began to cool then rose, dripping, to dry himself in front of the scorching leap of the fire.

A slight scuffle of sound came from the small room which separated his chamber from Elenor's and he wrapped the linen drying cloth around his waist and crossed towards the narrow doorway. He glanced briefly at his sword but did not bother to pick it up, thinking that probably Joan was searching through the boxes now stored in the small antechamber for something for Elenor.

When he jerked open the door it was to meet the wide brown eyes of Elenor herself, frozen in the act of inspecting one of her mother's old gowns. They stared at each other in silence and Elenor could not prevent her gaze from wandering hungrily to the broad muscular shoulders and the massive chest bared before her. Crazily she imagined her fingers sliding over the smooth muscle, and her lips planting kisses down the strong column of his throat.

"What are you doing?"

"What?"

He smiled devastatingly at her and she thought to herself that even if she should die right now she would at least have known the passionate pleasure of his kiss, his touch, and of course, his smile.

"What are you doing?"

"Oh! These things were my mother's. I was just looking for something to wear."

She hardly knew what she was saying she was so stunned by his half - naked presence and she felt a prickle of sweat on her upper lip which was ridiculous when you considered how cold it was in that small room.

"I see. Well I shall see you downstairs."

"Yes."

Neither of them moved, however, then Armand found himself, instead of retreating back into his room, taking a step towards Elenor.

"Have you found anything my lady...? Oh!"

Joan could have kicked herself for interrupting them - if only she had known he was there!

"I shall see you downstairs." This time his body did as he bade it and he retired hastily into his own room to finish drying himself and to dress ready for the evening meal.

Elenor did not know how she, herself, got ready considering the fact that her whole body had virtually turned to jelly.

"I do not think I can stand it Joan. Did Erland have this effect on you or am I bewitched?"

"Only bewitched by love, lady. Take pleasure in it for I tell you, this is what makes life worth living."

The magic was still there as he helped her to her chair almost an hour later and Elenor found she had no appetite for food, hungry only for his touch, the sound of his voice, his smile.

She hung on his every word as he talked, opening up to her as he never had to anyone else, telling of his ideas and dreams and hopes for their future. The wine went down so smoothly that she found herself in a fit of the giggles several times before realising that although she was not eating much, perhaps she was drinking a little more than she was used to.

In their absorption with each other all thoughts of Gerard de Beauvrais faded into insignificance. The shock was all the greater, therefore, when Gyrth, who had taken out the last patrol of men searching for signs of the escaped lord, made his sodden way to where Armand and Elenor laughed together.

He was reluctant to disturb them yet he knew his news may be of some import.

"We have found two horses, my lord, running loose yet fully saddled and bridled. They must have broken free from their tethering, frightened by the storms."

Elenor felt the colour draining from her face and the fear, in its return, was more shocking, more intense for the fact that for a while she had been without it.

"Could you not tell which direction they came from? Surely two frightened horses would leave a crashing trail a baby could follow!"

"We back - tracked them as far as the river, lord, but in the dark and the storm we lost the trail after that."

Gyrth was agonised at his failure and normally Armand would have been more understanding but he was so conscious of Elenor's white - faced terror beside him that he was harsher with the serjent than he might otherwise have been.

"Perhaps I should send out someone who can do the job properly. We could be overwhelmed before we knew it... and to lose the advantage of such a clue! Curse it, Gyrth, you should know better!"

The serjent was shivering with cold, soaked to the skin and exhausted trying to battle his way through the forest following the horses' tracks.

"My lord, please. Gyrth has done his best. Show me the man who can follow a trail in the blackness of the night and in this weather."

Her touch on his arm calmed him and he sat back and sighed.

"You are right. I am sorry Gyrth. Double the guard and make s ure no-one sleeps at their post. If de Beauvrais is out there, I want him!"

"Yes my lord."

"Gyrth. Make sure you dry yourself and get some hot food - you and your men."

"Yes my lady." His glance was grateful.

"I am sorry. But I want that bastard so badly!" Armand rubbed at the bridge of his nose, a habit she had noticed he had when he was agitated.

"I shall not feel safe until I see him dead before me, until I can feel him cold ready for the grave."

The flat bleakness of her voice made him reach out and take her hand and she could feel the strength in his fingers, the callouses caused by hours of wielding the heavy battle sword and the coldness and fear receded somewhat.

"I think I shall retire now. I have drunk too much wine and my head is not steady." She smiled at him with an effort and he stood and pulled out her chair, taking her hand again and raising it to his mouth to kiss her fingers.

"Have no fear. I shall keep you safe."

"Thank you my lord." She moved close to whisper and it seemed that only the two of them existed once again, all danger, all fear locked out.

It was the hardest thing she had ever done, to turn and walk away, yet she knew he would not be far from her while she slept and that thought comforted her.

Nevertheless, her sleep was restless, disturbed and nightmare-filled and as the storm crashed and howled about Fernrean she dreamed that Gerard was chasing her, chasing her down a long, dark passageway from which there was no escape. Eventually he cornered her.

She could go no further and he was laughing that obscene laugh and waving an object in his hand which she desperately did not want to see. He thrust it forward, into her face and it was Armand's severed head!

Blood poured from it, the eyes stared in accusation and she screamed - and screamed - and could not stop. Could not stop until she woke herself, sobbing and crying out his name hysterically.

And suddenly he was there. The connecting door flung wide and he was ready, almost snarling, to defend her. Clad only in a hastily wrapped cloak, sword in hand he sought the foe and she flew to his arms, clutching at his warm solid flesh, crying his name still, reassuring herself that he was alive - and she was in his embrace.

"Hush now. Hush now my love, I am here. Calm down. It was a bad dream you had. Hush now."

He cradled her tightly against his broad chest, wrapping his cloak about them both and raining kisses on her hair, her face - and her mouth. Her frantic terror turned to passion as his kiss, meant to calm and reassure her, merely lit the flame of her desire.

Neither of them noticed the door open. Neither of them noticed Joan close it again quickly, barring the way for Thomas and for Gyrth and his men close behind.

"All is well. My lady rode the nightmare but my lord is with her and all is well."

They dispersed sheepishly to their posts again and Joan hugged herself with glee before returning to her own bed.

Inside the room all reason had fled. There was only passion and the flames of love and desire to consume the two who had denied themselves for so long. Armand lifted Elenor in arms which barely noticed her weight, and with his kiss still crushing her mouth he carried her to the bed.

Tangled in his cloak he realised he still carried his sword and cast it away from him impatiently.

It clattered across the floor to the other side of the room and he forgot it as he slid the straps of Elenor's shift down over her shoulders and caressed her soft skin with a hungry mouth.

Elenor knew not what to expect, and when her night-mare induced panic had subsided she found herself half - waiting for a violence and pain which, for her, had always been what passed for the act of love.

She could not have been more wrong.

She looked up into grey eyes which were smoky with desire, into a face which held only love for her. He kissed her brow and her temple, sensitive where the skin was so delicate.

He traced the line of her cheekbone and hovered agonisingly for a moment before his kiss descended to caress her mouth, tenderly at first, then with a growing passion which he fought to control.

The last thing he wanted to do was to frighten her but her slender arms came up and about his neck and she raised her body up from the bed to press her softness against him.

He groaned and rolled over onto his back pulling her over on top of him and wrapping her in a tight embrace.

Her hair fell in a soft curtain each side of her face and he slid his fingers through the silken strands to cradle her head in his hands, not breaking yet that kiss which she wished would never end.

The straps of her shift were snapped with ease and his kiss slid down her throat to her shoulders then after one brief hesitation, to her breast. Throwing back her head, she whimpered, the sensations he aroused almost an agony, but when he stopped at her cry she pulled his head back against her, the spiky roughness of his cropped dark hair a heightened sensual pleasure against her skin.

He rolled over again so that she lay looking up at him.

"I love you." He whispered the words against her mouth.

"I love you." He whispered again at her throat.

"I love you." The whispers went on, preceding each kiss. She raised her knee and her shift slid up, baring her thighs. His battle - roughened fingers worshipped the silken skin and she raised her hips as he sought the velvet of her stomach, his tongue caressing her navel, her hip, then the inside of her thigh.

Elenor felt as if she was melting beneath his touch. Her thighs quivered uncontrollably and the pit of her stomach ached with wanting.

Armand did not know how much longer he could wait. Sweat beaded his brow and his upper lip but he so desperately wanted this to be right for her that he almost sobbed with the effort of control.

His tongue gently touched her nipples and she gasped and clutched at his shoulders, pulling at him, begging him to come closer.

In the end it was so easy, so totally beautiful as he entered her that the tears gathered at the corners of her eyes and she clasped him to her with all her strength, rising to meet his demands as he lost himself in her sweetness.

Undreamed of pleasure swept Elenor's body. Heat and shivers took their turn of her sensitised skin and each rhythmic stroke inside her brought soft sighs of ecstasy which added to the tension building inside Armand.

"My love, my sweet love...." The words shuddered from him as he sought the beckoning paradise she offered. His heart pounded like a drum and his breath caught in his throat, silencing his words of love for a brief moment as he reached his goal, then his great strength deserted him and he briefly crushed her beneath his weight before he rolled to one side and pulled her close into his arms, her head pillowed on his shoulder.

Elenor was still blind and deaf with the intensity of the sensations still pulsing through her body yet the sheer heaven of the strength of his arms about her only added to her bewildered joy.

She breathed in his warm scent and rubbed her cheek against the hair - roughened muscles of his chest, murmuring his name softly as the beat of her heart steadied and slowed.

Their legs were still tangled together and she wished they could stay thus entwined and not have to face the outside world with its constant threat of Gerard de Beauvrais She understood how Joan felt for Erland and what a tragedy it would be if he should not survive to come home and love her again.

Armand's kisses were tickling her skin and she tilted her head back against his arm to look into his face.

"I never dreamed that love could be so sweet."

He laughed softly. "Nor I, sweetheart. I do not know how I existed before I met you. You understand that now you are mine I could never let you go?" He was teasing yet she knew that beneath it all he was deadly serious. "Never try to leave me for I would die before I set you free. Even if we never find de Beauvrais I could not dream of parting from you and I would defy the King himself in this matter."

"Ssh! Have no fear." It seemed strange that she was the one to soothe him. "I love you so much, your worries are foolish."

Wonderingly he stroked the soft skin of her arm, then ventured further, his rough palm amazed at the silken quality of her curves, the long graceful sweep of her thighs, the tiny span of her waist.

"You are so beautiful, it hurts."

He tilted her head and kissed her with such passion she felt the salt of blood on her tongue.

She did not care a whit for that, for her blood was racing again at his touch and she revelled in his weight and strength, caressing the long, iron hard muscles of his back with a hungry fervour which drove him wild. This time she knew what pleasure awaited her and she was intoxicated by his desperate hunger, pulling him to her with all her strength, clutching his hair and holding him to kiss him wildly and passionately.

It was almost a battle, their lovemaking, a battle with both sides the victor and as the sweat slicked their bodies and the climax left them shaking and weak Elenor found herself weeping with the emotions which raged within her.

When finally he pulled his cloak across to cover them both she rubbed shaking fingers over her cheeks then clasped his hand tightly in hers before they drifted away, exhausted yet totally content.

Outside there was a brief lull in the storm and the few sentries unlucky enough to be on duty wrapped their cloaks more closely about themselves, glad of the respite from the noise and confusion of the wind and lashing rain.

Not a man of them would see the dawn.

The darkness and the rain provided perfect cover for Gerard's men. In all they murdered twenty - two of Armand's soldiers, taking prisoner those who were off duty, disarmed and sleeping, and forcing them down to be imprisoned in the very dungeons which had provided entrance for the enemy. The wind and rolling thunder covered any sounds of the odd attempt at resistance and the capture of Fernrean castle was the most silent conquest ever achieved. It helped Gerard that Armand still had large numbers of men out on patrol, scouring the forest and all the surrounding area for the very man who now crowed with triumph as he saw his own small company at the walls, their numbers swelled by those who had been Gerard's men in the past and were now given the chance to rejoin him. They shrugged fatalistically. One master, to them, was much the same as another and at least with Gerard the discipline was not so tough.

Only the keep remained silent, all within ignorant of the changes taking place outside.

De Wulfe slid inside the great hall, sword at the ready, and gestured to his men to fan out, quickly and efficiently, waking the servants and herding them at swordpoint into the kitchens.

The huge Saxon cook, Anulf, picked up a meat cleaver and in a short, bloody struggle accounted for two of de Wulfe's men before he was cut down, hacked to the floor to lie staring sightlessly upwards, a terrifying lesson to anyone who might try to resist. Gerard chortled gleefully as he strutted once more the length of his own hall to his chair, beckoning to his two knights. "There remains only the bedchambers and that slut of a wife and her paramour. I want them both alive. Silently now, and make sure you have sufficient men to do this job properly."

Armand and Elenor were both in a deep, dreamless slumber, still wrapped in each other's arms. The deafening crash as the bedchamber door was kicked open, sent Armand de Carrefour, warrior that he was, hurtling from the bed, wide awake and searching for his sword. It lay where he had cast it away from him so impatiently not two hours before, and the enemy was between him and that longed for weapon. Gerard's men poured into the room as Armand fought, all naked and unarmed as he was, like a lion.   It was hopeless.   They bore him, still fighting and cursing, to the ground and they bound him up, trussing him like a chicken and throwing him down at Gerard's feet.

Elenor heard someone screaming insanely from a distance and it was only when her husband slapped her backhanded across the face, snarling "Shut it, you bitch!" that she realised it was she who was screaming.

"Well now. Is this not cosy?" Gerard smirked at the helpless Armand who sucked up enough blood stained saliva to spit on his enemy's shoe. "Tut, tut. What's this? A poor loser then? Surely it is I who should be so contemptuous? After all I do find you abed with MY WIFE." He shouted the last two words in Elenor's face as she stood, naked, with her arms held cruelly behind her back by one of Gerard's men. She was pushed forward, bent like a bow, her breasts thrust out, her head dragged back by her hair as Gerard's fingers encircled her throat and squeezed until she could not breathe.

"Leave her alone you evil bastard! I'll kill you with my bare hands. Fight me! Fight me! You can have any weapons you like! I'll kill you - Christ I'll kill you!" Armand screamed his threats, straining furiously at his bonds and Gerard raised his brows, amused and delighted at the situation he had discovered.

He turned back to Elenor, releasing his throttling grip so that she heaved for air, then he made her cry out again in agony as he gripped her breasts and twisted them hard in his filthy fat fingers.

Armand went berserk!

He lashed out with his legs sending two of Gerard's men flying and he lunged and fought frantically to protect his love from her husband's cruel attentions, almost snapping his bonds as he exerted every ounce of his considerable strength against them.

"Hold him! Hold him! Watch out - don't let him loose!" Gerard was hopping about like a great fat toad with excitement and apprehension, seeing the chance for a fine revenge which could also be vastly entertaining.

Armand was finally subdued. Blood poured from his nose, badly broken by a well aimed fist and he was having difficulty breathing with the pain of three broken ribs, the result of a vicious kick by de Wulfe.

Elenor had gone strangely quiet. Her head drooped and her hair fell forward, hiding her face, partially covering her nakedness and this did not suit Gerard at all. He grabbed at the long silken tresses and snatched his dagger from its sheath. In several violent, slashing strokes her beautiful hair lay in tormented coils upon the floor. Still she did not react, although Armand groaned and cursed.

Suddenly a scuffle at the door distracted them and all eyes turned to the group of figures there.

Joan stood calm and relaxed, her blue eyes showing no emotion, her arms folded across her bosom.

"My lord." She inclined her head.

"'Tis good to see you back." The hiss of Elenor's indrawn breath was barely audible but Armand's" You traitorous bitch!" was clear to all. Gerard was still, his eyes narrowed for a moment then he smiled. "How is it with you? Have they treated you well?"

She shrugged"I survived lord. As always."

He accepted that, then turned his attention to the other figure, struggling in the grip of the knight, de Grace. "And who have we here?"

Armand groaned.

"The Lord de Carrefour's squire." Joan's voice was off hand.

Thomas was fighting as hard as he could to free himself yet he was held easily by de Grace, who was grinning happily.

"Ah yes - just your sort of meat - young, tender - and a boy! You can have him!"

"Thank you my lord."

"Nooo!" Armand's cry was only echoed by Thomas's screams as he was dragged away by the laughing de Grace.

Elenor looked straight at Joan - brown eyes meeting blue in one long steadfast stare before her head drooped again.

"And now, gentlemen."

Gerard walked to the table by Elenor's bed and picked up the flagon of wine, pouring himself a cup and taking a long draught.

"Bring them down."

They had to carry Armand. Not an easy job, for in spite of his injuries he still struggled to free himself.

Elenor was cool.

She walked proudly in spite of her nakedness, in spite of her raggedy - shorn hair, in spite of the leers and comments made by Gerard's men who sensed that there was to be some entertainment involving her and possibly the badly damaged but still raging Lord de Carrefour.

They truly did not know how right they were.

Gerard settled himself in his chair at the table and poured himself some more wine hastily provided by a trembling servant then he turned his evil regard on Elenor.

"So, my sweet wife and is this your latest lover?" He indicated Armand with his cup. "And how many more have there been? Hey? Tell me - William himself perhaps? Although I doubt he would be interested in such a scrawny bitch as you. But de Carrefour here - it seems he is most interested." Gerard picked up a chicken carcass and wrenched off a leg, biting into it with relish. "Yes. Most interested. Perhaps we should show him some of your talents." He laughed again, hysterically and Elenor felt so afraid that her lower stomach and her legs seemed turned to water.

She knew Gerard.

Oh, how she knew him - and the things he was capable of. But Armand did not know. Aye, he had heard the stories, but none of them did any justice to the evil pervert that was Gerard de Beauvrais.

"You!" Gerard pointed at random to one of his men.

The chosen one looked around, half grinning and his comrades fell back, leaving him standing alone.

"Yes lord?"

"D'you fancy a piece of this?" Gerard indicated Elenor.

"Well..."

"Do you or don't you?"

The man slid a sideways glance at Elenor and swallowed hard. "Yes lord."

Armand was uncomprehending but Elenor could not hold back a whimper of denial.

"Sorry? You have something to say?"   Gerard was almost comical in his play acting.

"I have nothing to say - nothing to say to you - except - I hope you burn in hell!" The venom and deadly seriousness of her reply shook the fat bastard for one brief second, then he surged to his feet and grabbed her by her hair, flinging her forward over the high table.

Elenor clenched her teeth and closed her eyes. She knew what was coming - only too well.   But Armand did not. He watched uncomprehending as Gerard unlaced his chausses and bared himself, ready to assault his wife in front of everyone.

"I'll kill you if you touch her - I'll kill you, you vile bastard!" He was almost sobbing as Gerard paused and spread out his hands, totally uncaring that he was standing half - naked in front of everyone.

"But this is my wife. - My wife!   What objection can you have? You are nothing to her." And he advanced on Elenor.

She uttered not a sound, not a protest as he thrust into her. Clenching her teeth she suffered the pain and humiliation in silence although her heart was breaking that Armand should be witness to her degradation.

Armand was a madman.

The pain of his ribs was forgotten as he struggled desperately to escape the hard men who held him and get his hands on de Beauvrais.

A warrior who had never known tears in his whole life, he tasted now the salt which drenched his face.

Elènor was in agony, not only from the animal thrusting of her husband and the scrape of the rough unyielding wood of the table on her stomach and breasts, but from the fact that Armand should see the brutal acts she suffered at her husband's hands.

Gerard finished with her quickly and she sighed softly - nothing more than she was used to - in fact it was not the worst she had suffered.

"You!" Gerard stabbed a finger at the man - at - arms he had singled out before, and the man jerked to attention. "My lord!"

"Your turn!"

There was a dumbfounded silence.

Gerard was fastening his clothing and after a moment he looked up.

"Well?"

The man - at - arms looked round at his comrades, then as they realised what was toward, they gathered round, urging him on, pushing him forward, helping him with his unlacing and even holding Elenor's legs and arms while she set herself to endure more torture.

Armand de Carrefour was on the verge of losing his sanity. That any man should offer his wife to his men for the taking was totally beyond belief.

Gerard walked casually over to Armand.

"Enjoy, my lord. And when it's over you and I will have our own little party."

Almost before the words were out of his mouth he staggered back, blood spurting from his face, a shrill scream of pain causing heads to turn.

Armand showed his teeth in a shark's grin, Gerard's blood staining his forehead where he had head-butted him, hard and fast.

Gerard's men lit into their prisoner, kicking, punching, beating him with sword - pommel and axe handle.

"Stop!" Gerard staunched his bleeding mouth with his sleeve. They looked at him confused. "I want him conscious. I want him to watch. I don't want him to miss a single thing!"

Thus began what seemed an unending nightmare for Elenor.

One after the other they took her, in brutal, merciless fashion, until her mind closed down - called a halt and she passed out, her abused body lying limp and bleeding across the table, her shorn head sticky and grotesque with blood and sweat and God knows what other foul spewings of Gerard and his satanic crew.

Armand was numb with horror.

He could hardly see out of eyes which were blackened and swollen with the beating he had received and the several broken bones in his body caused deep searing pain.

But it was Elenor who filled his heart and mind. He felt so helpless in his rage.

He remembered his oath to her that he would keep her safe and he felt an overwhelming shame and grief and despair that he was forsworn. And in such a grotesque and terrible fashion.

When finally it was over, Gerard gave him a vicious kick in the ribs, eliciting an involuntary scream of pain. "Take him down below. We'll have more sport with him later."

Dragging him callously along the floor, they hauled him through the door and shoved him down the steps. He could not hold onto his cries of agony, making them laugh, then they threw him into the cell beneath the keep where others of his men were imprisoned, some mortally wounded, some already dead. He lay with his face in the dirt and sobbed, harsh, racking sobs, unashamed in his grief, not for himself, but for his tender, fragile love who sprawled broken and bleeding in the hall above.

Upstairs, Gerard stretched his bulk and yawned, then dismissed his men. "Get some sleep. We may have some trouble tomorrow if any of de Carrefour's patrols return."

Joan stood silently until he beckoned to her.

"Come. I have need of a soft pillow for what is left of the night."

"Yes lord."

Joan walked past Elenor's unconscious body without a glance and Gerard, watching her closely, was satisfied.

He wrapped an arm about the Saxon maid's neck and pulled her along with him towards his chamber, fumbling her gown away to fondle her breasts. She leaned back and smiled up at him.

The whole dreadful thing had taken barely more than an hour to accomplish.

It was the cold which woke her. Elenor's eyelids fluttered reluctantly open, yet she continued to lie, unmoving, her senses questing, alert for the presence of the enemy. The silent darkness, the lack of any movement finally convinced her that she was alone. They had left her, contemptuously sure that she could do them no harm. How could she? Bruised, abused, bleeding, weak, she lay like a discarded toy where she had slid from the table onto the floor.

Slowly, agonisingly she raised herself on her hands and dragged herself towards the thick, heavy leg of the table, using it as a support to struggle to her feet. Shivering with cold and with shock, Elenor hobbled towards the dying embers of the fire, her nerves jumping in fearful anticipation of being discovered.

Her appearance was grotesque in the extreme. Her dagger - shorn hair stuck out in every direction, stiff with blood and sweat, a fitting halo for her bruised and swollen features.

Knife thrusts of pain stabbed at her vitals, and it was almost as though she had been ripped apart, each step she took eliciting a stifled whimper of pain, terror of being heard and caught stopping the sound at its birth.

The dogs made way for her and she huddled against the warm stone of the fireplace trying desperately to come to terms with what had happened to her.

Shuddering breaths which could scarcely be called sobs, tore at her aching body and she fought to calm her rising hysteria.

Fernrean was as dark and silent as the grave and it occurred to Elenor that if she was to escape, then now was the time to do it. If only her body would obey her. If only she was physically able to move fast enough and silently enough, she would brave the dangers of the forest - anything to get away from Gerard!

But then what of Armand?

She did not even know if he was still alive.

What of Thomas?

The boy's fate could easily be more hideous than her own.

Joan?

God forgive her, but she did not know what Joan would do. She hated Gerard, that was the one thing Elenor was certain of, but what action she would take, it was impossible to guess.

A whisper of sound behind her made her cringe down amongst the dogs, her heart thudding like a drum.

"Lady! Lady Elenor, where are you?"

Joan's whisper sounded so loud and Elenor rose up and shushed her instinctively. The maid was by her side in an instant.

"Sweet Mother of God! How can you stand up? That vile monster has surpassed even himself in this!"

"What of you?"

Joan shrugged." He was never violent with me, we both know this. He trusts me - the fool!"

Elenor's mind was tumbling with the desire to put as much distance between herself and Gerard de Beauvrais as possible - yet she knew she could not run. The ogre had to be faced. He had to be dealt with. Somehow.

"Listen!" She gripped Joan's arm like a vice.

"We have to kill him."

Joan stared at her and swallowed hard, the pain of Elenor's tight grasp barely registering."I know."

"Is he asleep?"

"Aye. Drunk and snoring like a hog."

"Come then."

Elenor kept her mind focused solely on Gerard's death. She ignored her injuries. She ignored the abominable pain and the fear which threatened to turn her into a gibbering, mindless idiot. That had certainly been Gerard's intention - to inflict so much agony and humiliation on her that her she would go insane.

As silent as wraiths they made their way up the stairs, hugging the wall and praying that they would reach their goal before anyone awoke and discovered them.

At the door to Gerard's room they stopped.

"How will we do it?"

Elenor chewed her lip. If they were going to kill him they must do it now and be away, yet here she stood, naked, powerless.

Suddenly she remembered.

"Quickly - in here." She dragged Joan to the door of her own room and slipped hurriedly inside. It was pitch black and they dare not kindle a light of any kind.

"It's here. It must be here. Oh sweet Mary, please let them have forgotten it."

Joan stared as Elenor scrabbled about on the floor, the whispered prayers making her wonder whether Elenor was really going mad.

The wonderful blessed feel of cold steel under her fingers brought a surge of triumph which gave her all the strength she needed. She lifted Armand's discarded sword with both hands and swung it aloft as though she were, herself, a warrior used to wielding the mighty weapon. She almost beheaded Joan.

"Lady! Careful! Silently now, come on."

They crept up to the communicating door between the two bedchambers and opened it carefully, crossing the small anteroom and tip - toeing to the door which opened directly into Gerard's room. Joan was close behind her mistress as she took a deep breath and opened that heavy barrier between the two women and the man who had been responsible for so much misery for so long.

The fire was still lit and the flickering flames cast their dancing shadows on the ceiling as they took their courage and their determination towards the vast snoring heap on the bed that was Gerard de Beauvrais. Briefly they froze as he muttered and turned in his drunken sleep, holding their breath until he settled again then easing their way forward until they stood beside him, staring down at him. Elenor felt empty, emotionless. The great sword hung heavy in her fingers yet strangely, she could scarcely be bothered to raise it for the blow she most desired to deliver. Joan nudged her from behind and, almost in a trance, Elenor bent to lift her weapon. As her face dropped level with that of her husband, he suddenly opened his eyes and stared straight at her.

There was a moment of stunned amazement and incomprehension before he came upright with a growl and swung his legs off the bed in an attempt to stand up.

He was knocked backwards, flat on his back as Joan hurled herself at him, pushing Elenor to one side and smashing at Gerard's face with her clenched fists, hissing urgent low - voiced commands to her lady.

"Hurry! Hurry or we'll fail! Kill him! Use that blade or we all die and he lives!"

Elenor awoke and lifted the sword high. The firelight gleamed along the steel and Gerard screamed, a high - pitched squeal which elicited a grim laugh from Joan before she was sprayed with Gerard's blood.

The chopping blow almost severed his arm but it did not kill him. He rolled away to the other side of the bed, sobbing and whimpering in pain and terror, trying frantically to escape the two blood - stained harpies who came after him.

Joan picked up the heavy silver wine flagon and crashed it down onto the fat man's skull. Still he would not go down. Elenor was panting, panic making her clumsy as she dragged the heavy sword after her, swinging it round in an arc at her husband's head. She missed the killing blow again, slicing his ear and laying open his cheek to the bone. He screamed in fear and agony.

"Again!" Joan looked around for a weapon of her own and her glance fell on Gerard's knife, stuck into a haunch of venison on the table beside the bed. She laughed gleefully and snatched it up before joining Elenor in the desperate attempt to end Gerard's life. Clutching at his hair, she pulled back his head, intent on cutting his throat.

He grabbed her ankle and pulled her over on top of him. Still it did not stop her and she stabbed and stabbed and stabbed again as he rolled, pinning her beneath him and grasping the wrist of her knife hand.

His blood was everywhere, thick and warm and slippery and Joan screamed out her hatred and lust to kill. He struggled with her for possession of the knife until suddenly he stopped and his chest sprouted a monstrous growth of steel, pushing further and further outward in front of him almost impaling Joan as well on its lethal point.

She pushed him away from her and he toppled sideways leaving her free to scramble out and throw her arms round Elenor as she swayed, white - faced and huge - eyed her hands still stretched out where the hilt of Armand's sword had been snatched from her grasp by the weight of Gerard's falling body.

He struggled to live, to draw the steel from his chest, his eyes bulging, his fingers desperately scrabbling at the swordblade, then his head jerked back, blood gushed from his mouth and he fell still.

They stared in silence.

Several moments ticked by before Joan pushed tentatively at his body with her foot. He did not move. She lifted her head and listened, expecting footfalls, shouts of alarm, violent capture. Nothing. Fernrean stayed silent.

Softly she laughed. "Of course. They are used to hearing screams and the sounds of struggle coming from this room. They would not dare disturb him. They would not dare to interrupt his games of pleasure. We are safe for the moment."

Elenor could not tear her gaze from his body. Joan shook her gently.

"Come lady. Get dressed. We must get out of here before we are discovered."

"Yes." It was all she could whisper just then, but as Joan found clothes for her mistress and for herself, Elenor's thoughts swung to Armand.

"We have to find Armand - and his men. Our only chance lies in freeing them to deal with Gerard's soldiers.

And there is Thomas. We cannot leave him."

"Very well then. But are you fit for this?" Joan was worried. Elenor was weak and in pain from her ordeal. Only her spirit was strong. Only her heart was brave. Her body was so frail that Joan was amazed she could still stand.

"I have to be. We cannot fail now. Help me with this." She crossed over to Gerard's body and with scarcely a hesitation she bent to grasp the hilt of the sword which jutted from his back. Joan added her strength to Elenor's and they pushed at the body with their feet, pulling, heaving at the sword until it slid free with a thirsty reluctance. Gerard's own weapon lay across the chair in its scabbard and Joan took possession of it before the two women prepared for the next vital step in their survival.

Carefully Joan opened the door and peered out. It amazed her that all was still and silent but the fact was that Gerard's men had drunk themselves into a stupor. Now they were sleeping off their excesses. Even the few guards Gerard had posted were half senseless with drink and fatigue.

Elenor followed Joan, gripping the hilt of Armand's sword, the blade hidden in her cloak.

No-one meeting her now would have guessed that she was the Lady of Fernrean, rather some half - demented whore who had fallen foul of some of her customers.

As she passed the last chamber before the stairway, she was halted by a trace of a sound from within.

She caught hold of Joan's cloak, pulling her back, motioning silence with a finger to her lips and nodding at the doorway from behind which she could hear a faint whimpering.

Joan took a firm grip of the sword she carried and gently, oh ever so gently, she lifted the latch. There was a dim light cast by the few guttering candles left in the room and they could make out the hunched up form of a boy, cowering against the fireplace, and the spread-eagled body of Gerard's knight, de Grace.

The two women moved as one, gathering Thomas between them, not giving him a chance to explain or protest, not even glancing at de Grace as he lay unmoving in a dark, glistening puddle of what had to be blood. They were out of the room in seconds and moving swiftly, down the stairs and towards the great doors.

It was that silent moment before dawn. The storm had completely cleared away and the sky was black and cold, setting them shivering again as they edged their way down the steps into the bailey yard.

"They'll be below, but they are sure to be well - guarded."

"Leave the guards to me." Joan passed her sword to Elenor and quickly pulled open the lacings of her bliaut beneath her cloak before ducking to the heavy door beneath the steps where lay the entrance to the cellars.

Elenor and Thomas pressed back into the darkness, trying hard to become invisible as Joan's knock was answered by a shaft of light and the deep rumbling voice of the single guard left on duty.

"Only one guard, it seems. Gerard has too few men to keep a grip on Fernrean. And he has only one knight now."

Thomas' gasp made her turn and take him by the shoulders. "You killed him?"

"Aye lady." He could hardly speak the words.

"You have much courage, Thomas. My lord would be so proud of you although I know how hard it is to take a life so, sometimes it is the only possible thing to do." She kept her voice steady, trying to give the boy reassurance although God only knew she could have done with some of that very stuff herself.

"Now come. There may be deeds far worse to be done tonight."

A faint shaft of light showed where Joan had made certain to leave the door unlatched and Elenor slid forward on thistle down feet.

She stopped and passed Joan's sword to Thomas, ignoring his hesitation, pushing the weapon at him until he was forced to take it.

Peering carefully through the gap in the door Elenor half smiled with satisfaction at the sight of Joan, doing what she did best and flirting outrageously with the one guard in sole charge of watching over Armand and his men.

Their carelessness was hardly surprising really for they certainly did not expect anyone to attempt a rescue, never mind slaughter the Lord de Beauvrais and one of his knights.

Elenor softly pushed the door open and Joan made certain that the man she was charming had eyes and ears only for her as she allowed the shoulder of her gown to slip and her breasts to strain tantalisingly at her neckline.

He was dead before he hit the floor as Elenor's blow with the huge sword severed the vertebrae at the back of his neck, almost decapitating him.

The two women scarcely spared him a glance for they were too busy heaving at the heavy catches of the storeroom doors. For several moments nothing happened and they looked at each other in consternation. Had the garrison been slaughtered to a man? Were there none left alive to rescue?

Elenor ventured slowly into the darkness then gave a scream as she was grabbed by a multitude of hands, intent on her death.

"Fools! You fools! Get back! It is my lady Elenor! It is I, Joan. You are free!"

Joan was in their midst like a whirlwind, shouting and pushing at them until they realised their mistake.

Elenor had lost her sword, Armand's sword, and she was hysterically begging for its return, overwhelmed by this attack on the part of those she sought to rescue.

"Joan! My lady! Dear God in his mercy, how is this? Get back you - back!"

Gyrth flung his men away frantically until Elenor's cowering, terrified figure was revealed. In the darkness she was but a shapeless hump on the floor and the hard bitten soldiers were silent, mortified and distressed at their blunder.

"My lady?" Joan did not touch her and Elenor responded to her voice, uncurling and rising unsteadily to her feet.

"The sword!" It was handed to her quickly and she closed her eyes for a moment, thankful for its cold confidence.

"Where is my Lord de Carrefour?"

The one thing uppermost in her mind, closing out all the fear and horror, was the urgent desire to see him alive, to touch him, to reassure herself that he was alright.

The men at arms stood back and for one awful, heart stopping moment she thought he was dead.

He was so still, and in the darkness it was impossible to see the rise and fall of any breathing.

Then he groaned and Elenor was beside him in an instant. Armand was unconscious and rambling, his injuries many and severe; broken ribs, fractured cheekbone, broken collar bone, but worst of all a broken arm - his sword arm, broken in not one but two places!

Despair flooded her heart as she crouched over him. "'Tis through me that he has come to this sorry state. My fault, all my fault..." Her heartbroken whisper aroused pity in them all, but Joan was desperately aware of their danger still and she urged Elenor to her feet.

"My lady we must decide what to do.

Do we try to escape or do we stay and fight?"

For a moment Elenor's spirit failed her and she wanted to scream at Joan to leave her alone, to leave her with Armand. He needed her, could they not see that? Gyrth added his plea to Joan's. "Aye lady. Once the Lord de Beauvrais notices you have gone..."

"Hah! He'll never notice anything again!" Joan's voice held triumph.

"How is that?"

"Dead! The filth is dead. By my lady's hand - and mine. As is de Grace. Thomas saw to him." She looked around in fierce challenge. "Will you leave all the battle then to women and boys? We have set you free and there are weapons for the taking. The drunken sots are senseless - easy prey for you dogs of war!"

"She is right." Gyrth took charge. "De Wulfe will be the one to watch for. He was ever the warrior in that pack. Rold! Hakell! Pick two men to stay here. Bar the doors behind us, for we go hunting this dawn - hunting for rats!"

Their weapons were few to start with but their hearts were burning for revenge as they sought what was left of de Beauvrais' men and showed them no mercy, gave no quarter.

For the second time within a single night Fernrean keep changed hands and as the sun came up, the patrols of men who had been searching the forests for Gerard de Beauvrais started coming home.

The bodies of de Beauvrais and de Grace had been unceremoniously dragged away for burning with the rest of the enemy dead and Elenor and Joan left Armand's side to watch, to make certain that the monster was finally gone, consumed by the flames.

Gyrth was self - appointed commander, his authority supported by Elenor and it did not take him long to restore order and ensure that all would sleep safely within Fernrean with the guards doubled on the walls and the whole company alert against any further threat.

Only de Wulfe was left alive at the end and him they saved to answer to Armand de Carrefour, and to the King.

By the time the sun was high, both Elenor and Joan were on the verge of collapse and it was Gyrth who supervised the construction of a stretcher for his lord, so careful of those broken bones. He was carried upstairs to Elenor's room and Gyrth watched as Elenor ignored her own hurts and took such tender care of the still unconscious warrior.

"Excuse me, my lady, if I presume, but you need help. There must be women from the village who could be trusted, who would be glad of employment here at Fernrean. Especially now that de Beauvrais is no more!"

"Aye, my lady." Joan urged her mistress. "There is a good woman, Hedda, and her daughter Alyss. They are alone, no man to care for them or for them to care for. I can vouch for them, for I have known them all my life and you will kill yourself if you do not rest."

Elenor knew Joan was right and although she was reluctant to leave Armand in other hands than her own, she would be no good to him at all if she was sick herself.

"Very well. Bring them up and I'll see them."

She stood by the bed staring down worriedly at Armand. It was not the broken bones which concerned her but the fact that he had still not regained his senses and she gently stroked her fingers across his brow, willing him to open his eyes, to look up at her and smile that heart - stopping smile of his.

But then, she thought desolately, after the things he had seen, after watching her degradation and use by so many men, he would probably never smile at her again. He could certainly never want to marry her. What man would want a woman to bear his children after she had been used in such a fashion?

Heaving a despondent sigh she turned away to sort through the herbs and remedies contained in the large box Gyrth had brought up for her.

A brief knock heralded the arrival of Gyrth with two women, obviously freshly scrubbed and smiling, who bobbed their nervous curtsies to Elenor.

Suddenly her ordeal hit her in full force and her legs gave way beneath her. Before she realised it, she was sitting on the floor, her face in her hands, her shorn hair sticking out, shaking in every limb with shock, exhaustion, despair. Taking great gasping breaths, she fought back the tears and the shimmering threat of blackness which threatened to overcome her.

"My lady, drink this!"

A cup of foul smelling liquid which made her gag was shoved under her nose, and recognising one of her own herbal remedies she took it and swallowed it quickly.

The heat coursed through her burning away the shivers and calming her, restoring her. She gasped and steadied herself.

"Thank you. Hedda is it?"

"Aye my lady." The woman was pleased at Elenor's use of her name.

"Hedda, ask Gyrth to send hot water, plenty of it - and a pallet bed for me to sleep in here. Also, get some men to clean out the other bedrooms. Burn everything that belonged to my husband and his men and use lime to cleanse the boards and walls! I want no trace of Gerard de Beauvrais left within this keep."

Hedda stared for a brief moment then, a little frightened by the lady's fierce expression, hurried away to do as she bid.

Joan took the empty cup from Elenor and bumped down onto the floor next to her.

"He will be alright my lady. His heartbeat is steady, he has no fever and he is strong - very strong."

They were both silent for a moment thinking of Gerard and the misery and destruction he had wrought in both their lives.

"At least he is here and I can care for him but Erland, we still have no news."

"I am too exhausted to think."

Hedda's daughter moved quietly about the room, in awe of these two women.

Fernrean buzzed with the tales of how they had slain Gerard and set free the Lord de Carrefour and his men and Alyss was already picturing herself queening it in the village on the strength of waiting on Lady Elenor herself.

The arrival of the tub and the buckets of hot water was welcome to both Elenor and Joan and once again Elenor found herself washing away all traces of Gerard and, this time, his men as well. She was raw and bleeding still and the hot water stung as she lowered herself into it. If only it were so easy to wash away the memory of it all. Gently she washed off the blood and sweat and filth, wondering what would happen to her now. She could not imagine that Armand would still want her and William could not afford to leave her in charge of Fernrean without a commander he trusted to order its defences.

It would be impossible for her to marry Armand knowing that he had watched her being raped in such a fashion.

Her shame would be too much to bear and he - he was such an honourable man. How could he possibly take to wife a woman who had gone through so much?

Perhaps it was as well that he was still unconscious, for she found she did not want to face him.

Fresh water was brought for Joan and Elenor dried herself quickly, finding her hair drying fluffily around her head in minutes.

"You look like a nun, lady, with your shorn head and that pallor."

Joan's comment hurt at first, but then slowly it started the germ of an idea. The more she thought about it, the more it seemed to be the only solution. York was near enough for there to be half a dozen endowed convents who would be glad to take the Lady de Beauvrais. It would leave Fernrean vacant for William to enfeoff a lord of his choice - whether that lord be Armand de Carrefour or not would not matter. All Elenor wanted was peace and a chance to hide her shame and dishonour. To try and forget the brief glimpse she had been given of a life of love and happiness - a glimpse cruelly obliterated by Gerard and his men.

Checking on Armand before she allowed herself to seek her bed, she was glad to see his breathing was normal, his colour good.

Hedda and her daughter had bathed him carefully and dressed his wounds, strapping up the broken arm with expert ease.

A bed had been set for Thomas in the small chamber next door and Elenor was glad to see him sleeping peacefully after his own nightmare ordeal.

Finally she sought the low pallet. Within seconds she had plunged into a deep slumber, a slumber in which her body set about healing its hurts and her mind set about the consideration of a life without her love, a life of broken dreams and hopes.

While she slept Gyrth was a busy man.

He sent out messengers on the road to York with the story of all that had happened at Fernrean.

He descended once more to the storerooms beneath the keep to question de Wulfe about the method of their entry into Fernrean. He was a stubborn man but so was Gyrth and the serjent already had a fair idea of how it might have been accomplished. Eventually they found the secret passageway.

"Sweet Jesus. I should have guessed. What a fool I was." He blamed himself and was sorely tempted to destroy the whole construction. He really did not have the authority, however, and the fact that it was no longer a secret took away most of the danger.

Anulf the cook and those others who had died in the sneak attack on Fernrean were given a veritable Viking funeral and as dusk returned once more Gyrth was satisfied with his day's work.

As he entered the hall, the woman, Hedda, met him. "Serjent Gyrth, shall I wake my lady for the evening meal?"

"No. Let her sleep. Have some broth ready if she does wake. She has been through so much has the lady. Her rest is well - earned."

"Is it true that she slew the Lord Gerard? And the guard? They say she near took his head off!"

"You guard your tongue! You're here to serve my lady - not to gossip about her."

"I'm sorry." Hedda was affronted. "'Twas not gossip I wished for. I have only the greatest admiration for Lady Elenor. She did what many a warrior had not the courage for. Such a brave heart is not often found in the weak frame of a woman."

"Aye. Well be sure where your loyalties lie - or you'll be out of here so fast, you'll be dizzy!"

Hedda swished away to prepare the broth for Elenor, feeling suitably chastened by Gyrth's telling off.

Elenor did not wake that evening. It was as though her body and mind needed the oblivion provided by sleep to complete their healing processes. Hedda and her daughter cared for her quietly, cared for her and the Lord de Carrefour.

Joan's recovery was faster, but then she had not suffered as Elenor had. She went down to the kitchens to find herself something to eat and there she encountered Gyrth.

He was nervous of her. Grateful for her part in setting them all free, nevertheless he knew she had gone with Gerard to his bed, albeit to cause his down fall in the end.

So what of her man, Erland? Did she not care that he lay near death while she played the slut - whatever the reason?"

Joan sensed his disapproval, his wariness and she smiled sardonically.

"Lost interest then, serjent? Why is that then?"

He shrugged, changed the subject. "How is the lady? Still sleeping?"

"Yes. She needs this time. I could not have survived as she has done - the cruelty, the abuse, the pain. Then to taste of heaven possibly to lose it..."

"And what of you? Your man lies close to death they say..."

"He will not die! He will come back to me - I
know it...and anything I do... anything I have
done... 'Twas only for him. So that we could be
together!"

Gyrth backed away holding up his hands to
ward her off.

"Steady! I'm sure you are right. He must be
very special."

"He is. Oh he is." Suddenly the tears choked
her and for a brief moment she allowed herself the
luxury of giving way to the fear and uncertainty
which she had held at bay so successfully until
now.

Gyrth was helpless in the face of her distress
and he patted her shoulder, then pulled her against
his chest to offer comfort. Gently he stroked her
hair and shushed her as he would a child,
forgetting his earlier doubts and cursing himself
for his lack of understanding.

Joan's clenched fists beat at him - hating him,
briefly, for being there, strong and alive, when
Erland was not. He took the punishment stolidly
until she slowly calmed, sniffing and wiping away
the tears with her fingers, pushing away from him
and making great play of smoothing down her
skirts.

The kitchens were dark and silent, the great
fires banked down for the night. The dark warmth
heightened the sense of intimacy.

"I'm sorry." Her apology was defensive.

"No need for that. If you need me - If you need
help of any kind, I am here."

"Thank you." She still would not look at him.
"Food is my need for now." She tried to joke and
he went along with it, finding cold meat and bread
for her.

"I must go back to my lady. Goodnight
serjent."

"Goodnight."

He watched her go, then squared his shoulders.
The responsibility for the defence of Fernrean lay
solely with him just now and he was determined
that his lord would find naught amiss when he
finally regained consciousness. He walked the
rounds of the keep and bailies until he was
satisfied that there was nothing more he could do.

The messenger he had sent out towards York
met with a small heavily armed cavalcade
escorting a litter carrying a wounded man.

He kept his distance until something familiar
about the huge barbaric figure leading the band
made him relax a little.

"Where are you bound?" The Saxon words
were hard to understand, but the voice confirmed
the identity.

"You are one of Erland's men?"

"Aye. Erland we have here, returning to
Fernrean."

The messenger kneed his horse closer.

"I ride to William. Fernrean was attacked by de
Beauvrais in the night."

"Christ! What happened?"

"There was a secret passageway unknown to
anyone and before the night was over, half our
company was dead, my Lord de Carrefour
imprisoned and the Lady Elenor sorely abused."

The litter rocked violently and Erland forced his way out, cursing."They treat me like an old woman.   I am not at death's door, Erik you savage, get me a horse!   For Christ's sake we must get to Fernrean!"

"No hurry, Saxon. Gerard de Beauvrais is just ashes on a pile of rubbish now."

"But how is that? Who succoured the keep?"

"'Twas my lady and her maid!" The messenger waited for the open-mouthed amazement, enjoying the disbelief and consternation.

"They sliced de Beauvrais like a sucking pig between them, slaughtered the one who guarded us and set us free to wreak revenge!"

There was silence.

Jaws sagged open, then Erland started to laugh, holding onto his sides as his wounds gave him a sharp reminder that he was not yet fit.

"Joan!" He gasped. "The vixen!"

"And my Lady de Beauvrais - 'Twas she who dealt the death blow."

"But how? Erik we must get home. If they are short - handed they will have need of us anyway."

Erland turned back to the messenger. "The King is not far behind us. He aims to be home with the Queen by Easter but he will be calling at Fernrean."

"I had best be on my way then. Safe journey to you."

"Aye and to you."

They watched as the stones kicked up behind the messenger's horse and he headed for York and the King.

"So! No need for us it seems, at Fernrean. The ladies hold the day."

Erland laughed again."Joan, my Joan. De Beauvrais never knew that when he took her, his death became a certain thing, with her awaiting only her opportunity."

The litter was abandoned like some giant broken toy and Erland gritted his teeth against the hot stabbing reminder of his wounds as he mounted a horse given up by one of his men.

"To Fernrean!"

They needed no second bidding, and the man left behind started the long walk home, in the dust of their thundering departure.

Elenor was so stiff and sore when she awoke that she could not stifle a gasp of pain when she tried to sit up. The burning fire between her legs was almost unbearable and there was not a part of her body that did not bear bruises or scratches.

Collapsing back onto the pallet she did not give way to tears. The time for that was past, but she could have screamed with frustration and despair.

"My lady." Joan was there, her eyes puffy as though she had been crying hard herself, but composed and concerned. "This will make the pain easier.

"On a tray which Joan placed on the floor was a collection of creams and a steaming cup of herbal tisane. "Lie back, lady, and I will tend to your hurts."

"Armand?"

"He is fine, do not worry."

"Is he conscious then?"

Joan did not answer and Elenor struggled to sit up again.

"No, no, lady. He still sleeps and you can do nothing if you do not let me attend to you first."

Elenor sighed and gave in, but only because she was in such agony. Adrenaline and fear, and the desperate need to kill Gerard and free Armand had kept the pain at bay before. It was as though her body had produced its own barrier against it and now that the need was past she suffered in full force.

Gentle as she was, Joan could not avoid hurting her and Elenor stuffed her fist in her mouth to stifle her moans of pain. When she was smeared from head to toe in sharp - smelling unguent, Joan held out the cup of herbal brew which was now cool enough to drink.

Elenor and Joan stared at each other over the cup for a brief moment.

"To stop you conceiving lady." Joan whispered the words and Elenor nodded once, then took the drink and gulped it down as fast and hard as she could. She could not even consider the nightmare possibility of bearing a child as a result of that night of rape and abuse. She quelled the heaving of her stomach against the bitter brew, then forced herself unsteadily to her feet. Shivering in her shift she stood at the side of the bed, staring down at Armand with tragic eyes and as if he sensed her there he moved restlessly, muttering and frowning, his fingers pulling at the covers. She caught his hand, feeling its rough strength and remembering his touch on her body with a quiver of her heart.

"He will mend my lady. Slowly, perhaps, but surely."

"Yes. But my heart will not, Joan. He will not want me now - what man would?"

Joan was outraged."What did you say to me my lady, when I thought such a thing of Erland? - Rubbish, you told me. He loved me - and I knew it was true. Is this lord, then, any less a man than Erland? I think not. I think you do him injustice."

"You only lay with one man. Not ten or more. It is different, and for him to watch! No! I could never face him."

"You were forced, lady. Beaten. Abused. And at the end you sent your tormentor to hell! What more could you have done?"

"That is not the point. Even if he said he still wanted me, I would be watching him to see how he looked at me. A simple disagreement would bring the thought that he was remembering my shame. The dishonour it would bring to his name when his fellows knew of it. No. I could not bear it. I could not. Not after all I have suffered with Gerard. One glance of contempt from him would kill me, whereas I did not care what Gerard thought of me."

Joan was silent, seeing how Elenor's mind was working.

"But he loves you. He would not treat you so!"

"I could never be sure. It would be torture. No. I shall ask William to let me retire to one of the convents outside York. It will leave him free to give Fernrean where it would benefit him most."

"I still think you are wrong."

Elenor sighed. "Perhaps. But how do I find out? Once we were wed I could not escape if I was proved right.

At least I have one night, one sweet heavenly night of love to remember. I could not bear it if that was ruined, obliterated by his disgust."

She shivered again and Joan scolded her, hiding her own sadness at her lady's dilemma.

"Come now. You must get dressed or you will catch a chill on top of everything else."

A knock heralded Hedda's fussing entrance into the room, bringing food for Elenor and fresh linen for Armand.

"My lady there is a commotion at the gates. Some say it is a company   returning from the King!"

"What? My God, where?"

Both Joan and Elenor ran to the window.

For several seconds there was stunned silence, then Joan gave a shriek.

"Erland! 'Tis Erland."

And without excusing herself she ran from the room and down, down to the bailey where a cheering crowd prevented Erik and Erland from even dismounting.

"Erland! Erland!" Joan's cries were finally heard and they parted to let her through, falling silent, grinning foolishly as though each man of them had personally managed this miracle himself.

There was one of those moments in time for Joan when everything seemed to stop.

Erland was having difficulty controlling his horse amongst the shouting crush of people and it was only as he clenched his teeth against the lancing burn of his wounds that he suddenly looked up and saw her - standing there - scarcely able to believe it was him.

"Joan!" The word came out between gritted teeth and his laugh was almost a sob.

She ran forward to him, beneath the horse's dancing hooves and he reached down to draw her up into his embrace, hard and demanding. Joan threw her arms about his neck, hysterical in her joy and disbelief.

"Erland, Erland. Sweet Jesus, Erland!"

Their kiss was a hungry singing affirmation of their love and cheers rang around Fernrean in a celebration of life and happiness as embodied in these two reunited lovers.

Elenor watched from her window.

Tears ran, unchecked, down her cheeks.

They were both tears of happiness for Joan and Erland, and tears of grief and loss for her own fragile love, destroyed, at the last, by that fiend Gerard de Beauvrais.

Turning away she met the distressed features of Hedda.

"Now, now, my lady. Your lord will recover. 'Tis only shock and broken bones which will surely mend."

Elenor choked out a parody of a laugh.

"If only that were all!"

She tried to gather control and dignity. "Bring me my clothes, Hedda.

Joan will be fully occupied for a while, but then I must talk to Erland and Erik and I can scarce do that clad in this shift and with a face like a gargoyle."

The attempt at a joke was pathetic but Hedda smiled and started to fuss around the Lady de Beauvrais, trying her best to lighten Elenor's deep sadness.

At last, warmly dressed and a little more composed, Elenor stood next to the bed and bent her head down close to Armand, her mouth feathering light kisses on his face, closing her eyes, breathing in his scent and his warmth. To commit his very essence to memory was her purpose, to brand him on her senses for the lonely years she knew would lie ahead.

"I love you. Oh how I love you."

Then she was away, down to greet a joyful ecstatic Joan and Erland, and that beloved barbarian, Erik.

They had eventually reached the relative peace of the hall, away from the cheering excited throng of castle folk and villagers, all gaping, welcoming as they were.

Joan poured drinks, her hands shaking, her heart a - tremble with happiness.

As she handed the two men their cups, she followed the direction of their gaze to see Elenor descending the stairs.

"My lady!" The two men bent their heads to her.

"Erland! Erik! How good it is to see you here. There is so much to tell you."

"We heard something from your messenger, lady, met on the road to York."

"We heard you were lying near to death." Elenor looked Erland over.

He laughed.

"It takes something more than Gerard de Beauvrais to kill me, my lady."

There was a brief silence.

"Where is my Lord de Carrefour?" It was Erik who asked the question.

Joan frowned and grimaced at him behind Elenor's back, but it was too late.

"He lies unconscious, badly beaten and with many broken bones thanks to my husband and his evil henchmen." Elenor's voice held not a tremor. She was reviving all her old abilities at self - control.

"And you, my lady? How goes it with you?"

The bruises and cuts were the obvious signs of her abuse but the inner anguish, the hidden turmoil were all beautifully cloaked by her apparent calm, by her careful composure.

"I survived, thank you Erik, in spite of my husband's best attempts to destroy me. But I would rather forget all that, put it all behind me if I can. So. You must be exhausted and in spite of your bravado, Erland, I know that you have wounds to be attended to."

"I've hardly noticed them since entering Fernrean my lady!"

Erland smiled at her and she cocked a disbelieving brow at him.

"Joan. Take him away and make him behave!"

"Not much chance of that, lady." Joan's comment earned her a playful slap.

"The King is not far behind us. You know when William decides he wants to be somewhere, then his company almost has to sprout wings."

"Good. I need to speak with him." Elenor turned away as she spoke and Erland glanced askance at Joan. She shook her head and then took her leave.

"Are you sure you don't need me my lady?"

"Go Joan. Hedda is more than adequate for my needs just now."

"Very well my lady. Thank you."

When they had gone, Elenor went to sit in the heavy chair near to the fire.

She was moving more easily now but the smell of the creams with which Joan had anointed her was still strong in her nostrils.

She would leave Joan to recount the happenings of the last few days to Erland, for she herself was too tired, too deeply dispirited to go over it all again.

Leaning her cheek on her hand she let herself dream of Armand.

It was several hours later that she was gently awoken by Hedda.

"My lady, your lord is awake. He is weak but his eyes are clear. He has asked for you."

"What? What?" Elenor was confused, slightly panicky, still half in the land of her dreams.

"The Lord de Carrefour. He is asking where you are."

"I cannot." She was distressed. "Say I am still sleeping, please, Hedda, make my excuses."

Hedda was surprised, taken aback but placatory. "Do not upset yourself my lady. I shall tell him you had not slept and I do not think it wise to disturb you now."

"Thank you."

She watched as the woman departed and cursed herself for a coward.

If she saw him, spoke to him, her resolve would weaken and she would accept any crumbs from his table just to be near him.

No. It was best if she left Fernrean without seeing him again if she could.

She would only stay long enough to assure herself that he was on the mend.

Erland had said that William was not far behind. She would have to find out from him exactly how far behind. She could not leave without William's permission.

Gradually Elenor regained her calm composure and her determination to follow the course on which she was set. She would be unable to use her own room now and so she must give instructions for the third of those chambers, built by Gerard, and previously occupied by de Wulfe, to be prepared for her.

As the evening drew in she found it so difficult to walk past the room where Armand lay. Hedda had reported back to her. "He accepted the excuses my lady. Indeed he is still very weak and does not even seem to be aware of what has happened or how he has come by his injuries. I slipped a soothing powder into his broth and he is resting peacefully once more."

"Hedda you have done well. I shall go and check on him later."

It was better for her if he was still confused, if he did not really know what was going on. Time was so important. She needed to be away from Fernrean and well settled before he was able to dissuade her from her plans - that is if he wished to...

Elenor made herself very busy moving into her new quarters. She did not see Joan or Erland until it was time for the evening meal, but she was startled by Erik leaning suddenly in the doorway as she fussed over fresh coverings for the bed.

"So! How is my Lord de Carrefour, lady?"

She avoided looking at him,. smoothing her pillows.

"He will mend. His sword arm may not be all it was but it will do well enough."

"And you? What of you lady? Will you mend?"

Elenor gave a short laugh. "A few bruises Erik, a little dishonour, nothing life - threatening."

"And do you think he will stand for you leaving?"

"That is not your concern." She took a haughty tone but Erik just laughed.

"I thought better of you lady. I thought you had courage, that you would fight for your man."

"Not if he does not want me anymore." She turned to him using every ounce of self - control to keep back the tears.

The barbarian shook his head. "You are making a foolish mistake. He loves you, and I'll warrant he'll come after you - and he won't take no for an answer."

"He will have to! I could not bear to live under sufferance again. Oh he may feel obligated, he may even truly love me, but he would not be able to stop himself thinking of all those brutes taking his wife, one after the other, and it would show. It may be only in small ways, but each time it would be as a knife in my heart. No. You are right. My courage has run out. I am not a warrior, I am a woman, a weak, soft female who has had enough of men! So. Out, barbarian! Seek out Joan and Erland and tell them I expect them at my table this evening. At least there is one happy ending in all of this."

Erik bowed his head and left without another word.

Elenor plumped the pillows with a vengeance, taking out her doubts and frustrations on the feather - filled sausages.

The truth was that she was not certain that what she intended to do was the right thing at all.

All she could think of was the pain and humiliation she had suffered just when she had thought that happiness was to be hers. She simply could not bear it to happen again for she really did not know Armand well enough to be sure how he would react to all that had occurred.

Cowardly it may be, what she intended, but as she had said to Erik - her courage had run out. She wanted to hide behind cloistered walls, safe from cruelty and heartbreak. Safe from the pain that men could inflict, physically or emotionally.

Two days went by in a strange charade of creeping into the room when Armand was asleep to check on his progress, and of making excuses to avoid seeing him when he was awake and asking for her.

Both Joan and Hedda became adept at turning aside Armand's questions until the time came when he totally lost his temper.

"Enough of this! Where is she? What are you hiding from me? Get me Gyrth! Perhaps I'll get a straight answer from my serjent - at - arms!"

He was raging so violently that they flew to do as he bid. Joan sent Hedda to find Gyrth while she herself went to fetch Elenor.

"He will not take no for an answer, lady. I am worried that he will injure himself for he thinks that something has happened to you and we are afraid to tell him."

Elenor's heart sank. She should have foreseen that this might happen as he got better.

"I'll see him, but Joan, don't leave me too long with him - arrange an interruption - some emergency that requires my urgent attention."

"Very well, my lady. If you're sure."

"I'm sure." She sounded as if she needed to convince herself.

It took all of the courage which she had told Erik she had lost to enter that room with a calm and even expression.

Unfortunately, when she got inside, the sight of him, struggling upright with his arm still strapped up and the pain - induced sweat sheening his muscles, totally destroyed that hard fought - for composure.

"No! No, Armand, you must not. I am here. Lie down. I am here, please lie down."

His breathing was heavy and rasping , the pain of his broken ribs a burning agony which robbed him of his power, took the strength from his body so that he was glad to do as she told him and lie back, eyes closed. He fought each breath until slowly he calmed and the pain eased.

"Where have you been?" he whispered. "What has happened to Gerard? Who was it who came to our aid? " He opened his eyes as the pain subsided and fixed her with that silver stare. "They tell me nothing these women of yours. What are you up to?"

"We did not want you to become agitated. You need to rest, to heal those broken bones."

He reached up with his good arm and grasped her by the back of the neck pulling her down to him, searching her face as though to read there the answers to his questions.

"Tell me. Tell me what happened."

She was trembling now, so badly, at his touch, at his nearness.

She wanted to stay where she was for ever, here in his arms. She wanted to forget everything that had happened to her and go back to that night when they had shared this bed with such tenderness and passion. But she could not. She was too afraid of being hurt again.

She had to be strong.

"We killed Gerard."

He let her go.

"We? Who?"

Elenor got up and turned away from him.

"Joan and I."

There was a disbelieving silence and Elenor started that pacing of the floorboards again as she had so many times in the past.

"His men were all drunk. I found your sword where you had flung it - here, on the floor." She gestured jerkily. "We crept into his room, and when he awoke, we did it. We attacked him. We - I - killed him with your sword."

"God's mercy!" he whispered, and she carried on with her tale, frightened to stop now, not wanting to give him the chance to speak.

"We found Thomas next door. He had killed de Grace, so we three slipped down, no - one was about, no - one to stop us and Joan distracted the guard so that I could slay him.

Then we set everyone free and Gyrth and his men re-took Fernrean."

"Just like that!" He could barely murmur the words.

"Erland and Erik are home, William not far behind. So you see..."

She turned back to him holding out her hands appealingly.

"There has been so much to do... I... I could not have come to you as I would have wished..." She stammered to a halt, running out of words and nerve.

"So. You had no need of my protection in the end. It is I who am in your debt for saving my life." His voice was strangely flat.

Elenor was shocked for she had not thought of it in that light before.

"I shall rest now, my lady. My thanks for your tender care." He had closed his eyes again, shutting her out, she thought. She continued to stand for a moment staring down at his pale face then she sighed softly and left the room.

As soon as she was outside the shakes hit her again. She had been dreading seeing him, speaking to him, and now that the suspense was over, she suffered a kind of delayed shock.

It was Hedda's daughter who came to her rescue."Steady, my lady. 'Tis only natural after all you've gone through.

Come and lie down and I'll bring you a hot drink and some food."

Truth to tell, Elenor had never felt less like eating, but she did desperately want to lie down, before her unreliable legs gave way beneath her.

The dark quiet haven of her room restored some peace and calm to her shattered nerves and easing her bruised body onto the bed, she lay back and closed her eyes against the weak, burning rush of tears.

Determinedly she fought them away fixing her mind on the tranquillity she hoped to find in some gentle shaded cloister. Wanting to sort out her feelings, the chaos and confusion, the heartache and desire, all the myriad emotions which churned in her breast.

Slowly exhaustion stole over her and she sank into a deep and heavy stupor. Only the barely perceptible rise and fall of her breast betrayed the fact that she was not dead but merely sleeping.

William's advance guard arrived amidst a fair cacophony of noise, but Elenor slept on. Joan, after softly checking on her mistress, would allow no-one to disturb her.

"Surely you do not need my lady to wet nurse you in preparation for William? Just make sure we have enough food in the storerooms and on the spit to feed him. He cannot expect lavish entertainment in view of all that has happened."

Erland agreed with a nod.

"I must talk with my Lord de Carrefour for he will wish to be well informed of all that has happened before William reaches Fernrean."

"Aye. Well that is for you men to order, for I have my hands full just now with worrying about my lady. Just make sure you do not undo all our care and attention for the lord. The sooner he is mended the better for us all."

"Whatever you say, sweet wife."

Erland mocked her bossiness, yet he knew she was right for with Armand de Carrefour down, Fernrean was Masterless and with Masterless men, trouble often lay not far away.

Joan hurried back to Elenor.

As she passed Armand's door a shadow detached itself from the gloom, making her jump.

"Gyrth! You scared me half to death!"

"I'm sorry." The burly sergeant's voice was low.

Joan made to push past him but he caught her by the arm, not roughly, but enough so that she could not escape easily.

"So your man has returned safely?"

Joan was not sure how to reply. She was careful.

"Thanks be to God. I cannot tell you how happy I am."

He took a moment to digest her reply. Then he sighed and released her.

"Ah well! Some you win. Some you lose."

Hesitantly, not sure of herself for once, she looked down. "I want to thank you."

He was taken aback.

"Thank me? For what?"

"For your sympathy. Your understanding when I was... when I was so sad."

Gyrth lifted his hand to touch her blonde hair, gently.

"I meant what I said. If ever you need me."

"Joan?" Erland's voice startled them. Made them jump apart guiltily.

"Erland! I am just going to my lady. I shall be down soon."

There stretched a few moments of tense silence, then Gyrth backed away.

"I must check the guard." He left without even glancing at Erland.

Joan was at a loss, feeling Erland's bewilderment yet not wanting to give the incident any importance by defending herself.

"You will have to wake your lady. William will be here for the evening meal."   Erland determinedly put aside the images of that obvious tension between his wife and the Norman serjent and Joan gladly followed his lead.

"Very well. Until later then..."   She walked quickly away, knowing he was still standing there, watching.

When she reached Elenor's room, she slipped quickly inside, closing the door behind her and leaning back against it, glad of that barrier between her and Erland's gaze.

She listened for him, not wanting him to follow her, not wanting to have to explain anything or deny anything.

"Joan? Is that you?"   Elenor had awoken and Joan quickly moved forward to the bed to tell her of William's imminent arrival.

Galvanised into action, Elenor dismissed her injuries and her pain and fixed her mind on what she intended to say to the King.

"Get all my things together Joan I need to be ready to leave as soon as I have William's permission. Armand is mending fast and I could not face him if he should try to stop me."

"I still think this is wrong."   Joan said the words, but she remembered the look on Erland's face when he had caught her talking, just talking after all, to Gyrth.

At least she had known Erland since they were children and she knew that deep down he trusted her. Elenor did not have that basic security and where she had given her heart she was more vulnerable to the daggers of suspicion and mistrust.

Elenor ordered the meal held back that evening until William and his force once more crossed the threshold of Fernrean keep.

Travelling with only his closest and most trusted men, including Ragnor de Louberon and Reynald de Cercy, he was pleased with the success of his rescue of the garrison at York, and was determined to be back with his Queen, Mathilda, in time for Easter.

He intended to stop in Fernrean only for one night, hopefully to give his blessing to the union between Elenor and Armand and to confirm Armand as the new lord of Fernrean.

Elenor stood to welcome him at the bottom of the steps to the keep.

The torches, by the dozen, lit the scene almost to daylight as she curtseyed stiffly before him.

"Lady Elenor, 'tis I who should bow the knee to you, I think Once again, it seems, you saved the day here at Fernrean, and in spite of the revenge de Beauvrais took on you."

"I did not do it alone, my lord King. Without Joan, once more my ally, I could have done nothing."

"My mistake in not disposing of de Beauvrais when I had the chance has caused everyone here much pain and could have been one of my more tragic misjudgements. I am glad all here are alive and set fair for recovery including your Erland." He spoke the last words to Joan who dropped her curtsey more easily than her mistress.

"And your serjent - at - arms? He who sent out messengers to reach me? Where is he?"

Elenor looked for Gyrth who was trying to avoid the attention.

"My lord King." Gyrth dropped to one knee and William bent to raise him.

"Faithful men are beyond value, serjent. I know I shall be looking for knights from Fernrean as part of the lord's dues. You have proved yourself to be a true servant to both the Lord de Carrefour and Lady Elenor. It will not be forgotten."

Gyrth was stunned. What William seemed to promise was beyond a mere sergeant's dreams and Gyrth was not sure he had the right of it.

"Erland. You seem much recovered." William called forward the Saxon.

"Well enough Sire. Thank you."

William missed Erik.

"And that giant companion of yours?"

"Erik will turn up Sire. He comes and goes as he pleases. He will be here to welcome you."

William was satisfied, yet he noticed Elenor's haunted expression and the nervous twisting of her fingers.

"How is my Lord de Carrefour?" He thought perhaps she was worried about Armand.

Elenor swallowed hard. "He is recovering Sire. Indeed I need to speak to you privately..."

He could see her distress. "Certainly, lady.   I shall be at your disposal as soon as you wish."

"Forgive me.   You are all hungry and weary. My needs can wait..." But not for too long, she thought edgily.

Aware that she had virtually ignored the lords de Louberon and de Cercy, Elenor pulled herself together enough to welcome them and while their squires saw to the stowing of their gear, the men eased their hunger with food provided in abundance by the Lady Elenor.

"And how is your horse my lord? He survived I hope?" Elenor asked the question which she knew would amuse the company.

Ragnor de Louberon rolled his eyes to heaven. "The beast saved my life, lady. So it seems I am under an obligation to care for him as long as he lives."

The mournful, long suffering attitude fooled no-one.   They well knew that he idolised the idiot horse.

"My Lord de Framois is not with you?"

Elenor liked Baldwin de Framois and missed him from among the gathered lords.

"He stayed in York. He will be returning to his own lands from there rather than trail all the way back to London with us and then back up north again. I need him up there to watch out for more trouble."

The conversation turned quickly to the problems of the threat from Scotland and northern England and an involved discussion was soon under way with Erland contributing more than a fair share of his opinions.

William leaned to Elenor.

"And now, my lady, I can see your distress. What would you have of me? What help can I give?"

The King's blue eyes were kind and sincerely sympathetic but Elenor wondered if they would stay so when she explained what she wanted.

"Did the messenger from my Lord de Carrefour reach you Sire?"

William nodded. "Concerning your intention to wed? Yes, certainly. I was most pleased and happy for you."

Elenor almost groaned aloud. "Well, Sire, much has happened since then..."

William became still, attentive.

"I cannot describe what occurred here.

Suffice it to say that what I suffered was so shameful, so utterly abhorrent... and in front of my Lord de Carrefour's very eyes..."

Her voice broke and it took a few moments to fight down the tears.   William was silent, still totally sympathetic, but waiting.

"I do not feel that my honour, or rather lack of it, would allow me to marry the Lord de Carrefour." The words came out in a rush and she waited with bated breath for William's reaction.

"I see. And what is his view of the matter?" His voice was gentle.

"I... I have not discussed it with him."

"Do you not think that perhaps you should?"

"Oh please, Sire, just listen. You know what an honourable man he is. How could he have a wife who had been used by so many men, treated so shamefully... everyone knowing what had happened? Each look askance of his would be a dagger in my heart... I would be looking for contempt in his every word and gesture, even though none might be there."

"I think you undervalue your man, lady. I know Armand de Carrefour better than anyone else and I tell you that rather would his honour be brightened by marriage to such a woman as you. Such courage, such strength is only to be admired. No. You are wrong. I know it."

He was going to deny her and she did not think she could bear it. She pushed back her chair and fell to her knees and everyone slowly grew silent at the sight.

"Sire, you swore you would not force a man on me who was unwanted. Will you now forswear that promise?"

There was a concerted gasp as she challenged William's honour, yet the King was not offended, realising her agony and despair. He sighed.

"You do not need to remind me, lady. You are right, but you realise that I need a man at Fernrean I can trust...?"

"I have considered that Sire." She was eager now, her plans tumbling from her tongue. "I shall retire to a convent. You may dispose of Fernrean as you will, as is your right." Her eyes held such appeal as she gazed up at him that he could understand how Armand had lost his heart to her.

"And what of your people here?"

"I know you will choose someone just and honourable as their lord Sire. I just... I need to get away. I need peace and quiet to order my thoughts, to restore my sanity, to come to terms with what has happened. Please say you understand?"

He pulled her to her feet, gesturing to her to sit back in her chair.

"And will you tell him?"

She knew of whom he spoke.

"I cannot. My courage is all used up. I do not know what I would do should he try and dissuade me. I must flee before he can stop me."

"I still think you are wrong, but what can I do? I wanted to continue on my way tomorrow, but I shall wait one more day until you have left. Then I shall go and see him. Tell him."

All the stuffing went out of her. She collapsed back into her chair, eyes closed, face pale.

"Thank you Sire. Thank you."

William compressed his lips. He did not know how this would end. Things had not at all turned out as he would have wished, but she was right. He had given his word. He must let her go, but one thing he was sure of ; The lady was badly underestimating Armand de Carrefour and he did not think she would be able to escape so easily.

Erik demanded the honour of leading her escort the next morning. William had given her a letter to introduce her to the Abbess of the Convent of the Holy Rood not far along the road to York.

"I do not think you should be too far from those who can protect you if we have more trouble from the north."

"But Sire, the farther away I can get, the better..."

On this point, however, William was adamant. It was to this convent she must go, or she did not go at all. In the end, she had to agree.

Joan stood with Erland to bid her farewell.   "I wish I could go with you my lady."

"Impossible. Well you know it. What of Erland?"

"Aye. I know that. I may visit though?"

"God help you if you do not." Elenor looked up to the window of Armand's room."How is he?" She had not even dared to sneak in to whisper goodbye.

Nothing must stop her now although she knew full well that when she left she would be thinking of him, only of him, every step of the way.

"He is mending fast. You know he will come after you?"

"I will not see him. Once I am behind those walls there will be nothing he can do."

"Don't count on that, lady." Erland disapproved completely and had been all for going up and telling Armand what was intended. Only Joan had prevented him.

"'Tis for the best Erland." Elenor's voice was almost pleading.

"I don't agree." Erland was unyielding and Elenor turned away, not wanting to argue just now. Lifted to her palfrey by Erik, Elenor bowed her head to the King in farewell and with a last glance up at that familiar window, she bid goodbye to Fernrean and its folk.

It was two days' ride to the Holy Rood Convent and they travelled with a large escort. These were dangerous times and when the huge rambling walls of the convent, which had been there since before the time of Alfred, appeared in the distance, they all heaved a sigh of relief.

William's letter was presented at the postern gate, and the huge barred doors were not long in opening, the welcome they received most gratifying.

"We are honoured, my lady, that you chose our humble house for your stay. Our lodgings are simple but clean and wholesome, and we hope that you will find here whatever it is you seek."

The Abbess was short and stout, but her blue eyes twinkled incongruously beneath the spotless coif and Elenor felt herself warming to the other woman and relaxing slightly.

Shown to a room which was somewhat larger than she expected, Elenor was pleased with the spartan comfort.

Erik was not at all at ease with the soft female atmosphere of the place and as he showed his men where to put Elenor's belongings he shrugged his great shoulders uncomfortably.

"I shall head straight back, lady. This is no place for a warrior." He glanced sideways at her."No place for you either is my opinion."

"I did not ask for your opinion. And you are not to tell him where I am!"

"I thought William would do that."

"No! He has promised he will not."

"How long do you think it will be before he comes after you?"

"He won't!" But a touch of uncertainty shivered her voice.

Erik smiled, showing large uneven white teeth. "He will!"

"He will not be allowed in here. There will be nothing he can do because the King gave his permission for me to retire here."

"Well then. It seems you have thought of everything."

"You may go. I am very tired."

Indeed Elenor was so pale that Erik did not argue further, but bowed his head to her and left the room, chivvying his men to their mounts before they had even finished the food and drink which the sisters had provided for them.

Standing at her window, Elenor watched them go, raising a hand in farewell as Erik glanced back to her.

When they had gone she continued to stand for a while, staring out at the sun - dappled cloister, letting the peace and the silence steal over her.

****

At Fernrean William had broken the news to Armand de Carrefour.

"She said she needed time to herself. That after what had happened here with de Beauvrais, she felt she would never be able to face you again."

Silence stretched out between the two men, and William shifted uncomfortably.

"I'm sorry." He felt so much sympathy for the badly hurt warrior before him.

"And you let her go!" The flat statement made William protest.

"I had given her my word that I would not force an unwanted husband upon her."

"She said she did not want me?"

"It seems she thinks you would not want her."

"Hah!" Armand's mirthless bark made William blink then the King moved forward to support his commander as he struggled to sit up.

"So Sire..." He paused to regain his breath."What do you intend to do with this holding?"

William raised his brows. "Is the lady forgotten so soon then?"

"Oh no Sire. You should know me better than that."

"But you want Fernrean?"

"I want the lady - and if I have to buy her to get her, then I shall do so."

"You are asking me to put a value in dues on Fernrean and the hand of its mistress?"

"Right! It is a common practice."

"I do not see how I can do this without being forsworn."

Armand could see that William was not against the idea, merely worried that if he broke his word it would reflect badly upon his credibility as King.

"Did she actually say she did not want me?"

William thought carefully for a moment before smiling slightly. "I do not believe she did in so many words. She merely reminded me that I had promised not to force her to wed an unwanted man."

"You say that she thinks I would hold her in contempt for what was done to her?"

"That is so."

Armand shook his head in disbelief. "How could she think that of me?"

"You must not forget that her experience of men has not been such as to instil confidence in their treatment of her. Also she has only known you for a very short time."

The two men, King and commander, stared bleakly at each other.

"Are you sure you will be doing the right thing by buying the rights to her hand? After all, that is what happened to her before."

"This is different."

"Is it?"

"I love her."

William sighed."I know.   Believe me, I understand."

Armand knew that the King was thinking of his own wife Mathilda, and how he had struggled also to win her hand.

"Then you must do this - for both of us. If I can just present her with the deed accomplished - then I know I can win her trust."

William shook his head. "You know little of women, my friend. However, if this is the way you want it - if you think you can make her happy - then I'll do it."

"Thank you Sire."

"But only because I am convinced that you love her, truly - and that she loves you."

"That will do for me."

"I have only one small problem still."

"And that is?"

"I promised I would not tell you where she had gone."

Armand smiled. "You may safely leave it to me to find that out. One way or another, she will not escape me."

William grimaced, hoping that he was indeed doing the right thing. But then he knew in his heart that Elenor could not ask for a better man than this.

"I must go."

 William turned brisk and business - like.   "I have stayed longer than I intended as it is. I shall have the dues on Fernrean prepared and sent to you.

I shall expect you to provide me with two knights for now, but I hope I can expect five men from Fernrean eventually. You know your serjent - at - arms has a good head on his shoulders and the way he organised the recapture of this keep shows a rare grasp of tactics and leadership. It would be worth considering him for knighthood, although I know he is not of noble blood. The Saxon, Erland, would be a good choice also, for it would ensure loyalty from those Saxon fighting men under your command."

He stopped there for Armand had closed his eyes and his breathing seemed laboured once more. Those ribs would take months to heal to the point where the Lord de Carrefour could start working towards battle fitness, and the arm may never have its former strength. Yes, it would be a while before Elenor found herself confronted by a determined suitor and perhaps by then she would be in a calmer, more receptive frame of mind.

It was obvious that Armand had slid into sleep and William left the room, closing the door quietly behind him.

Impatient now to be away, the King ordered his lords to make ready and at dawn the day after Elenor had left, Fernrean once again stood to bid farewell to William and his men.

Before he left, William spoke quietly to Erland.

"Your lord is now Armand de Carrefour. He holds Fernrean directly from me. You are a free man, free to go your own way, but if you stay and swear to him, you will find much honour. Will you stay?"

"Sire, I was born in the village here. My father and mother are buried here. What else do you think I would do but stay?"

William smiled that hard smile of his.

"I am glad, for Fernrean and its lord will need faithful men in the years to come. This will not by any means be the last of the fighting and rebellion and I need to know there are men who can be trusted, relied upon to stay true to me."

Erland bent his knee. "You can rely on me Sire."

Clapping the kneeling Erland on the shoulder he urged him to his feet and put his mind on the journey ahead - the return home and his waiting Queen.

It took some time for the departing force to clear the gates of Fernrean and Joan came to stand next to Erland as he watched from the walls of the upper bailey.

"Who would have thought, just a few short weeks ago, that we would be standing here, man and wife, waving farewell to the Norman King?"

Erland put his arm about her shoulders and pulled her close to him.

"He is our King now, and I find him fair and just, although a hard man in some ways."

"Will we be staying here? Now the lady has gone, there is no need for me at Fernrean. Thomas can see well enough to his master, although the lord may look for a wife and it may be that she will need a maid."

Erland smiled down at her, still unable to quite believe that she was his, truly married, together until death might part them.

"William has asked me to swear to de Carrefour, to stay here as his man."

"Are you then to be Sir Erland?" Joan mocked him gently.

"It seems so, my lady. What think you of that? You will no longer be a maidservant, even if a lady for Fernrean should be found."

Joan shook her head. "Well, I think I have the way of it after serving here these last years." She looked up questioningly. "Do you think he will look for another woman as his lady?"

A snort from her husband showed his opinion of that suggestion."Not a chance! He will be after her as soon as he can ride. I thought you would have realised that."

"She is so stubborn! It will take a good deal of coaxing to make her agree."

"From what I have heard, she has no choice in the matter. De Carrefour is to pay full dues for Fernrean and the hand of the Lady de Beauvrais."

Joan was stunned, staring open mouthed at Erland.

"But the King promised that she would not be forced to wed."

"She would not be forced to wed a man she did not want! But we both know that it is not that she does not want him - far from it - she is but afraid that he will consider her dishonoured by what happened here - Fool of a woman!"

Joan was already missing Elenor and the thought that she might be brought back, willing or not was glad news to her.

"I shall be visiting her at the Convent so I mean to do what I can in the way of persuasion so that when he finally comes to claim her, she may be more willing, more inclined to accept the inevitable."

"Do not tell her, though, that her fate is sealed. Leave it to him." He cocked his head towards Armand's window. "The power of love, they say, conquers all."

"Aye. I can believe that."

She turned full into his arms and he bent to kiss her, hard and fast , on the mouth.

When he released her, she was dizzy and giggling.

"We must see what we can contrive to bring the two of them together, to make my lady see sense and to ensure that he does not go at it like a mad bull, frightening her away."

"It would be a shame for them to miss out on such happiness as is ours. We must do what we can."

"Now. I feel suddenly tired."

"But we have not long been awake."

"It must be the spring air."

Joan and Erland sought their quarters like the two young lovers they were and neither of them noticed Gyrth standing, staring wistfully after them.

After a week he was out of his bed. Despite the protests of his squire, Thomas, and indeed Erland and Joan, he fought the pain of his broken ribs and when he was finally on his feet, he grinned in triumph.

"So. Now we begin."

He was forced to take it slowly however, for Hedda had sharp words with him when she found out.

"My lord, ribs are the devil to heal. You'll have more pain from them than any wound you've had before - and if you pierce a lung, then you're a dead man!"

The truth of her words soon became obvious for he could not even walk to the door of his chamber without each breath causing agony. He fretted and fumed, desperate to be up and about and his snarling bad temper had the castle folk avoiding him like the plague. It was several weeks, before he was moving a little more easily but he still could barely lift his heavy sword using only his left hand, without a great deal of pain.

Doggedly he kept on, until the sweat stung his eyes and his broken bones stabbed their protest along his nerve ends reminding him to go steady.

The tally of dues for Fernrean came through from William and Armand called into conference Erland and Gyrth.

"I am now confirmed in the title of Lord of Fernrean and as such I can raise to the rank of knight any man I wish. William requires two knights' service from Fernrean so I shall dub you both for your services to me and to the King."

Both men were red - faced with pleasure and embarrassment at the honour done to them and Gyrth put forth a protest.

"My lord, it is not right. I am no nobly born man to aspire to knighthood..."

"You'll soon have the way of it Gyrth - and Erland is as new to it as you are so you can support each other. So long as you can fight, that is all that concerns me - and I know you both can do that."

The ceremony was brief, both men swearing fealty to Armand, but the feast in their honour that night was long and noisy.

Lounging in his chair, Armand felt a sudden sweep of loneliness assail him. He pictured her sitting next to him, smiling softly, those brown eyes full of love and wonder as they had been on that magical night when they had lain together with such passion.

Then he stifled the vision of what had followed when Gerard had intruded into their world with demoniacal force, destroying their dreams and causing such horror and agony for his sweet Elenor.

And now - he jabbed at the table with his eating knife - now she had gone, without even giving him the chance to talk with her, to reassure her - even to thank her for her outstanding courage in saving them all.

When he had got himself fit he would go after her for now that he had paid the dues on Fernrean, she was his - and there was nothing she could do about it!

Slowly he mended and the day came when his great roan destrier, Renard, was saddled up and brought out for him.

"Careful, lord. Watch those ribs!" Erland warned.

There was no need for the warning for his body made it clear that it would not tolerate his impatience.

As he settled in the saddle he was sweating with the effort and he favoured his right arm which had healed crooked and stiff. He flexed the fingers of his right hand wondering if he would ever have full use of it again and determining to build up his skill with his left side just in case.

The sun warmed his back as he left the gates of Fernrean for the first time in almost three months and Armand felt his spirits lift and optimism fill his heart.

The summer was well advanced and all had been peaceful around Fernrean and its lands. Work had gone on clearing back more of the forest to create cultivated land, the crops were well under way and the people of Fernrean, both Saxon and Norman, seemed well content.

All they lacked was the lady.

Armand glanced at Erik who rode beside him.

"How did she seem to you?"

The Viking smiled. He had wondered when the lord would start asking about her and when he had been invited to accompany him this morning he knew the time had come.

"She has suffered greatly..."

"Don't think I don't know that!"

"She needs time and peace to think, but you hold her heart that is certain."

"Have I done the right thing in forcing this upon her?"

"You have done nothing yet. She does not know that she belongs to you."

Armand cursed."I'll never have the way of it! If I don't force her, then she stays at the convent and I'll never see her again. If I do force her then she will be with me but will she hate me?"

"Oh I don't think she will ever hate you. Rather she loves you too much, She is afraid you will hurt her even more than she has been hurt already."

Armand was bewildered. "But I have never hurt her. I know I was unable to protect her from Gerard when I had given my oath. I shall ever be forsworn for that..."

His voice held pain and regret and Erik was exasperated that two people could be such fools. Their love was strong and certain, but pride and fear held them apart.

"Go and fetch her. Tell her how much you love her and then prove that love to her. There is no quick answer to all of this, for two people need to stay together and know each other's heart."

"You are right. Now all I need is to find out exactly where she is." He gave again that crafty sidelong glance to Erik.

"Oh no!" The Viking laughed. "She made me promise not to tell. You will have to find out some other way."

"Barbarian!"

Erik jostled his horse against Armand's Renard and the huge warhorse laid back his ears and bared his teeth.

Armand was forced to calm the animal before it attacked, and the lancing pain in his ribs caused by his exertion soon silenced him.

They were out for several hours before Armand had had enough. Renard was more than a handful in normal circumstances for a man who was battle fit and in Armand's present condition it was a constant strain on both mind and body to keep control of the huge beast. Still, at least it kept his thoughts off Elenor.

When they returned to Fernrean Armand was exhausted and his ribs were so painful he had trouble getting a decent breath.

Gladly he slid from Renard's back and handed the reins to his groom before making his laboured way back up to the keep.

When he reached his room Thomas was waiting for him with hot water and fresh clothes.

Hedda and her daughter had taken charge of the domestic chores about Fernrean and Joan, as Erland's lady now, saw to the ordering of the meals and the general discipline of the servants.

He was well looked after, that was certain, but his spirit craved for her presence. In her haste to leave, Elenor had forgotten a few personal items and Armand had made sure that they lay about the chamber as if she had only gone away for a brief visit somewhere. If he had his way that would be the truth of it and it would not be long before she was back, sharing this room - and the bed - with him.

Sometimes he could not believe that everything had gone so wrong so suddenly and so quickly. Who would have thought that Gerard could be clever enough to create that secret passageway into Fernrean.

And they had been so close to it in the old ruins, he and Elenor, on the day they had sheltered from the storm.

"Hell's teeth, she haunts me at every turn!" He slammed his cup of wine down then looked around to make sure Thomas had left the room.

He wondered longingly how she was faring, and wished that he had been well enough when last he had spoken to her to guess that she had this crack - brained idea that he would not want her after what had happened.

He felt his gorge rise at the memory of Gerard's filthy revenge on his wife and he cursed himself for being such a careless bloody fool in not taking more care, more precautions against de Beauvrais. If anyone was to blame it was he and she should be blaming him not herself for what had occurred.

Thinking of that way into Fernrean, that passageway still lying dark and brooding beneath the ground, galvanised him once more into action. He pulled on a leather gambeson and fastened his belt, taking it in a few notches with the weight he had lost, then thrust a heavy knife into his short scabbard and left the room. He needed plans and action to keep her image at bay and what better action than to destroy what Gerard had so painstakingly built?

Gyrth was in the upper bailey, practising with a great two - handed sword he had taken a fancy to in Gerard's armoury.

"Gyrth! Join me in a little healthy destruction. I may need your expert advice for I don't want to send the keep plunging below ground."

Gyrth grinned, realising what it was his lord intended.

There was a gaping hole still left untouched where Gerard and his men had dislodged the heavy stones to open an entrance into the storerooms of Fernrean.

"Torches!" Armand peered, amazed, down into the passageway which had been their downfall.

"Sweet Mary, they must have had some courage to have come up through that demon's lair."

"Either that or they were so terrified of de Beauvrais." Gyrth agreed.

"You are not going down there my lord?" Erland had heard what was afoot and was as curious as his lord about the passageway.

"Only a little way. I do not fancy being buried alive after surviving de Beauvrais' best attempts on me."

There were a few grins at that, but just as many shudders.

As Armand slid his way below, closely followed by Gyrth, he found himself disbelieving the fact that the brain behind the project had been that of Gerard. Gyrth echoed his thoughts."The man was a genius, lord. Look at the way he has set the supports. No chance here of an accidental falling - in."

"The point is - how do we create a non - accidental falling-in without affecting the buildings above us?"

"We need to measure it out above and then make a fall outside the line of the outer wall. It does not matter if we have a stretch of tunnel here, so long as there is no way through."

Armand grinned. "I knew my faith in you would not be misplaced. See to it then Sir Gyrth. I leave it all to you."

The newly - dubbed knight grinned back, still not used to his title of respect, and then both men turned as Erland called to them a little anxiously.

It was good to be back in the sunshine again and Armand felt that he had, in some measure, gone a little way towards destroying the traces of Gerard which still haunted Fernrean.

The next step was to destroy that part of Gerard which still haunted Elenor.

A hail at the gates attracted his curious attention and he strolled down to see who was asking admittance to his holding. That fierce surge of possession he experienced was merely an echo of the feelings he had for Elenor.

As he walked through into the lower bailey, he suddenly stopped and slipped back into the shadows. Joan was talking animatedly to a one - armed man who stood holding the reins of a dust - covered pony which seemed too fat to have travelled any distance. When the conversation ended, Joan turned to walk hurriedly up towards the keep where Erland was still talking to Gyrth.

Armand stayed where he was until she was out of sight then he walked casually towards that one - armed man.

Joan was breathless when she reached Erland. "I need to speak with you."

He turned quickly at the low urgency of her tone. "What is it?"

She shook her head. "Not here."

He followed her out of earshot of the others and she quickly explained what she wanted.

Sighing, he nodded his head."If she needs you, then you must go. Take a good escort and be careful."

She smiled at him and leaned up to kiss him briefly, then she swirled away to prepare for a journey to the Convent of the Holy Rood.

There was no sign of the Lord de Carrefour when she rejoined the one - armed messenger and gathered an escort to see them safely on the road to York.

The lone figure watching from the upper walls smiled in satisfaction as they left.

"We are ready, my lord." Gyrth's voice behind him made him start.

"What? Oh, good." He followed Gyrth down to where the group of men detailed for the destruction of Gerard's tunnel waited. Keeping his mind on the task ahead of them, Armand, nevertheless, felt an elated surge of triumph resulting from that brief, informative conversation with the messenger who had left with Joan.

Elenor was sick. Almost three months had gone by in a blur of gentle activity, helping the nuns tend to the sick and lame, growing and brewing herbal remedies and in long moments of quiet prayer and meditation which had been balm to her soul.

Until she was sick. Sister Ansela clucked and fussed about her, gently wiping her face with a cool damp cloth between the spasms of retching.

"Now now, my lady. Rest easy. It was probably the fish. It does not agree with everyone."

Elenor knew it was not the fish.

She needed Joan. Desperately.

When the sickness had subsided and she had stopped shaking, she pulled herself together and spoke to Sister Ansela about sending a message to Fernrean.

"Easily done my lady. We shall send Rollo."

The manservant was an ex - warrior who had been badly crippled at Stamford and he lacked an arm, but continued to praise God that he had at least survived. He attended to most of the chores about the convent and it did not take long to send him on his way with a message for Joan.

The four days of waiting went by in a swelter of misery and sickness which had Elenor once more wondering what she had done in her life that was so evil she must be punished so.

On the fourth day after Rollo had left on his errand, Elenor spent her time watching anxiously for Joan, or being sick or kneeling in the chapel praying for mercy.

Joan's eventual arrival, in a jumble of dusty escort and squawking chickens, scattered by the horses' hooves sent Lady Elenor sobbing into the arms of her maid as soon as Joan's feet had touched the ground.

Taken aback by her mistress's deep distress when she had seemed to be recovering so well. Joan murmured reassurance and coaxed Elenor towards her room, away from the curious eyes of both the escort from Fernrean and the assembled sisters who had come out to greet them.

Elenor was almost hysterical by the time the door closed behind the two women and Joan forced her to sit down and held a cup of water to her lips, making her drink, choking and spluttering between her sobs. Slowly, hiccuping, gasping, Elenor calmed down.

Joan waited, letting Elenor take her time, tell her when she was ready.

"I am with child."

The bald statement dropping into the quiet made Joan close her eyes briefly.

Several seconds passed without another word as each woman wrestled with the idea, then Joan took a deep breath.

"So am I."

"What?" Elenor forgot her tears and stared.

"I said, so am I." Shrugging, she turned to the table beside Elenor's bed and poured wine this time, two cups - one each.

"I have not seen my courses since we left Fernrean, you and I, to warn the King of Gerard's treachery."

The question had to be asked.

"Is it Erland?"

Joan smiled slightly. "'Tis hard to be sure. I lay with Gerard the night before we left, then on my marriage night only three days later, it was Erland. Even if we forget the night that Gerard recaptured Fernrean, the possibility of either Gerard or my Erland being the father of my child is too close to guess."

"As with me. Gerard's abuse the night before we left was a possibility, when...when Armand..." Her voice quivered. "What happened after that... It could have been any of those devils."

Elenor's predicament was much more complicated than Joan's.

If the child in her womb was acknowledged as Gerard's, then he or she would be Gerard's heir.

As such, the child could complicate the situation at Fernrean.

Elenor knew that Armand had been made lord of Fernrean, but she did not know, for Joan had been warned not to tell her, that Armand had paid William, full dues, not only for Fernrean, but for the hand of Elenor herself.

"There must be something I can do, someone who can help me." She stared appealingly at Joan. "You must know someone, a wise woman, a herbalist, whatever you call them."

"To get rid of your child?"

"I must. I am in no position to bear it."

"It could be done. But lady, it could mean your own life too."

Elenor put her hands to her head, the picture of despair. "I care not. I cannot live like this."

Joan heaved a sigh. "I will see what I can do. As soon as I have some news, I shall return for you, for if you truly mean to do this, it must be done soon."

Elenor leaned across to grasp Joan's hands.

"It seems I always turn to you when I am in trouble."

"You would do the same for me."

"Aye. I would. You can be certain of it."

Joan ordered her escort to be ready to leave again at once. They were surprised and disgruntled, but Erland's woman was to be obeyed.

"I shall be back as soon as I can. Be ready, lady."

"I will be ready."

Joan nodded and was away leaving Elenor standing alone at the gate.

She lay in her bed in the dark that night and she placed her hands on her stomach.

"Oh Armand, my love, if only things had been different and I, as your wife, was expecting your child. How wonderful life would be."

But life was not wonderful. She was alone, and sick, and afraid.

After two days Joan returned late in the afternoon. "Come lady."

She needed no second bidding but held up her hand to be pulled up pillion behind one of Joan's escort.

The sun was hot on her cheeks as they forged steadily eastward. Within an hour they had entered dense forest following a narrow track which forced them into single file.

Where they finally halted, the sun could not reach.

The trees were so close together, the thicket so dense that they had to dismount.

"You men, stay here with the horses. We should not be long. Come after us if we have not returned by sundown."

"Aye my lady." Joan stifled a smile at being addressed so, but she knew she would have to get used to it since her man was now Sir Erland.

Elenor heard the respectful reply, but she was so scared that she took no notice just then.

Joan took her hand and the two women pushed their way deeper into the forest.

The going was hard and Elenor was still weak.

Clinging to Joan's fingers as though to a lifeline, she followed blindly until they reached a small clearing, perfectly round with a rough hut set exactly at the centre.

Elenor felt the hairs stand up on the back of her neck and her heart was hammering with her fear, but bravely she walked forward with Joan until they stood before the low doorway of the hut. Several seconds went by as they waited, unmoving, and Elenor was on the point of turning around and running away, when a figure stooped out of the doorway. Surprisingly it was not the old crone that she had expected but a young woman, clean and comely with a gentle smile.

"Come inside. You are welcome."

It seemed light inside the hut and a pot hung over the fire, something bubbling away, giving off a spicy odour which made Elenor's stomach gurgle.

"Sit."

They sat on the wooden stools she indicated and were subjected to a thorough examination by the wide blue eyes of the young woman before them.

"You are both with child." It was a statement not a question. "Why do you need me?"

"It is my lady. Her husband is dead and the child could be the result of a rape involving more than one man." The facts, bald but true without giving any details.

The young woman nodded. "Very well."

She turned her full attention to Elenor and Elenor felt as if that wide blue gaze could see to her soul.

"And what of the man who loves you?"

How could she know that? Elenor felt again that prickle of superstitious warning.

"There is no-one." She lied.

A smile was her answer and then the woman indicated a low rush bed.

"Lie down here while I examine you."

Wishing desperately that she did not have to do this Elenor did as she was told and gentle hands moved over her stomach, probing, assessing.

When she stood again the woman sighed. "It is not too late, but it is almost so. I do not know whether I can do anything without an element of risk to yourself."

Elenor also stood and tidied her clothing. "Please. You must. It does not matter if I die - I could not go on with a child such as this at my breast..."

"Do not say that! You have lied to me. Your man loves you and he will come for you. I urge you to reconsider."

Elenor felt the demons of panic tearing once more at her mind - What did this woman mean? How could she know?

"No. Truly, it is impossible. Even if you are right about this man I could not bear this child. Please, help me. I can reward you well."

A sigh, then finally a reluctant nod

"Very well."

Elenor felt the relief wash over her although there was still that fear, that tingle of doubt.

Busying herself amongst bottles and pots, the wise woman soon had a small vial of clear liquid to give to Elenor.

"Take this tonight before you lie down to sleep. Tomorrow will bear results. Expect pain because this remedy is not an easy way out and I cannot guarantee success. However, it is all I can do."

"Thank you." Elenor fumbled for a gold coin.

"No." A shake of the head refused the reward. "There may come a time when I shall need your help. Remember me then. Now go."

Clutching the small container in her hand, Elenor followed Joan back along the way they had come. Their escort was glad to see them.

"I like not this place, lady. I am relieved to see you safe." Their leader was edgy, hurrying them on their way until, with darkness closing in around them, they saw the lights of the convent once more before them.

Dismounting in the dark, Elenor caught Joan's arm. "You will have to stay. You cannot journey back to Fernrean in the dark."

"Do not worry, lady. I will not leave you."

They shared a meal in Elenor's room and then they both stared at the small vial of liquid.

"Think hard. You are sure this is right?"

Elenor shook her head. "No. I am sure it is not right, but I have no choice, no choice at all."

Quickly Elenor pulled out the moss stopper and tilting back her head, swallowed the liquid.

She had expected bitterness, but the taste was rather over-sweet on her tongue and when it was gone she felt light-headed.

"Well, now the die is cast. We shall see what tomorrow brings. I shall stay until it is over.

One of the men can ride back to Fernrean to tell Erland you are sick and I am staying a while to care for you." "And have you not seen the sickness yourself?" Joan laughed. "No. Nothing. Strong as an ox with no sign of the usual symptoms, like my mother and her mother before her."

"You are lucky."

"Aye. I am. In many ways." Joan thought of Armand. He would come for Elenor as soon as he was fit and she wanted to warn her.

"Your lord will come for you. He will find out where you are and come to fetch you."

Elenor shrugged, weariness and a slight numbness taking hold of her.

"He can come, but I shall not go with him."

Joan watched as Elenor's eyelids drooped, then closed and she lifted her mistress's legs up on to the bed, covering her up and smoothing back the curls which were starting to grow again, soft and unruly where Gerard had hacked at them.

"You will have to go with him, sweet lady, willing or not."

But Elenor did not hear her. Perhaps it was as well.

The pain woke her before it was dawn. Gasping for breath, clutching at her stomach, she called for Joan.

Her maid crouched next to her. "Hold on my lady. Try not to cry out. I have heated some stones and I'll wrap them up to place on your stomach. Hopefully it will ease the pain."

But it did not. Nothing did.

Time passed in a blur and she felt as if demons were clawing at her vitals. She burned and sweated and wept as the spasms shook her body. Joan bathed her brow and held her hands and cradled her in her arms. On and on it went until she thought she would go mad with it.

When the first rays of the sun lightened the sky the agony eased, finally, the pains becoming weaker, the spasms shorter.

Soaking with sweat, trembling with weakness she lay back and let the tears fall without effort. Joan wiped her burning skin with cool cloths and stripped away the sweat - stiffened shift to replace it with another, soft and clean. Then she offered her some broth.

"Drink this. It will help."

The broth went down slowly and Joan insisted that she finish it.

"What happens now?" Elenor wondered, but Joan shook her head.

"I do not know, lady. Perhaps you will see bleeding soon - I can only guess."

"As long as the pain does not return."

Joan silently agreed.

Elenor had surely had enough of pain to last a lifetime. It was a wonder she had survived it at all.

There was no sickness for Elenor that day, or the next day and they were convinced that the remedy had worked.

"I must return to Fernrean. I shall come again in a week or so to see how you fare and to give you any news."

Elenor asked the question she always asked. "How is he?" "Mending fast." "Has he asked for me?" "No."

It was true. Armand had not asked Joan about Elenor, although he knew that she had visited her. It was as if he was waiting, waiting until he, himself, should be fit enough to seek her out.

"I see." The tone was forlorn but Joan was brisk.

"It was your choice."

"I know, and I still think I was right."

"Then you must live with it!"

"My thanks!"

"'Tis the truth. You could always come back with me."

A vehement shake of the head. "I could not!"

"Then you must wait. Wait until he fetches you."

"You are very sure that he will."

Joan shrugged, not wanting to give too much away. " I have other news if you want to hear it?"

"Yes?"

"Erland has been knighted - and Gyrth. The King hinted as much. Now the Lord de Carrefour has confirmed it."

"So." Elenor smiled. "We are no longer mistress and maid. Yet our friendship will be stronger than ever I hope."

The two women embraced, then Joan prepared to leave.

"Goodbye, my lady."

"Farewell Joan."

A lone figure, left standing at the gate, waving until Joan and her escort were out of sight, Elenor pulled at Joan's heartstrings and although she knew that the remedy lay within Elenor's own power, she pitied her so much.

Elenor was not sick again. But she still did not see any bleeding. Another month passed without a sign and Elenor was worrying herself to a shadow. The old Abbess finally came to her room and tried to coax her into confidence.

"Lady Elenor it grieves me to see you so sad. You have been a wonderful help to us here and we hoped you had found peace and some small happiness with us. But all seems to have changed and I would help you if I could."

The kindness and sympathy almost broke Elenor's heart and she found herself pouring out her tale of woe to the gentle old Abbess.

She told her everything, from the moment she had learned that she was to wed Gerard, up to the visit to the wise woman deep in the forest.

The Abbess sat and listened, and when Elenor's story was finished, the woman was weeping. "Oh, my dear!"

Elenor was enfolded in motherly arms and rocked to and fro gently, soothingly. "How you have suffered.

Here you are safe, you know. You can be at peace, even if you bear a child you would not be turned away. You will be safe here."

The gentle reassurance filled Elenor's heart with the deepest gratitude and she raised her head to thank the Abbess.

"Now, hush Lady Elenor. You need to rest and feel secure. You need to look after yourself." She gently led Elenor to the bed and made her lie down.

"I shall put this cushion under your feet. It helps the blood to circulate." Her smile and the brisk way she pottered about the room made Elenor feel cared for the first time since her mother had died.

"I shall send Sister Ursa to have a look at you and when we know a little more of your condition we will know what to do."

After the Mother Abbess had left, Elenor dozed off. The feeling she had was of floating along without any more conscious effort. Telling of the events of the past few years had been a cleansing experience and she realised that the idea that she, in some way, had been guilty, was gone.

Sister Ursa arrived, a tall brisk nun, who was nevertheless gentle as she examined Elenor. "'Tis certain you are still with child, my lady. You must rest, take care of yourself and eat such things to aid the carrying of the baby. I shall prepare a raspberry leaf drink for you, then all we can do is wait and see how you go on."

From then on Elenor found herself cosseted and spoiled as she had never been in her life before.

The next time Joan came to visit, she was surprised and pleased at the change in Elenor.

She had put on weight and the dark, haunted circles had vanished from beneath her eyes.

"My lady, you look well." Joan's gaze travelled her body. "Any sign of...? Any sign?"

"It seems the potion did not work."

"I see. So what? What will you do?"

"Nothing. I shall do nothing. I shall stay here and be looked after by the good sisters. Then when the child is born...well. We shall see. I am a wealthy widow with a freedom granted to me by the King himself..." A sound from Joan made Elenor pause and look piercingly at her ex - maid. "What is it?"

Joan shook her head. She not only could not tell Elenor because she had been told not to, but she now did not want to set the lady back just when it seemed she had found a measure of peace.

"Well. Never mind. How are you?"

"Blooming. I have never felt better and Erland fusses round me like a mother hen."

"You have not said anything about me?"

"Of course not. Do you take me for a fool?"

A moment of silence. The two women walked slowly together through the rows of sweet smelling herbs tended by the nuns.

The summer was moving on, and the two of them carried new life within them, and it did not really matter who the father was, the fires which had forged the mothers had been fierce and strong. They had come through it all and steel was in their souls.

"How is he?"

Joan smiled. "You always ask me that. He is well. His arm has mended crooked but he can handle his weapons and he has been out on that great horse of his lately."

"Has he asked about me?" Once again she needed to know.

"He has spoken to Erik, but he will get nothing from that one, believe me."

"So he still does not know where I am?"

"He keeps his own counsel but you know he is not one to let things go so easily."

Elenor bent to pull at a weed, keeping her face hidden. "Perhaps you are wrong. He will not come after me. He will find a new lady for Fernrean and I shall be left in peace with my child. I am glad. It is best this way."

"If you think that, you are dreaming..."

Elenor suddenly got up and caught Joan by the arm, staring into her face. "You are too sure. You know something more yet you are hiding it from me. I thought we were friends, nay, more than friends, sisters more like. Tell me what it is."

Joan was taken by surprise and could not hide a guilty expression. Elenor shook her.

"Tell me!"

Wrenching her arm away Joan hissed.

"I cannot. I want to, but I cannot!"

"Oh God, Joan, you cannot do this to me. If you do not tell me now what my fate is to be then I shall suffer all the more for wondering. Why are you so sure he will come to fetch me back?"

Rubbing a hand across her brow Joan finally burst out... "Oh this is impossible, lady!

He will come for you because he has paid the King the dues both for Fernrean and for you!"

Elenor was stunned. "But... but he promised. The King promised!" Her world had turned upside down once more and she seemed to reel from one shock to another.

"Here. Sit down lady." Joan was in a determined frame of mind."Listen to me, and listen well. The lord loves you and you love him. The situation is ridiculous for you were meant to be together. I tell you he will come for you soon and you must set your mind to it for it will be the best thing to happen to you."

"No! I will not be bought again like some - some piece of furniture. And what of my child? He will not want a child whose father none of us could name for certain."

"It could be his."

"And more likely not. No. I knew this place was too close to Fernrean. I shall have to leave here and seek another haven where he will never have a chance of finding me."

"Have you lost your wits? A woman alone and pregnant? How far would you get in safety, especially in these dangerous times? Where would you go?"

"I may go back to Normandy. Armand de Carrefour may have been granted Fernrean but my father's land is still mine by the King's own words."

As she thought about it, it seemed to be the perfect solution. To return to Normandy and bear her child where she, herself, had been born.

But she must leave immediately, before he had
a chance to come to the convent and either stop
her, or discover she had fled, and chase after her to
fetch her back. The only problem was that she
would need an escort and where would she find a
trustworthy band of men to see her safely out of
England?

"Joan! Can you ask Erik to come out and pay
me a visit? I need to speak with him. I have not
seen him for some time and there are some things
I would like to discuss with him."

Joan looked at her suspiciously."Now what?
You cannot ask Erik to become involved in this.
Will you come to your senses? How can you
possibly turn your back on the love that awaits
you if you return to Fernrean? Once I urged you
to have a brave heart and reach out for love..."

"Yes! And where did it get me?"

"It got you a man that any woman would give
her soul for! And you are just throwing him away
when you know he would die for you!"

Elenor gnawed her lip and paced the stones of
the Herb garden much as she had been used to
pacing the boards of her room - it seemed
centuries ago now.

She had tried to put him from her mind these
past months, tried to block him out, forget him,
but how could she? She felt so alone without him,
wanting him to hold her in his arms and keep her
safe, smile down at her with those soft grey eyes
and kiss away her fears.

"Curse him! I wish I had never met him!"

"How can you say that?" Joan sensed that in
some strange way she was winning the argument.

"I never thought that another man such as Erland could be found, but if any man comes close, it is the Lord de Carrefour. Oh lady, he was so badly hurt! His injuries have taken so long to mend and he is so thin. He hungers for you and I watch him looking to see you at his side."

Elenor stifled a sob. "He will not want me when he sees me like this." She indicated her short hair and her stomach which was just starting to show signs of the child, and which would soon become swollen and ponderous.

"Lady, think of how you looked when he first saw you, with those blackened eyes and the broken nose - you look a thousand times better now than you did then."

Joan was scenting victory.

Elenor was uncertain.

She had thought she knew what she wanted when she left Fernrean, but Joan's description of Armand and how he was suffering tore at her heart.

"I need to think! I am confused and I must decide soon what to do before he forces me into a position where the choice has been taken away from me completely."

"I think - that if you truly love him, the choice has already been taken from you."

"But the child! What will he think? What will he do? This is a complication none of us could have foreseen, even if I had stayed. Even if I do go back the child will make a difference and I would not want my baby to be scorned and unloved as either some soldier's bastard or the child of Gerard de Beauvrais."

Suddenly, both women were distracted by a commotion at the gates of the convent. Shouts for entrance, nuns running in confusion and Joan's escort tumbling out into the courtyard caused them to clutch at each other in a moment of fear. Were they being attacked? Had the rebels come down from the north again?

Rollo fumbled, one handed, at the bars of the gates and some of Joan's men ran to help him, pulling back the heavy bolts and opening wide the gates to allow entrance to a dust - covered force of mounted men who clattered noisily into the courtyard disturbing the peace and sending scattering chickens, pigs and people alike.

Sunlight glinted off mail, horses whinnied and reared, the big roan destrier in the lead snorted and danced.

Elenor and Joan peered cautiously through the archway which led from the Herb garden to the main courtyard and as the dust settled and it became apparent who had disturbed the peace and serenity of the place, Elenor gave a moan and collapsed in a heap at Joan's feet.

Armand de Carrefour was off his horse in an instant and he scooped up the unconscious Elenor in strong, careful arms.

"This way my lord." The Abbess was there indicating to Armand that he should follow her and he ducked his head to enter the room which had been home for Elenor in the four months since she had left Fernrean.

Joan trailed close behind him, not sure whether she was sorry or glad that he had followed her.

It should have been obvious all along that he would do it eventually and Joan suspected that that had been King William's intention when he had given Elenor no choice but to stay at Holy Rood.

Armand laid his burden gently on the bed, then reluctantly stood back to allow the Abbess and one of the sisters to attend to Elenor.

He could not take his eyes off her and was forced to rein in his impatience as the nuns made her comfortable. Finally they stood back to allow him near her, although the Abbess's stare was uncomfortably piercing as she looked him over.

"You are the Lord de Carrefour?"

"I am." He did not look at her, for all his attention was focused on the still pale figure of Elenor.

"You took your time coming to fetch her."

"What?" She had his attention now.

"You should have come sooner. She needs you."

"I could not come before this." Why should he excuse himself to her?

Those steady blue eyes made him uncomfortable but he had no reason to feel guilty. He had come as soon as he could.

Elenor sighed and stirred and he was by her side in an instant, taking her limp hand and holding it as though he feared she would try to escape him again.

The Abbess's face softened as she watched him and she gave a little satisfied nod before reassuring him. "She will be fine, you do not need to worry. We have looked after her for you."

Armand, however, was totally absorbed by Elenor, and gave scarcely a sign of having heard anything the Abbess had said to him.

She knew he was there even before she opened her eyes. Deliberately she kept them closed as long as she could, trying to gather her wits, trying to prepare herself to face him. Imagine making such a fool of herself as to pass out at the mere sight of him, although surely she did have some excuse?

"Will she be fit enough to travel?" The sound of that soft, husky voice made her stomach dissolve.

"I would not leave today my lord." The Abbess sounded anxious. "Stay until the morning. We have plenty of room for you and your men and it will give my Lady Elenor time to collect herself."

There was a pause and then she heard him sigh. "Very well. You are right. We need to talk anyway, she and I. Thank you."

"Good. Good. I shall go and make the arrangements."

The door closed and Elenor wondered if they were now alone.

The edge of the bed dipped as he sat next to her and she could not stifle a tremor, could not still the flutter of her eyelashes.

"Elenor." His voice was low, coaxing, and she could pretend no longer. With a soft, intake of breath she opened her eyes.

She was totally unprepared for the heart - stopping fall of emotion which assailed her at the sight of that dark lean face with the silver grey stare bending so close.

"Why did you run away from me?"

There was a quality in his voice she could not define. Was he pleading? This warrior so used to battles without mercy. Could he possibly be pleading with her? Raped, abused, pregnant with the child of God knew who? No. It was unbelievable.

Yet she could not answer him.

Still dressed in his chain mail, the coif pushed back to reveal the close - cropped dark hair with its shots of silver, he seemed so invincible.

"You bought me!" The accusation made him flinch.

"I could see no other way of keeping you with me. You believed I would despise you, reject you because of what that evil swine did to you. How could you believe that?"

She recognised the pain in that question and the thought that she had hurt him so much only added to her misery. He stood up suddenly, running his hands over his short hair, shrugging those wide shoulders, then easing his arm over his ribs.

The headlong journey after Joan to find the convent where Elenor was hiding had sapped his strength.

"Will you be able to travel tomorrow? I know you have been ill. Joan said you had been sick."

Elenor was shocked.

Of course. He did not know she was pregnant!

"Yes. Yes I have been sick." Tell him! Her mind screamed at her. You must tell him!

"My lord..."

"My lord?"

He whirled back to the bed, put his hands either side of her head to stop her turning away and leaned down, his mouth close to hers.

"Was it 'my lord' that night?" His lips grazed lightly over hers and she closed her eyes, her heart thudding like that of a frightened fawn.

"Do you remember that night? - I will never - never forget it. The rest of it - the shame, the pain, your pain and agony, burns my soul. But the sheer heaven of that night haunts my dreams." His voice dropped to a whisper. "I love you. What will it take to convince you that I love you so much my heart may break."

His voice was hoarse with tearing emotion, unable to handle the depth and strength of his feelings for this woman.

A whimper escaped her throat and she turned her head away from him, so that he would not see her distress. She must tell him!

"Elenor, please, do not turn away from me," he begged.

He pulled her up and into his arms, cradling her against his chest pressing kisses to the curls growing all awry about her face.

"You must forgive me for forcing you but I could not bear to lose you without a fight and this was the only way I could be sure of keeping you."

Willing her to understand, he could sense her reserve but did not know the reason for it.

Elenor was where she wanted to be most in all the world - in his arms and for a few brief moments she revelled in his strength, in the glory of his words.

She would tell him later.

For now she needed his embrace. She needed his kiss. She needed his love.

His breath was warm on her skin, his mouth creating havoc with her nerves as his kisses travelled her throat, his fingers tangled in her hair. He tugged gently to pull up her face for his caresses and Elenor closed her eyes so that he could kiss her eyelids, her temples, her soft, flushed cheeks, and finally, her mouth.

With that passionate possession he broke down the last of the barriers she had flung up and she curled her arms about his neck, her soft lips parting beneath the demand of his. Their bodies were so close, so hot for each other that they burned and Elenor shook as if she had a fever, so weak at his touch she scarce could breathe.

They were so lost in each other that at first they did not hear the knock at the door and when they did, when the second rap came, they tried to ignore it.

However, it would not go away, and finally, reluctantly they came back down to earth.

"Come in." Armand was exasperated, but there was little he could do in the face of a smiling, apologetic Mother Abbess.

"Do forgive me, my lord, but your room is ready and Sister Ursa needs to see to Lady Elenor before the evening meal."

Sister Ursa stood behind the Abbess with the jug of steaming raspberry leaf tea and Armand wrinkled his nose at the tart smell of it. He was a little curious but assumed that it was something to do with Elenor's illness.

Elenor was red - faced and confused trying to calm her rioting senses. Now that he was here with her again, she could not have enough of him. She saw him glance at the jug which the nun carried and she felt a bump of dread.

She should have told him. While she had the chance and while he was so softly inclined towards her, she should have told him. Too late just now, she would have to choose another moment, when they were alone.

The two nuns stood waiting, looking at Armand expectantly until he realised they were waiting for him to leave.

"Oh! I shall go then."

The Abbess smiled and nodded.

"Rollo is there to show you to your room, my lord. You may wash and rest and we shall see you at the evening meal."

Effectively dismissed, he bowed his head and left them.

As soon as the door closed behind him Elenor panicked.

"Oh, what am I to do? He has paid the dues to William for my hand, yet he does not know I am carrying a child! How can I tell him?"

"Hush now! This outburst will not do the child any good." Sister Ursa was severe.

"I think you can tell him." The Abbess's soft voice captured Elenor's attention, and even Sister Ursa glanced at her Superior curiously.

"What do you mean?" Elenor was uncertain.

The Abbess came close to the bed and indicated the drink which Sister Ursa had placed on the small table. "Drink up." She would say no more until Elenor had finished the raspberry leaf drink.

"I think that you underestimate this man..."

"But you have barely met him," interrupted Elenor.

The Abbess held up a hand. "I think you may rely on my ability as a judge of character. You do realise how much he loves you?"

The flushed cheeks and averted eyes of Lady Elenor answered her question.

"I see you do. Well then you must trust him. You must trust his love for you for without trust between two people, love becomes stifled and may finally die. You must have hurt him very much when you ran from him, yet still he came after you as soon as he was able."

"But he bought me. I was promised my freedom and he has taken it from me."

In spite of her resentful words, there was uncertainty in her voice.

"Ah yes. Your freedom. And tell me what did you plan to do with this precious freedom? Spend it in tears and regrets for what might have been? In longing for the voice, the touch, the presence of a loved one?"

There was a certain quality in the old lady's voice which took Elenor aback. It was as if she knew - as if she had been there herself.

Elenor drew up her knees beneath the bedcover, resting her elbows on them, her fists supporting her chin, remembering. Remembering these last months of misery, worrying about him, wanting him, missing him - oh how she had missed him!

"Very well." As if she stood on the edge of a cliff she felt that she was diving out into the unknown. "I shall tell him tonight, as soon as we can be alone together."

"Don't worry. That is easily arranged." The Abbess clapped her hands lightly together. "You will not be sorry. Now let us see how we are getting on here."

Elenor had put on weight and her waist had thickened to the point where she wondered how Armand had failed to notice her condition.

Her mind turned to the child within her and as Sister Ursa gently pressed her stomach, the question of whether it was a boy or girl occupied her to the extent that she did not see Sister Ursa frowning. The Abbess saw, however, and raised her brows in question, receiving a shake of the head in reply.

When the two nuns left the room, they met Joan, waiting to see Elenor.

"How is she?"

"The lady is doing well, but..." Sister Ursa hesitated and Joan felt a flicker of concern

"The baby? Is something wrong?"

"No, no. Nothing like that. There is just something a little odd about the way the child is lying. All the worry and strain of the past few months may be to blame. When she leaves here you must make certain that she rests adequately and takes the brews I have prepared."

"So she is coming home." It was not a question. Joan was relieved.

"I do not think the Lord de Carrefour will give her any choice, and it is as well for it is what she really so desperately desires."

"Do not worry, she will be very well cared for. Does my lord know about the child?"

"Not yet. She will tell him though, this evening I should think." Sister Ursa shook her head and sighed."It is at times like this that I am glad I am in Christ's service, away from men and their demands."

"Away from love and life and passion, sister." Joan reminded her.

"Yes, well. I think I am too old for that thank goodness."

The tall nun hurried away with that and Joan prepared to enter Elenor's room.

Elenor was in something of a daze. Life seemed to be taking her by the neck and shaking her as a dog shakes a rat.

The only constant thing just now was the babe inside her and she felt suddenly ashamed that she had tried to get rid of it.

It! Was it a boy or a girl? The only thing she could hope for was that she had not hurt it with the potion she had taken.

Joan's knock startled her. Was it Armand? If it was she would tell him now.

It was both a relief and a disappointment when it was Joan who came in.

"How are you?"

Elenor suddenly felt exhausted. "So tired. So very tired." She let her head fall back on the pillows and allowed Joan to fuss over her a little.

"Then rest. Just go with the flow of the tide for there is nothing you can do about what is past. There is no profit to be found in worry or regret." You are right, as always. Armand followed me here and he wants me enough to have paid for me, so he must take whatever baggage I bring with me."

Glad that Elenor seemed to have accepted her fate and was prepared to make the best of it, Joan hastened to further reassure her."Also, do not forget, you are, and will be, surrounded by friends, by people who love you now so you will never have to face anything alone again."

Those words came back to Elenor that evening and gave her courage as she entered the dining hall with Joan and saw Armand seated next to the Abbess, talking seriously of some matter, a chair empty at his side, obviously waiting for her.

The walk down the length of that long table was the most nerve - wracking Elenor had ever made.

He had fallen silent as soon as he saw her, not even finishing the sentence he had started, a discourtesy to the Abbess which was totally unlike him. She saw his throat move as he swallowed convulsively and in surprise, she realised that he was as nervous as she. Getting to his feet as Elenor reached him, he smiled, and suddenly she felt that swirling lift of the spirit, that bubble of joyful anticipation which his mere presence aroused in her heart. Suddenly certain that this man, this hardened, battle scarred warrior would never hurt her - even unintentionally, she cursed herself for a fool, a cowardly, spineless fool for leaving when she did, for leaving him lying injured and unknowing without a word. Truly she did not deserve him.

There was scarcely a sliver of space between them yet that desirous tension shimmered there unbearably, Elenor's head tilting up to him, her long curling lashes sweeping to hide what he might read in the soft molten depths of her eyes.

"My lady."

There was a certain quality in the huskiness which sharpened her awareness of him, focusing her attention on the gauntness of his face, the hollows beneath his cheekbones and the haunted shadow in his grey eyes. Guilt and remorse made her bite down on her bottom lip, drawing a trace of blood. Was she the cause of the misery she saw lingering there?

Armand's hand came slowly up to cup her cheek, his thumb moved softly against her bottom lip, erasing the spot of blood which trembled there and almost making her faint with the sensuousness of his touch.

"Do not bleed for me, lady. Do not weep, do not fear. I would have died to save your pain and shame. Instead it was you who were my saviour. I am ever in your debt."

Elenor shook her head, denying his words, then a soft cough from the Abbess made the two of them aware of where they were and of the many watching, for the most part benignly approving, eyes.

Armand hid his embarrassment behind a clenched jaw and cool grey gaze, but Elenor's flushed cheeks and tremulous smile were too obvious a sign of her shyness to hide.

The meal was simple but plentiful and Armand and his men tucked in with a will, their usual boisterous banter kept to a minimum by the presence of the gentle nuns.

Unused to such company, for visitors usually dined in the guest house, the sisters kept their eyes downcast and spoke only amongst each other.

The Abbess, however, was under no such constraint, enjoying the novelty of so many visitors from outside the sheltering walls of Holy Rood.

Armand was engaged in a charming yet in some ways, annoying hour of conversation with his hostess.

Annoying because all he wanted to do was revel in the presence of the woman he desired so much, Elenor de Beauvrais.

Elenor, herself, was glad that the Abbess kept Armand occupied for a while, because she needed time to think of how she was going to tell him that she was pregnant.

The opportunity presented itself so suddenly that she was almost caught unawares.

The food was good and Elenor had been eating as heartily as any of them, when the appearance of a large haunch of boiled bacon, swimming in globules of fat, caused a gurgling sensation in the pit of her stomach. Determinedly her jaw was clenched, her eyes averted, but it did no good. The scent of meat wafted to her nostrils and she felt the rush of sickness rise in her throat.

Her chair tipped back behind her as she made a frantic bid to escape before heaving the contents of her stomach up in front of everyone. Narrowly she made it outside with Joan, Armand, Sister Ursa and the Abbess in concerned pursuit.

It took several minutes for the bout of sickness to subside and Sister Ursa was ready with a moistened cloth to wipe her face.

Armand was confused and worried.

"How long have you been ill?" he demanded. "What is wrong? Please tell me what is wrong."

Elenor's eyes met those of the Abbess and a silent message passed between them. Within a second Elenor and Armand were alone in the soft scented twilight of the summer evening.

Armand felt a pang almost of fear as he became aware of that diplomatic withdrawal.

Waiting for her to speak, he watched her hungrily, unable to express his feelings for her, unable to find the right words to reassure her. He tried. "Elenor..."

She turned on him in virtual attack.

"I have something to tell you."

He was silenced, taken aback by her sudden fierceness.

Elenor searched those lean, beloved features, committing them to memory so that if he spurned her after hearing what she had to tell him, she would be able to conjure up his face in her dreams.

"What I have to say is..." She took a breath. "I am carrying a child."

Her voice was defiant but her eyes were pleading, pleading for him not to turn away from her, not to leave her.

After all she had been through, after thinking that she could run from him, could live without him, now she found that if indeed he did not want her - it would break her. It would destroy her.

As her words sank into his brain, he found himself thinking, without any relevance, that he really rather liked her hair curling softly about her face like that, then when he saw that those huge brown eyes were fastened on his face as though he held her very life in his hands, he realised what she had said.

She watched him close his eyes and turn away and a despairing sob escaped her throat.

Armand de Carrefour was a hard man.

He had spent his life fighting, using his strength and courage, his ability with spear and sword to fight his way up to the position of honour he now held. But before this woman he found himself helpless, without weapons of the kind he might need to win her. Faced with that bald statement she had thrown at him, he experienced such a surge of love, a deep overwhelming love and a desire to protect her and the child she carried, that he almost choked.

When his ears caught the faint thread of sound she made, he whirled about, his grey eyes alight with determination. Before she could move or protest, he enfolded her in arms whose strength would brook no denial.

At first she fought him, struggling to escape, so wound up in the belief that he did not want her that she did not understand what he was saying.

"Dear heart, how could you believe that I would not want you? You and the child. If you want me to go down on my knees and beg, then I will do it. Just come home with me. Be my wife. Bear our child in love and safety."

Those words stilled her as nothing else could have done. She stared up at him in wonder.

"Our child? You said, bear our child?"

He frowned, not understanding her question.

"Of course. What else would I say? Come home to Fernrean and let me love you both. I swear you will never regret it."

Elenor de Beauvrais quivered, clutching at the tall warrior who held her, whose mind had not even considered for a moment that her baby might be other than his.

With a sigh she melted against him, raising her face to offer her mouth for his kiss.

He did not hesitate, but took the gift she gave with an exultant groan, rejoicing that the brave heart of this woman was finally his to treasure forever.